STORM SEER

D Wild

Wild Books

First published in Great Britain in 2020
by Wild Books

A CIP catalogue record for this book is available
from the British Library.

ISBN: 978-1-9164111-0-4 (paperback)
ISBN: 978-1-9164111-1-1 (ebook)

This edition is presented in British English

www.wildbooks.ltd

Cover design and layout by
www.chandlerbookdesign.com

Acknowledgements

The author is grateful to:

Gale Winskill (winskilleditorial.co.uk)

Hal Duncan

Gina Rathbone, Proofreader

Cover and illustrations by Maggie Downer

For Mum & Dad

CONTENTS

DAY 2

DAY 3

DAY 4

DAY 5

Map of Sealand

Sealand

Shingle
Beach

Cove

Landing

Sealand Wind Scale

Wind Strength	Wind Force	Description
Mild	1	Flurry
	2	Drier
	3	Pummel
Moderate	4	Blow
	5	Breeze
	6	Strong Breeze
High	7	High Wind
	8	Gale
Storm	9	Strong Gale
	10	Storm
High Storm	11	Rage Storm
	12	Fury Storm
	13	Destroy Storm
	14	Rip Storm
	15	Cutter Storm

STORM RISING

Raider

Alfren slithered along the ditch in pitch-black night and fell onto the beach just as the surf tossed an open rowing boat onto the shingle. She hefted her bow and nocked an arrow, sure to strike. In the faint lamplight cast from the prow, a raider leapt out and turned to pull on a rope. Likely they wore body armour: thick leather and maybe steel plate. Alfren stood and, in a snap, took aim and loosed the arrow at her target some 50 yards away.

The wind gusted, the raider slipped and struggled upright ... and yet the arrow stabbed on target, through leather sleeve and flesh of arm into chest.

The raider cried out and fell into the surf.

Alfren's watch partner sprinted past, lamp held high in one hand and knife drawn in the other. Alfren nocked another arrow and ran forward, ready to shoot should the raider fight back. Her partner dropped the lamp and crouched over the raider with knife raised. The raider called for mercy ... Alfren heard children's wailing screams, pleading.

Two children reached over the gunwale.

Children?

Her watch partner held up a hand to stay Alfren and pulled the raider roughly into the lamplight. The raider was a young woman, a girl.

Alfren looked up and down the darkness of the beach and out to sea. No one else lurked there. They were alone. She shouldered her bow and lifted the children from the boat. She saw her partner bind the raider, put a compression bandage around her chest and strap her wounded arm.

The children held her hands tightly as Alfren led them the few yards to the top of the beach. They stumbled over the shingle and whimpered.

'There, there. You're safe now,' was all she could say.

They were tough little lives – and innocent.

Alfren waited. It wasn't long before rangers arrived, who took the raider and children away.

As she watched them leave, she felt a pull to go with the children, to look after them ... so that they would know they were safe.

She thought how sudden this was when the day before had been an ordinary day within the wall of her home burgh. The waves of energies she had seen with her mind had been the usual; bright, rolling, wonderful ... as they were every day, all of them.

There hadn't been any tremors.

Except for one.

Soup

Alfren

After midday Alfren tidied up in the laboratory. She set up her water samples collected that morning – from the reservoir high on the fell above the burgh – to percolate slowly through tins containing sand and charcoal. Then, she put away the microscope used to examine residues, as well as the gas burner which she used to boil and distil samples, her very own hour glasses and mercury thermometer, and her record sheets – real paper on which she wrote neatly in the finest script she could manage. The chief scientist laughed because he couldn't read her writing, it was so small.

But she shouldn't waste paper, it cost so much!

It was great to work in the laboratory. There were several small rooms and often she had one all to herself where she wasn't disturbed. The stone walls were washed white with lime, bright and clean. The small windows looked over the market street, from which she heard the stall-holders' calls and angry customers' shouts.

Most importantly, because of what the water lab crew (of which she was the youngest) strove to achieve, one day folk would be able to drink the water piped directly to their homes, not only use it for washing and sluicing. Imagine that: no more household drinking water butts that collected rain washed from roofs, filthy with residue from peat smoke and bird droppings. Instead, the burgh would have a clean drinking water supply, and not too soon in her view.

Had folk looked inside their own water butts recently? They were disgusting. She drained theirs regularly. It didn't take long to fill again with rainwater that fell on their burgh. She had rigged a filter too, but her mum complained it blocked, overflowed and flooded the backyard, but her mum needed to understand that development took patience and a few setbacks.

True, the many breweries in the burgh produced good beer which was what folk drank rather than water, but she remembered when as a child beer had tasted just too bitter. Instead her mum had boiled their drinking water taken directly from the reservoir yet still it had been cloudy and had tasted of peat.

Alfren took the back door from the lab onto steep steps, a dank passageway between high stone buildings that popped out onto the esplanade above the sea wall. At the ends of the quay were boatyards with hulls high on slipways. Below the esplanade, fishing smacks lined up on a stone pier lolled on the waves, one of them with mooring ropes too short and straining because the tide had fallen. She looked around but didn't see a fisherman nearby who could help. She took the steps leading off the esplanade down onto the pier intending to let out the ropes herself before the mooring cleats were wrenched away.

As she bent over to reach for the rope, a sudden heavy weight pressed down on her and a shout hollered in one ear. 'In you go, fishy!'

'Liffy! You lump of blubber!'

Alfren shook off her friend.

'And help me, you barnacle.'

Liffet laughed and jumped across to the other cleat. Together they let out the ropes and the smack levelled in the water, the rope-wrapped fenders hung free and the boat bumped gently against the pier.

'I saw you,' Alfren said.

She hadn't seen Liffet though; not at all. Strange.

'Let's shove off in it,' Liffet suggested.

'The bilge stinks. You can if you want to.'

'With this westerly for a few days, we could make it to the League.'

'Oh, alright, let's go then. You cast off,' Alfren said.

Liffet laughed.

'Let's make a plan of escape. Come on,' Alfren called.

It was said the best pantry shop in Wallburgh if not all Sealand - including the main island and all the other large islands, holms and skerries - was Finnie's on the market square at the end of the esplanade. There was no shop sign so no one but burghers knew of it and that way it shouldn't be robbed by traders. Alfren knocked on a green door and Finnie, in shawl and heavy dark dress, opened it with a greeting of, 'Aye, aye'. A high stone threshold, which stopped the drains running in off the square, opened into a small stone room with only a table and chair for Finnie to sit at under the window and there, on the stove under the chimney breast, was the soup tureen. Finnie gave a good stir with the ladle and filled a pewter tankard. Alfren handed over a copper tuppence for hearty white fish and mussel soup and a thick slice of bread for dunking.

'Mind, it's hot,' Finnie said as always, then, 'You girls watch out, you're only young yet,' which was the way with folk, a bit coddling.

The wind was only a fresh blow-force 4, so they walked along the esplanade, the sunshine on Whaleback the island across the sound, the sea's surface simmering, to sit on the bench of a tram stop, although there was no tram service that day or any day.

Alfren was fifteen years old, which was bothersome because folk teased her albeit kindly and yet young children looked up at her in awe at her old age. Like her, Liffet wore a smock with a high collar against the chill wind, bib trousers and boots, and a close-fitting hood at the ready to pull up and tie snug when it rained.

Liffet lifted her tankard to her lips and slurped.

'Liffy!'

'It's hot, missus!' Liffet retorted.

'Well, blow on it ... and dunk your bread first.'

'I like my bread last,' said Liffet. 'You can tear a crust to reach to the bottom to get the dregs and there might be a shrimp there ... you never know!'

Alfren sighed loudly, although no one and nothing but the wind heard her. She watched some few folk pass by along the esplanade, concealed under their hoods and headscarves, bent into the wind one way, bracing the other. One held onto the wall for respite, clutching where a stone protruded, before setting off again. None were League traders from towns far away, taking a stroll off their sea-going ships, dressed in their fine woven-wool clothes and storm capes. Definitely not raiders who, from the few she had seen clamped in the stocks on the green before the Burgh Hall, tended to be filthy, ragged and sly looking, although a raider could be anyone, so she had always been told. The point was, it took little observation to judge who was out of place. Real burghers were dressed in smocks of oilcloth, seal or lambskin. They walked with heads down, the better to shield their eyes from spindrift. They knew their way through the lanes and how to bend with the winds, yield or lean, rest or push on.

Now that the season was ending there would be few, if any, trader ships before winter, and Alfren noticed that although she was just as watchful as ever, she wasn't so wary. *Don't drop your guard*, she reminded herself. Traders brought fine goods but sometimes trouble too. There were none just then. Everyone knew when traders were berthed in the harbour from the list posted at the Burgh Hall. The last one had brought only iron scrap, but before that, a regular trader from Great Dam had arrived with salt, steel bar, fabrics and grain. The market street had been packed that week with folk ruffling through the cloths, while the grain mill on the market square had run every day, grinding spelt. Aloft on duty on the watchtower above the burgh, she had seen the highway north to Floodburgh, Fell Garth and Stonewick busy with pony-drawn carts and fuel-oil tractors towing trailers.

Liffet was usually unruly, but today she was quiet – she hadn't a message ready at all; a message by mind, that is, and nothing remarkable if a fellow knew how to do it ... and evidently few did.

Actually, Alfren knew only of herself and Liffet.

Earlier, Alfren had sent an alert of readiness to her friend when she had finished at the lab to signify they should meet, and a sensation of wetness and cold when her friend had jumped on her at the pier, which meant, *I'll chuck you in, you fish bait*. Then a warm tummy and the aroma of turmeric as a suggestion they should go for soup. But there had been no joke from Liffet that she might have expected, such as the day before when Liffet sent alarm at a gull swooping for her bread, which had made her yelp and duck for no reason just as folk passed, who shook their heads, sorry for her madness.

'What're you doing this afternoon, Liff?' she asked, curious and a little bit suspicious.

'Nothing,' replied Liffet, fobbing her off. 'Aren't you going on watch tonight, Ally?'

'Yes. See you at midday tomorrow?' asked Alfren.

'Of course.' Then Liffet added, 'It's private.' Liffet looked down into her tankard and dipped her bread.

'What is?'

'Later this afternoon.'

'You've got a job!' Alfren guessed. 'Brilliant! You're great at cleaning windows. I knew it!' she said, to bait her friend.

'Do you think I'm a pickled egg? You won't spoon me out the jar easy, missus. It's private.'

It wasn't like Liffet to be so coy.

'You haven't decided on it, have you?' Alfren asked. Something had told her Liffet was waiting on a decision or taking time to make up her mind. Surely though, it would be better for Liffet to take whatever was offered and become more settled?

'Stop poking,' Liffet said.

'It's alright, Liff. It's a job, isn't it? Anything but the fish factory.' She paused. 'Or get thrown over the wall, so the scavengers will take you.'

The threat spoken to all wayward children.

'Good advice, Ally.'

Alfren laughed, but it was serious. It was good work at the fish factory, everyone said, but she was glad she didn't have to join the other folk on their walk each day to work at the shipwrights' quarter, where they gutted and salted the fish. If anyone didn't like the work, it wasn't unknown for some few to leave the burgh to try their luck elsewhere, at one of the other, smaller burghs or an outland farmstead. She wouldn't want that for Liffet.

Worse, Alfren had a concern that Liffet might one day simply jump on a trader with no time for goodbye, to leave Sealand forever. Alfren couldn't say she hadn't dreamed of leaving too.

'Liffy, I wish you were in the Watch with me.'

Just in case the job fell through.

Alfren had suggested that dozens of times.

'Yes, I know, Ally, but I wouldn't last a short shift on one of those towers before doing something daft, like swinging off the railings for a dare.'

There was some truth in it: her friend seemed determined to flout the rules.

There were many regulations in the Watch, but those were fine because Alfren knew them and stuck to them. More important to her were the watchmen who were fun, and she felt loyal to them.

Perhaps looking for somewhere to belong, she knew Liffet had got to know all sorts of folk around the burgh: all the characters and whoever had a story to tell.

'I'll be listening, Liff.'

'Alright.'

When Alfren searched the waves in her mind – waves made by all life and energies in the world – often she matched with her friend's mind. There could be a funny message ready, made up of small memories and sensations. She hoped she would hear thrill and for context she might hear a hint of something she was familiar with. She would put it all together and work out what the job could be.

'Don't be a clever-clogs,' Alfren said. She hoped Liffet wouldn't lose the job at the last hurdle.

'Ally!' her friend retorted and smiled. 'I might be nice, even polite. It depends.'

They returned to the pantry and collected the deposits on the tankards. Alfren sighed. All her silver, a few shillings only, was in her purse – she dared not count up because then she would know how poor she was – with nothing at all in the tin up the chimney at home. It was impossible to save because she gave her mum nearly every penny, leaving just a little for soup and beer, and not much of either. Liffet had a full purse because she did odd jobs like helping the roofers on the Burgh Hall or repairing the rigging on old steam sailing boats.

Liffet left, taking a line between the stalls in the market square and heading towards the South Gate. Alfren spied on her from the entrance to a passageway, unseen in the dark recess. Was that really where her friend was going, or was that intended to mislead her? What could there be at the South Gate besides the militia barracks and the highway out along the sound?

Alfren saw from the level of the ebb tide it was time to check that night's Watch posting. She snuck off the market square up a narrow passageway, dark with high steps. She turned onto a steep lane, which brought her to the Burgh Hall and the green, and then up another lane, rising in ramps and terraces. Out of habit from childhood, because children didn't want to be seen on the main ways – or anywhere out and about – she slipped through a ginnel, a narrow, arched way between houses, and then took the maze of back lanes up to the top of the burgh. Her favourite way over the wall was nearby; favourite because only she and Liffet knew it. It was a difficult climb, nonetheless one day a child's practised eye would pick out the burnished handholds and toe steps and several children would attempt it. Then, a careless child could be caught by a guard patrol or fall and hurt themselves. But before that happened, she would find another way.

She wouldn't have to. She was in the Watch; she had her own pass-gate. She could come and go so long as she carried a watchtower token too, although the guards never checked. Still, it was good to have an alternative way over the wall and out of the burgh when the gates were closed at night.

She ambled along below the wall to check if any children were following. They wouldn't be caught out. She hoped not, because she had passed on to some of them what they should do to stay hidden: it wasn't about simply knowing all the paths and rooftops and keeping your distance, in the shadows; it was about knowing your quarry and what they might be up to. Be ready to run; have a way out if your quarry turned.

It had happened to her knowledge only a few times over her years. A child, somewhere in and around the burgh, in the quiet of their backyard or playing on the scrap heaps at the shipwrights' quarter, had been snatched without sound or alarm, a raider glimpsed with a sack over their shoulder.

It was important for every child to know how to hide because no child wanted to be the one who got caught and taken.

And lost forever.

Duty

The Watch barracks were at the top of the burgh beside the West Gate, which opened out onto the fell above. That day the weather was fine and recently there had been no trouble with raiders. Perhaps folk were allowed up onto the gate to the lookout? Alfren approached the guards, head down, scuffing her her boots on the cobbled lane. All children should know how to pass unremarked. She nodded to the guard and pointed up. The guard shrugged. She raised her palm in thanks and bounded up the stone steps.

From the parapet she looked around at the hills covered by heather and moss bog, peat hag and couch grass where sheep grazed and, dotted around the fell, the stone-walled sheepfolds. High above on the hill tops were the three great watchtowers, with their magnificent steel-frame structures and top deckhouses. She waved. The watchmen might notice her. She turned her gaze down on the burgh roofs packed tightly within the wall, riven by the lanes like the ghylls cut into the fellside above. The grand buildings of the Burgh Hall and infirmary stood out tall and above them. The fall of the burgh, steep at the water's edge, concealed the market street and esplanade. Across the sound – a sea reach – was the island of Whaleback with, on its near shore, a broch: a round tower which housed a few families and their livestock.

The sound was the best shelter and deep-water harbour in all of Sealand, so folk said. She could appreciate that they needed respite from the storm seas, those ships and their crews that ventured this far from the League towns.

Wouldn't it be a fine adventure to sail away on one, some day?

Until then, the outland would have plenty to explore. Her transfer to the far watchtowers couldn't come soon enough. She would have to lodge in the eastern burghs on her way. That would be exciting. Imagine, tramping the highways, alert to raiders and scavengers, or to anyone up to no good, then on watch from the high towers for days on end. It would be brilliant. Would the waves be any different out there? Certainly, they could be!

She breathed in and because she was hidden by the parapet and no one was close she went to the waves in her mind. Her favourites were the wind waves. They were mostly blues, thin streamers and great blankets, which knotted, tangled and unwound, with some flitting by and others twisting around her. She dipped in among them lightly because she didn't have the time to fall in and float off with them.

Strange, she thought, but when she slipped away from them, they chased after her.

A tremor. That was odd.

She had been with the waves for only a moment but nonetheless she checked the moon and tide waves for the time. It was a moment's inattention and a half hour had passed. She should hurry.

Except for the enormous storm shelter deep underground, the Watch barracks were just an office and store. They weren't large and grand like the militia barracks, nor hidden down a dark archway like the ranger barracks. That was the Watch way, everything kept basic and she approved of that. Who needed grand barracks when you had the finest watchtowers in the League? That made the Watch the best service by far. She unlocked the door and stepped inside.

Strictly speaking she was still a novice, that is, almost but not quite a full watchman. She would be sixteen soon and expected to pass out then, one of the first in her intake, because she had passed all the tests.

As she had half expected, no one was there. All were out on watch duties. She collected her tower-token from her pigeonhole which would no doubt be for one of the three towers above the burgh, Angler, Barb or Cod, then went to the dispatcher's desk, lifted open the lid and searched down the duty roster.

She saw it wouldn't be a burgh tower. It had been her oversight not to notice straightaway. 'Check everything and check again,' the watchmen said. She cursed and turned over the token.

It was watchtower Dab. She went over to the great map on the wall. There was the eastern seaboard of Sealand with its many narrow geos cleaving the cliffs, islets and sea stacks, wide curving wicks, and finger-like voes, the long, winding sea inlets that reached far inland. The highway ran from Farewell, at the southern tip, through Wallburgh and other burghs all the way north, where the land became impassable bog and finally a ragged, wild coast.

There was Dab on Muckle Voe, a long, winding sea inlet, 5 miles south. She knew it. She had seen it many times from some distance as she had skirted by when over the wall.

This duty could mean only one thing: Watch command couldn't wait for her to pass out before assigning her a frontline duty. She had just become a properly active watchman because her watch that day would be at a tower new to her and to walk there she would be unescorted in the outland. She went over to the cabinet where the approved routes were filed, but she knew the way well enough. Could this mean that they knew she knew the way?

They couldn't suspect she had been over the wall so often.

She shouldn't fret. She had had almost three years of training and she knew she was ready. Command must be sure of that too.

Back at the desk, a lesser question was who would be her watch partner? If one of the older watchmen that would be great because they would ask her to sing songs which passed the time pleasantly, although they might tell their stories of the Extinction, which would be boring. She would listen because they expected her to learn all the stories.

There it was. *Ranger stand-in?* But, her watch partner would be a ranger?

She had heard it happened but only very occasionally. It occurred to her she could do the watch on her own if she could get a message to the ranger barracks to tell them not to bother. Although, maybe that would be just a bit too confident for her first watch away from the burgh.

Wasn't it odd though that a ranger would be her partner? It would be interesting to find out what he was like, certainly. Rangers were the toughest and hardiest, everyone said. No one wanted trouble with them. It would be no problem though. She would do everything right and she would do it well and that would be that and back to normal by morning. Probably she wouldn't have to speak much to the ranger. Some folk said they never spoke anyway.

She had caught glimpses of rangers in the lanes. They were sort of like outlanders, folk said – they belonged in the outland where folk were different because they dwelt in lonely farmsteads or on the off-islands, in their settlements without a wall as high as the one at Wallburgh to protect them. Rangers might be worse than outlanders some folk had whispered, more like raiders and all the other bands of folk that took to reiving except rangers didn't actually plunder settlements and steal livestock so far as she knew.

How can you tell the difference between a raider and a ranger? went the children's joke. *If you're that close to spot it, you're smoked.*

In a few minutes, her life had changed forever. She was as good as a full watchman. It was thrilling, but she would be steady because that was the watchman way.

She would still have her job at the laboratory and that was important.

She paused to check the tide waves in her mind. She had just time enough to get ready. Rather than send a message to Liffet, she would explain everything the following day. She had to put her mind to her job.

Voe

At home at afternoon tea with her mum, Alfren sat at their trestle table in the small best room to share soup and oat bread. Alfren didn't dare say anything about the new watchtower and especially not the ranger.

Upstairs in her tiny bedroom, with space only for a bunk and a chest, she dressed in her watchman's wind suit. First, she drew on fine undergarments, which were soft, itchy lambswool. The outer garments were sheep's wool dyed to a dark grey that had been shrunk to a dense weave. She pulled on bib trousers, which finished high on her waist, and drew the laces up the sides of her legs to pull the garment close so it wouldn't flap in the wind or snag on the climbing ladder up the watchtower. She pulled the smock over her head. Its hem finished at her upper leg, which she pulled close using a cord. There was also a tie which she fastened under the crotch to prevent the smock riding up.

She left loose the draw-cord at her waist and kept the neck open, then fastened a webbing belt around her hips and clipped on her snood and gloves, before attaching a small kit bag for her sit harness should she require rescue at height, and a chest harness to attach her bow and quiver. She was unusual among watchmen in that she carried a bow. A couple of other girls about her age carried crossbows, which had a fair range and were accurate, but she preferred the much lighter short bow, which was far quicker to draw and fire.

Inside the front door her mum waited to see her away. Her mum looked worried whenever she was on watch. It seemed untruthful not to mention she was a full watchman because she most certainly was. If she had mentioned the watchtower on the voe, her mum would have left for the barracks in a fury because she was a little young to be fighting raiders, but she was nearly sixteen and her mum should take that into consideration. She got a long hug, then her mum told her to shoot without a hesitation - as given a chance, raiders would strike first and mercilessly. They were a watchman's standing orders, so how could she not?

She pulled the house door closed and waited to hear her mum throw the bolts; it was a routine they had had since she was very young although they never talked about why.

She turned down the narrow passageway, skipped down a series of steps, passed through a ginnel and emerged into Waterfall Lane, which curved and descended to the market street. She didn't turn down to the esplanade but kept going across the market square to the South Gate.

She mused she needn't have gone this long way around to leave the burgh. As a child, after some waiting and watching from a hiding place, she would have simply climbed from a roof up the wall, over the parapet and down the outside, then freedom to roam. Those simpler ways over had long since been shut down by the guards. That couldn't be why children had gone missing in the past though – one or two, every other year or so. They couldn't have gone over the wall and got lost or captured by raiders. There was something wrong with that notion. For the most part, the missing children weren't wall-runners – they had been too young. In any case, children who could work out how to get over the wall would be quick and sharp, and well able to evade raiders.

Really, folk didn't know for certain what had happened.

The disappearances were never far from the minds of children: Who would be next, and when?

She cleared her mind. Under the South Gatehouse, she presented her pass-gate.

'Stick it to those raiders,' called the guard jovially and waved her through.

She stepped outside the wall onto the track to the open outland where there was slim chance of help in case of accident or distress unless a ranger passed by, and because they didn't patrol so near to the burgh and there were so few of them, that was unlikely.

That was the excitement of being a watchman. Watchmen were always on the move, each going to a different tower on different shifts. No one could recall exactly why it should be like that. Someone had told her that mixing up the watchmen and their shifts had proved the best way to keep everyone alert.

And watchmen were busy: she would spend her time both on the towers and at the lab, so her routine would never align with someone else's.

It was still daylight. She had an hour to reach the watchtower, 5 miles south, so she had plenty of time so long as she pushed on. She wondered about the ranger with whom she would spend a whole watch. What would he be like? Would he ignore her, sleep through because the duty was beneath him, or tell her gruesome stories about the outland?

Or get drunk and start a fight?

The wind had been pleasant for some days – a blow-force 4, the sort of gusting, pushing wind that whipped clothes from drying lines if not pegged properly. She saw from only a light glance at the waves in her mind that the wind would pick up to a steady breeze-force 5 within an hour or so, and to a strong breeze-force 6 overnight. No one would be at large in the dark hours in such heaving, tumbling wind.

She was watchful and checked all around as she ran. Although, being in the near outland close to the burgh meant freedom more than danger.

She trotted along the coastal path along the sound relishing the clear sea air, a relief from the burgh where smoke from peat fires whirled from the chimneys. Common seals perched on rocks watched her, ready to slide into deep water. Arctic terns and herring gulls wheeled overhead. She descended to a sandy beach and then climbed rock steps above sea cliffs. She crossed a bog to the head of Muckle Voe where she jumped a burn and approached watchtower Dab set high on a rise. She waved and signalled the watchmen, then climbed 50 feet up a ladder, where a hatch opened to the deckhouse.

A smiling young woman peered down and offered a hand to haul her up.

'Hi, come aboard!'

Alfren stepped onto the deck and stood to face the woman, dressed in a dark green storm suit.

Blimey, this is a ...

'I'm Lieutenant Handar of the rangers. How do you do.'

They shook hands.

'Watchman Alfren. How do you do,' Alfren replied, in awe of a real ranger officer. Up close for the first time, Alfren could see the detail in the storm suit, which was like her wind suit, but a close-fit, lighter material with wear patches of fine lambskin, and a full harness.

'I've never done a watch with a ranger before. I'll do my best.'

Handar smiled pleasantly. 'I'll be sure to do my best too! I hear you've learned everything you're supposed to!'

That was brilliant to know; better somehow than the encouragement from the vicar at the church who had sponsored her for the Watch; better than praise from the watchmen, who were quick to scold too when she forgot a story.

Thankfully Handar couldn't know of her night-time prowls over the wall and petty pinching from the quayside. It didn't matter anyway, not anymore; she was as good as a full watchman, except for the passing-out parade, and she should get used to that. She could relax in the company of this ranger, who seemed friendly, not at all like an outlander.

The off-going crew waved a cheery farewell, one to lodge with farmsteaders further south, another to take a short leave.

'Checks, please, watchman,' ordered Handar in a friendly tone.

'Yes, ma'am.'

Out on deck Alfren could see along the voe, curving to open sea, then along the coast to a headland with enormous sea cliffs. She turned to the deckhouse. There was a beacon on the roof, a search lamp on the parapet, plus a davit arm and chain block to lift up supplies. Inside, there was a map on the wall, telegraph apparatus to send signals to Wallburgh, a stove, bunks and chests for weapons and flares, as well as a telescope, various lanterns, harnesses, ropes, manacles, fuel cylinders, canvas sheets and a writing desk with log sheets. There was a rolled-up wire ladder, various hooks, pikes and poles, a water closet, sink, tool chest, and pots of paint and oil for repairs on dry summer days. Finally, there was a full water butt and alongside, a firefighting station. Everything seemed in order.

She joined Handar on deck.

'All correct, ma'am.'

'Could you do the watch briefing?'

'Yes, ma'am.'

All was routine so far, just like being with a watchman.

'Ours will be an overnight watch only, from the evening at 7 o'clock to the morning at 7 o'clock. There's nothing to report from the handover. Sunset is at a quarter to eight and sunrise at quarter past six. Temperature 10°C, expected low 6°C overnight. Barometer is falling, with a freshening south-westerly strong breeze-force 6 forecast.'

She spoke confidently because the waves had told her the same anyway. Too late, she hoped she didn't sound too sure of herself.

'Visibility, good. Tonight is a new moon, so with complete or patchy cloud cover it will be pitch-dark.'

'Thank you, watchman,' said Handar. 'When we're on duty together, please call me Handar.'

Alfren wouldn't dare to be so familiar, not with a ranger.

'Let's have a cup of tea, shall we, Alfren, out here on deck?'

They shared the watch as darkness crept in. Handar asked her about school and the Watch, the vicar and her mum. It didn't seem like prying and Alfren answered politely. She held back from asking questions herself because it would be a bit forward to question a ranger officer. She was curious to know where the ranger came from for it wasn't Wallburgh, as she knew almost all burghers by sight.

'When did you join the Watch, Alfren?'

'At thirteen years, ma'am, when I was still at school. The vicar arranged it. He said the outdoors would be good for me.'

'Do you like it?'

'Very much, ma'am.'

'What do you like?'

'Standing watch, ma'am.'

'What else?'

'I can see everything, ma'am.'

'Yes, we can this evening. What has the Watch taught you?'

'Besides the drills, ma'am, and the stories of the Extinction?'

Handar nodded.

They had trained her. They had shown her how to manage ropes and pulleys, stitch and repair, and how to hide high on the fell and low in the bog; how to evade a fight, and how to spring a surprise. They had taught her to fish and cook, and best of all, to sing.

'All's not as safe as it appears, ma'am.'

'Why not?'

'I don't know what's at the heart of it all, ma'am.'

'Good answer, Alfren. None of us know. We keep searching for what will make us safe though. Gives us a purpose, doesn't it?'

'Yes, ma'am.'

Alfren had thought rangers would know everything.

She went into the deckhouse to prepare soup before she took her turn on watch.

Trouble

Alfren trailed her gloved hand on the railing around the deck, ready to grab hold if thumped by a gust of wind. It was black-dark and strong breeze-force 6, but she wore goggles to protect her eyes and a harness and safety line to catch her in a fall. Here on the windward side of the deck, she held on to steady herself. She followed the routine, counting to make sure she carried out the watch from all four sides at the correct intervals. She was cold and time passed slowly, but she was content. Other watchmen had told her they preferred day duties when they could see the land and knew raiders hid from their watchfulness, but never did she mind the dark hours.

Blimey!

She was sure she had spotted the faintest lamplight out at sea. She rang the bell and Handar joined her. Looking again, Alfren was sure – the lamplight was there, but after several minutes still Handar hadn't picked it out.

'I don't see it.'

'It's there, ma'am. It's making for the beach.'

'No one sails so close at night. It's possible they could've taken bearings from the lighthouses.'

Handar searched again.

'Alright then, let's go. I'll telegraph the barracks. Alfren, make ready the boat.'

Her first encounter! There was no time to think. She collected her bow, pulled open the hatch, slid down the ladder and raced to the slipway. She heaved to turn over a boat onto a trolley and collected oars. Handar followed carrying a bright lamp and together they reeled out the boat. Alfren jumped aboard, took the bow oar, then rowed as strongly as she could in time with Handar across the voe against a battering wind. She stepped out, tied up to a stone wharf, sprang up steep steps and set off at a run along a track. Handar turned to cross the bog, while Alfren ran ahead over deep, soft heather but careful not to outpace the ranger. She slipped into a ditch that led directly to the beach where she saw a raider boat, pushed by wind and waves, lurch onto the shingle.

The action to arrest the raider and take the children into custody was brief and there was only an hour to wait until a ranger squad arrived on horseback. Nonetheless, she and Handar had remained alert to a surprise attack. Couldn't there be a shore party lying in wait for the raider and her bounty, the children? None came. Perhaps the raider had a trade arranged at a safer meeting place inland.

Alfren helped place the children together on a pony, and the raider onto a second. Rangers led them away into the darkness.

She and the Handar returned to the beach and together hauled the abandoned boat high up the foreshore before searching it, then Handar with her lamp led the way back to the watchtower.

Alfren paced the deck. She told herself that she had done her duty. She had had to, yet her shot had almost killed a girl not much older than herself and that was troubling. She felt quickened still from the dash to the beach yet relief it was over, and she felt a lot more experienced as a watchman.

Something niggled at her; something about everything she had been taught and was expected to do, and she didn't like it. Whatever it was that made her feel troubled, she wanted it to go away.

She was sure to feel strange, but the watchmen would dismiss her concern.

Dither and be damned!

The raider could have shot her given a chance! Worse, the raider could have been diseased. Handar had taken a risk by getting close. Yet clearly the raider was healthy and the children could have caught cold on the beach awaiting the slower militia to arrive to lead the way to quarantine in damp cells at their barracks.

It was odd they hadn't found weapons and it had been a relief to see that the raider seemed healthy, not starved and sickly – the children too. It was a worry that the raider might be mortally wounded.

The trouble would pass in time, Alfren told herself. It would have to. She would get to know nothing more about the raider and the children. Alfren was a watchman. Remorse, concern, sympathy were weaknesses. Give in to them and raiders would surge through.

The watchtower would stand forever and there would be other actions in years to come. She would be here for all her time, listening to the wind sing, watching her land through day and night in all weather, crusty with salt from sea spray, chilled by the winds.

She stopped pacing. On her own, she was free to go to her waves. She went to that part of her mind where the waves jostled all together like the voices of a hundred folk in the church at a celebration, seemingly inseparable. She teased out the wind waves and followed their pattern, then jumped into them and enjoyed being whisked along in their folding blue colours. She was reassured. How long had she been away? Let it not be ages! She found moon waves which told her only a few minutes had passed. That was alright. Handar, asleep in a cot in the deckhouse, hadn't stirred.

Alfren felt ready. She had heard sometimes a single watchman spent days on end on a watchtower and a good watchman, steady in the long, lonely hours of a night's watch, was hard to come by. They needed her. She was one of them.

She settled into her duty, pacing, counting and watching. All was well ... except a little trouble started. It happened every few weeks, sometimes when on watch; a sense that had lingered in her mind since a young child.

Something urged her on.

Another tremor.

She saw herself running from an unstoppable flood tide. The trouble would pass.

Watchman

Alfren and Handar returned in the morning, not by the pony track which was the long way, not by the watchman's path which she considered was open to ambush, not by the coastal path, the way she had come, because she didn't want to reveal to Handar the way she had used when over the wall and out hunting. Instead, Alfren led the way above the coves and across high ground, where she could see clearly all around – and any scavenger intent on surprising them both would have to chase up crags and across sinking bog. Handar had asked her to lead, which surprised her because the ranger traversed the outland every day and would surely know best. Walking in file, Alfren turned to her.

'Ma'am, I have a question, please.'

'Go ahead, Alfren,' Handar replied.

'Who are raiders, in your experience?'

'Good question, Alfren. The Watch don't stop to chat with them, do they!' Handar laughed. 'Raiders come from anywhere. Some sail here from distant settlements not aligned with the League. Some are our own who live here in the outland. Those are the ones we find peaceable when there's plenty to go around. They live in their hideaways and fastnesses and summer shacks. Some are bonded in some way with one another, through kinship or ties, pacts or deals, going back years or generations. There're tearaway packs of young from the families, cults and tribes that hide in the peel towers on the hilltops, or crannogs on the lakes, or brochs on the small islands. Yes, the worst of them strike out to steal and kidnap,' Handar sighed. 'Sometimes even the good ones turn to raiding. You can never tell because there aren't many years when there's enough to live on, or they've been raided themselves, leaving them short. It's simply that the more they raid, the more goods and silver they amass to trade in the lean years.

'You know, Alfren, that raider was an odd one. I didn't recognise her. I mean by clothes or jewellery – she had none. Or tattoos – she had none visible. We might never find out.'

Was Handar implying the girl might die?

'We don't ask too many questions, Alfren. We try to keep the peace, that's all. I guess the raider intended to trade the children. That happens and distressing it is too. I can't say if she's a Sealander. She could be. Maybe she knew of the beach, but it seems to me that she was driven ashore by the wind.

'She couldn't be one of the feral folk, who are few. You've heard of them: the scavengers in their wild bands. Certainly, she wasn't one of the drifters that pass by on their summer forays, as it's too late in the season for them. The raiders we have trouble with, I'm sure you know, are the League traders who steal or arrange crooked deals. She's likely to be one of them.

'Just so you know, we do catch sight of other folk, but they're not raiders. They're from the north and west, the far islands. They're settled and peaceable, it's said, and they go out of their way to avoid us Landers.'

'Right, thanks,' Alfren replied. She had only heard alarming tales of raiders, told to frighten children and folk alike, but Handar made them real and had described how desperate they were.

Anyone at large on her land could be a raider intent on theft, or carrying disease, or even a slaver ready to capture the unwary or vulnerable.

Around a headland, dark-green and brown hillsides rose from the sound and Wallburgh came into view. The burgh wall turned and cornered without order because that was how it had been built, a little at a time, adding to what was there – a house or barn wall – and then at some time made even more massive with great stones from the quarry. It was those bends and corners in the wall that had concealed her and Liffet when they had gone over. Closer, she could see the sea wall and the harbour buildings, and the stone roofs of the houses, the Burgh Hall tower and a clearing above the sound at the north side of the burgh where the fort stood, with its cannon emplacement. The next time the cannon would fire would be to celebrate the shortest day in the darkness of winter, when she and her mum, Liffet, the vicar and all the children would gather on the esplanade.

'Alfren,' called Handar, turning to her inside the South Gate, 'Well done. You're a fine watchman. I felt completely assured working with you. Could you pop along to the barracks this afternoon? I have a proposition.'

'Yes, ma'am. The Watch barracks?'

Handar smiled. 'I meant the ranger barracks.'

Blimey.

'Yes, of course, ma'am.'

'Alright, until then.'

At home, by the kitchen stove in her mum's rocking chair, Alfren slept for a couple of hours and dreamt she was on duty. She stood high on a watchtower, daylight and darkness passing, an expanse of land and sea below. The high winds blew, and she could hear the whistling and wailing of air whirling over hill and crag, through the lattice of steelwork under the watch deck. Then heavy hill fog concealed all from her sight. On deck, she heard a watchman beside her say, 'When we can't hear or see beneath us, raiders slip through.'

She awoke with a start. She sat up, put the kettle on the stove and let into her mind the sounds from the burgh.

All would be back to usual in a day or so.

Though, it niggled. Who was the raider and where from?

Remember the stories, the watchmen said. She wasn't sure about that. All the stories seemed to have the same message anyway. At the Extinction, everything of the Last People had been lost and afterwards, what they knew of their own folk had been passed by word, from one generation to the next. She knew why they told the stories: when the raiders came in great numbers to overrun them one day as surely they would, the watchmen warned, she and a few others might survive – and the memories of her folk in the stories she carried.

Erlo was his name. He lived three generations after the Extinction and spoke all languages because he had grown up with all folk-kind that had fled grief and destruction. He was one of the feral folk and there were many of those then. He was a lad when they found him on the beach, washed up after a storm, bodies of his kin strewn about. It was rare to take pity on such. He was made a slave to a smith and collected flotsam from the shore, dug the peat and scavenged for scrap. Those were the times when there was plenty of iron and steel, all of it abandoned. One day, he told folk in the settlement about what he had seen as he had fled. He talked in all languages and dialects so that everyone understood. He told the folk what he thought would happen. They didn't agree with him, but they listened because he spoke well. He told them gently, over and over again. He never tired. He was a good slave, a good worker. He made up stories to entertain them, now lost to us, and always with the same message.

One day, after a storm, after the loss of their stores in the destruction and theft by folk unknown, they came to him.

Erlo never worked at the smithy from that day on.

That same day, folk started work on their wall.

Pub

That morning, Alfren packed her sample tins from the lab then signed out at the West Gate and took a path which lay in sight of watchtower Barb. The wind had quickened to a high wind-force 7. She collected water samples from pools in the streams falling to the reservoir, which had white tops to the waves for the wind was so strong. On her way, as always, she checked that a sheep or this year's lamb hadn't got stuck in any watercourse, a ghyll or burn. It was hard going, as she was pelted with showers of rain and gusts that forced her to kneel and wait them out. It didn't matter. She let her thoughts go, her mind cleared. Her waves chased her playfully and she tripped down the hill back to the burgh.

As arranged, just after noon, she met Liffet on the green before the Burgh Hall. They went down Topple Lane to Four Winds pub and ordered one plate of lamb chops each and, to share, a large bowl of thick porage with toasted hazelnuts (which came all the way from Camp Bounty in the League) and a jug of beer. They sat by the hearth, a peat fire smoking.

'I wish I'd been there. I would've jumped her, like the ranger,' Liffet said.

The moment of arrest was no satisfaction, Alfren thought, and when you didn't know who it could be and found a girl not much older than her – it was a jolt. Yet, so it had to be, she and Liffet had been taught to fight off the unknown; that ruthlessness was the best way to survive.

'What about the two children?' asked Alfren.

'Better off with us. Someone will look after them.'

'And the raider?'

'You know,' said Liffet.

Alfren did. When – if – the raider recovered, the girl would be sent to gaol and later the burghers might give her a job. Some raiders were found to be a good sort once they had settled and saw that Sealanders might offer them a new life.

'That should be the end of it, but there's something not right,' Alfren said.

'What are you thinking?' asked her friend.

'Isn't it all a bit odd? It wasn't a raiding party was it, not really.'

'We'll never know what the raider was up to, will we, Ally.'

After a moment, Liffet spoke again. 'Alright, Ally, but what can you do? You'll have forgotten about her by tomorrow.' Liffet looked at her searchingly, then smiled just as when they planned some mischief. 'It's nagging you, isn't it?'

'I would like to know what she was doing there on her own with two children. I mean, there could be more to this and we should stop this trade, if that's what it is. Our children have gone missing from the burgh and here is a raider with two from somewhere.'

'Do you want to question her?'

'Yes. I know we're not really supposed to.'

'Do you want me to come with you?'

'Yes.'

'Where is she, at the infirmary?'

'I'll ask.'

Barracks

Alfren had left enough time to take an up and down way to the ranger barracks. It was good practice: never go directly from one place to the next; be nimble and quiet. All children should follow that simple advice, such that a kidnapper in pursuit would draw attention to themselves. There wouldn't be a raider chasing her that day or any day, but that wasn't the point – always assume there could be. Most likely, the children themselves might spy her as she passed and follow out of curiosity. As a tease, she darted away.

She turned up dank, slimy ginnels and down narrow, windy lanes, then held up in a small yard and waited.

Her night watch had been on her mind, but she hadn't forgotten about Liffet's new job. However, that day she had looked into her friend's eyes and seen only attention to her, which also told her she should put off enquiring. She was itching to know. She had hoped Liffet was expecting good news. It would have to wait but not for long.

She pulled herself over a high wall between backyards and in a corner, climbed up and over a low roof. She dropped into a narrow passageway, edged along and peeked out onto Slippy Lane running around the north end of the burgh. There was no one in view, but she heard the clatter of tackety boots as folk approached. She stepped back to wait. As soon as they had passed, she sprinted a few steps to a passage opposite and stepped under the arch.

Certainly, she didn't want anyone to see her enter the ranger barracks. It was her business only.

The passage was short and opened out into a walled garden, larger than others in the burgh but still only a few paces around. There were trained fruit trees on the walls, herb beds at their foot, and in the centre a stand of screens with trained plants that bore rich red autumnal leaves. It was nice that the rangers had made a pleasant garden to return to. Maybe they weren't as rough as folk said they were.

She hung back. Children apprehended by rangers had told her they asked one thing but were after another, they deceived and tricked with their questions and got you to say things you didn't mean to let out. She thought she had been fairly good at abiding by rules recently. She had gone over the wall with Liffet at dusk but only to shoot rabbits. Last week it was Liffet who had grabbed enough peat at the quayside to fill a basket, not Alfren, because it was her turn on lookout. She breathed in and stepped forward.

'Welcome, Alfren,' called Handar who stepped smiling from behind a screen. She wore the bib trousers of her storm suit, but the harness and smock had gone, replaced with a green, fine-wool jacket, which Alfren supposed was what officers wore in barracks.

'Thank you, ma'am. Nice garden, ma'am.'

'Thank you, we like it. I'm glad you're here. Please, sit here with me.'

There was a recess at the arched entrance to the barracks, door closed, sheltering a delicate-looking potted plant with large dark-green leaves, possibly from far away, probably taken from raiders. Handar beckoned her to sit in the alcove.

'I believe you've never before been here at the barracks, Alfren?'

Meaning she'd never been caught by a ranger in the outland and brought back for detention, was that it?

'No, ma'am.'

'I think you might be interested to see the base. There's not much, which is why we don't have open days like the militia. I'd like to correct any *views* you might have about rangers. We supply from here, but crew change is short and off we go out on patrol again. Folk in the burgh don't have a chance to get to know us. All the same, I think they trust we're out there in their service.'

'Yes, ma'am. I think so. I don't know any rangers. They don't live in the burgh, do they?'

'You may be surprised by how many do. We keep watch on things.' Handar hesitated. 'I mean, we like to know what's going on, so far as we can. In all the burghs and settlements, everywhere. I think what keeps folk in check and stops anything getting out of hand is the presence, sooner or later, of a ranger patrol. When folk turn away from us or avoid us then we know they just want to be left alone. If they hide or run, we have business with them.'

Alfren wondered if Handar was searching for some response. She looked up.

'Yes, ma'am.'

'I make the rangers sound much too serious, don't I? Well, I'd like you to relax and enjoy your visit. There's someone I'd like you to meet. Could you follow me, please, Alfren?'

Jin

'Marine Jin!' Handar called.

This must be about the watchman, Jin thought.

He set aside his soldering iron – he was repairing what appeared cracked and broken on a salvaged circuit board simply to find what worked and what didn't – replied 'Ma'am!' and slid from his stool at the workbench by the window overlooking the archery butts.

He hastened across the small workshop, around a pillar drill, lathe, bench and storage racks and smiled as he approached the recruit.

'Alfren, I'd like to introduce Marine Jin. Jin, this is watchman Alfren.'

'How do you do, ma'am,' he said, reaching to shake hands.

'How do you do, sir,' said Alfren.

'Would you mind showing Alfren around the barracks and telling her about what you do?'

With that introduction, Handar withdrew.

'Welcome to my home, Alfren,' Jin said.

'You sleep here?' she asked, looking at the shelves heaped with artefacts, all collected over many years which he added to occasionally.

'I would if they'd let me,' he replied. 'It's interesting stuff that we've recovered from the Last People.'

'Lieutenant Handar asked if I was interested to see the barracks and I am. It's not because I'm in trouble, just so you know.'

'Not been lifting peat or smuggling spirit.'

'No, never.'

He smiled. 'Come along, first let's see if we can't find a mug of tea and sit back.'

He led her along the corridor to the refectory; a small stone room with a stone-flagged floor and wooden-plank ceiling, where the window let in light from the south. He heard calls from workmen below who repaired roofs in the burgh. There were a couple of big wooden chairs with worn woollen seat cushions, a half fish-barrel between them for a table and a closed serving hatch opposite, from which he took his gruel or stew, morning and evening. Under a row of mugs on hooks in the corner there was a steel urn that bubbled with simmering water. Alfren had taken a teaspoon of dried leaves from a tin by the urn to mix in her cup; she was drawing in the aroma of camomile. It was always a surprise to Jin what supplies rangers acquired when out on patrol. He gestured to the chairs.

He saw that Alfren's oilcloth smock in deep blue was patch-repaired from wear and tear. Her eyes switched around taking in details; then for a moment they seemed to look far away, through the walls.

'I joined three years ago,' he said. 'They told me I could train for my craftsman's certificate, which was what I wanted, so I fix the radios and tinker about in my spare time. I go out on patrol a lot, which is alright.'

'Do you shoot raiders?' she asked, looking up at him.

'Occasionally. Usually though, they shoot at us.' He laughed and noticed how she relaxed.

'What do you do though?' she asked.

'We patrol, making sure folk are alright; we watch for incursions and question folk, and we arrest folk who don't belong here. Sometimes we send them on their way, or we help them if they want to stay. We investigate crimes and chase villains. Mostly though, we watch for raiders and when we find them, we drive them off and, if we can, we recover what they've stolen. But often they fight.'

'What about smugglers?' she asked.

'Smugglers?'

She blushed and dipped her eyes. 'I saw some once, from a long way off.'

The 'long way off' sounded like a fib, he thought. Perhaps the watchmen she served with had encountered smugglers and rather than report them, did a deal instead. It didn't matter. He gave the stock answer.

'They're a problem for the Watch and the customs, not us. We're here to keep the worst folk away, Alfren, and to watch for big threats to our Land.'

She nodded.

'When will the raiding stop?'

He could understand that, from folk understandably frustrated, cooped up inside their settlements.

'No one knows. The point is, Alfren, it's been like this ever since the Extinction.'

She frowned.

'Is the Extinction important still? I'm not sure, although the vicar says it is.'

'Who?' he asked.

'He has papers and drawings, stuff like that, from the time of the Extinction. The thing is, the vicar says the Extinction was when the storms came. Before that, it was always calm. I'd miss the winds, wouldn't you?'

A *vicar* looking for accounts of what happened at the Extinction? That wasn't allowed by the militia – who encouraged folk to look to their futures not dwell on the past.

'Do you go out expecting to fight?' she asked. 'I'm not sure I could do it. I shot a raider, you know. It was awful. How do you know what to do?'

'I heard. You did the right thing, at night and just the two of you. Don't ever take chances.'

He looked at her. 'You should always be ready for anything. Frankly, I prefer to have a good patrol when we sort out problems and go home without a firing a shot. But it can be dangerous.' He was silent to let that sink in. 'Any more questions?'

Alfren said nothing.

'Handar says you're a good shot,' he said. 'Would you like to see the archery butts? You could practise there as often as you like.'

'Here in the barracks?' she asked.

He led her from the refectory and turned to walk along a passageway.

'How old are you, Jin?'

'I'm eighteen. Actually, nearly nineteen,' he grinned.

He opened a heavy wooden door pivoted in its centre and led her outside. The high wind-force 7 whipped around them despite the shelter of the barrack walls. He braced himself, but Alfren yielded, stepping sideways to parry a gust, quick on her feet.

'Take your time,' he called over a whistle of wind, pointing to a door to the armoury. She heaved at the sliding door and reappeared with a longbow, a quiver with a half-dozen long arrows and a pleased look on her face. Handar was right: clearly Alfren took to archery and would have only occasional opportunity to shoot a longbow in the Watch.

Alfren strung the bow and went straightaway over to the longest practice butt of 50 yards. It was a narrow passage between buildings and the wall, so long it ran behind houses and workshops, but still the wind scooped and whipped. He saw her weigh the draw of the bowstring and sight on the target. In quick order, she loosed three arrows. They clumped dead centre of the target roundel.

He whistled softly. She had done that without getting to know the bow.

'You're strong.'

She looked down and made to retrieve the arrows. Then, as if deciding to tell something important, she faced him.

'I like to practise,' she called. 'It's a good bow,' not that he could see that was the reason for her accuracy. 'I started archery when the vicar put me forward for the Watch when I was twelve.'

Her eyelids dipped. Not all true, he thought. She must have been one of those kids who had roved outside the wall from a young age, taking a bow to hunt seabirds and rabbits. He had caught a couple of children himself when returning overland to the burgh, but rangers said there had been far fewer wall-runners since the guards had closed down their escape ways some years before. Still though, some children took small boats on moonlit nights; some climbed the wall; and some slipped the gates during the day and spent the whole night outside until morning.

He had been lucky. He had grown up on Furrow, an eastern island, where, when the weather was clear and the guards allowed them, he and his friends had explored freely, although he had often got into trouble for adventuring out of sight. He hadn't thought it was wrong. It was a small island; you could see all around from the top of the only hill. There were green fields for harvesting fodder at the coast, rising to heather-covered fell where the sheep grazed. The sea cliffs and rocks, the pounding waves and heaving swell, were natural defences. The curving, sandy bay with a wide strand and blue water was the only landing place, overlooked by the great broch, the round stone tower, where all the families lived. He missed his home, but he had found his role as a ranger, and was glad of that.

Alfren seemed to think about what to say. She hesitated, but he wasn't much older than her so maybe she felt at ease.

'It's not difficult really. Every shot is different. The target comes first, and then I become the arrow and bend with the wind until it hits.'

She talked openly with him despite being a ranger – he knew what the burghers said about rangers. Actually, beyond the wall, all sorts of folk did talk to him and openly too: the farmsteaders; the journeymen that chanced their luck on the highway, tramping between the burghs over summer; the shepherds and their sheepdogs hiding out of sight in their caves; the ship's crew hastening home on leave; the tinkers with their fine wares, glad of their freedom, but taxed by thieving scavengers; the doctors and nurses on their fine ponies. They talked because they saw that he tried to understand them and their ways in the outland, and whatever hazards they faced.

Rangers had to understand folk.

'Good answer,' he said.

It seemed to him that he should ask and maybe Handar had intended it.

'You know, I think you could be a good ranger. Would you like to join?'

She fixed a look into his eyes. It was brief but searching.

'Me? No, I can't. I'm a watchman, and I work at the lab.' She considered. 'It's nice of you to ask.'

There it was, the suggestion made, and the possibility opened in her mind.

Alfren

Meeting Jin was not what she had expected.

He was nice and not at all odd like rangers should be, although he wasn't from Wallburgh, he was an outlander; she could tell from his accent.

She would ask Handar if she could really practise there with a longbow.

She could never leave the Watch.

Jin had shown her the radio apparatus he was working on in the workshop and the Operations Room with the biggest maps she had ever seen on the walls – far more detailed than the map at the Watch barracks and showing all of Sealand, and also, the infirmary, library, mess, parade hall and gardens. It all seemed organised, but not too disciplined.

The Watch was disciplined, but not as strict as the militia, she had heard.

Jin returned her to an empty refectory, shook her hand and said he hoped to see her again. He was a good lad.

Her mind turned to imaginings. How would it be to roam the outland as a ranger? The great maps came to mind: Sealand was so much more than the east coast, which faced the League. It was barely believable that there was so much outland to see.

And there must be so many waves out there.

Chitty

Alfren looked up to see Handar enter the refectory.

'Well, Alfren, what do you think?'

'All good, ma'am.' She should say more. 'Jin showed me everything. I liked the longbow.'

'Let's sit, Alfren.'

Handar had said that firmly. Maybe she should have declined the invitation to the barracks, and she would have been spared what was to come? Although she would have to admit it had been interesting, and it would be news for Liffet.

She glanced up at Handar. The children said you should dread an interview with a ranger, but she wasn't a youngster anymore.

She was resolved; whatever was asked, she would deny she was a wall-runner and certainly she wouldn't mention Liffet.

'Alfren, I have something to ask you. We'd like to offer you a commission in the rangers.'

Jin hadn't been joking!

'A ranger marine, ma'am?'

It couldn't be. That wasn't how she had trained and besides, what would the watchmen say? They were counting on her. But, the problem was she had grown to like the rangers since meeting Handar only the evening before.

'Ma'am, thank you, but I don't think I could. I mean, I'd like that very much, but I'm a watchman and my work at the lab is so important.'

Handar nodded.

'I think you have a strong sense of duty, Alfren, but be reassured. I've discussed this with the Watch of course, and the lab, so it's up to you alone.'

Handar sat back.

'We have the authority to negotiate who we take as rangers. I take your point about working at the lab, but I think you need to progress from collecting samples and routine analysis.'

She knows all that?

'I'd be interested in the possibility of you testing water at the settlements. Rangers have specialities too, like Jin has. Yes, it'd be fair to say a ranger's role can be difficult. It's fascinating, amazing and sometimes truly awful, and physically tough too. It's why we've chosen you. We see you as adaptable; you have to be.'

This was serious. It would be a big leap, like jumping from high on the wall, trusting she would land in soft bog; or perhaps with no soft landing at all. What could the waves tell her? She wished she had time to see them right then; they would surely be the same as always, but it would be reassuring that they were. Unless, just possibly they weren't …

Handar leaned forward.

'Your friend, Liffet, has she told you?'

'Liffet? You know her, ma'am?'

Handar nodded.

This was confounding.

'No, ma'am, she hasn't said anything.'

What should Liffet have told her? She stiffened. Had Liffet told someone about the way they sent messages to each other? Almost certainly not, but what had Liffet done?

'As you're her friend, you should know we applied for her to be a ranger, but the militia have first pick. She will become a scout, not a regular militia trooper. I'm sure I can trust you with this news.'

So that was Liffet's new job! Liffet had kept an enormous secret from her! How could Liffet have kept secret something so important! Liffet, a scout? It sounded like a top role for only the most able. Liffet had leapt ahead of her when she wasn't looking.

It was a moment of jealousy although she felt begrudgingly pleased for her friend. She couldn't forgive Liffet for not telling her though.

Could she leave the Watch?

'Alfren?'

'Yes, ma'am?'

Handar was fixed on her still. It was clear to her the Watch must have been persuaded to give her up. Could she be a ranger? The way Handar had framed it, there was no going back. There was no choice at all.

'Thank you, ma'am, I would be very pleased to accept your proposal.'

She had done it and she wouldn't go back on her word, not to a ranger.

Had her Watch given her up so easily?

Had Liffet known she was to be offered a role in the rangers?

She stood to salute and shake hands with Handar. Almost straightaway Jin entered to congratulate her. Handar took her to the offices for introductions and then to the mess where a few rangers were either making ready for patrol or had just returned for debriefing. That was when what she had agreed to sank in. These were rangers in the raw and they were definitely outlanders – more outlander than Handar and Jin combined. She couldn't read them straightaway, not like she could the guards or even the watchmen. They gave nothing away except a friendly half interest in her. She would have a lot to learn about them, just as much as about the outland, she realised.

What had she done?

Already the mystery of a ranger's way felt more exciting than the certainty of the Watch. She followed Handar to an office where there would be a contract ready to read.

'Lieutenant Handar, ma'am, I have a question, please. It's not about my enrolment at all.'

'Go ahead, Marine Alfren.'

'Yes, ma'am, it's this. Could I go to see the raider we caught?'

'Do you want to?' asked Handar. 'We don't ask that usually, not once they're handed over to the militia. We await the report, but that isn't always passed on to us.' Handar continued on and turned again. 'It would be interesting to know where the raider and the children came from.'

'Maybe I might find out something,' Alfren said. 'The raider's not much older than me. She might talk. I'd like to know more about child-smuggling.'

It didn't take long for a clerk to read out the contract and for Handar and another officer to witness her signature in a great ledger.

'I prepared this chitty,' said Handar, holding out a small slip of paper, 'for an interview with the raider. She'll be at the infirmary, I'm sure. Take it across to the militia barracks for authorisation. Find out what you can and report to me.'

Alfren took it and stared. There was more to this than a simple chitty. It was a key. She felt a wave surge at her, a tremor. She felt dizzy for an instant and it passed.

'Thank you, ma'am.'

Under the archway, she pulled up the hood of her smock. A deluge of rain sluiced by and the drains flooded over onto the lane. The wind was rising. It would become a strong gale-force 9 that evening. Even she should be under cover.

She staggered a little as a gust pulled her from the archway. She set off feeling she had a new life ahead ready to fill with adventure, as she picked a way home to avoid lanes that funnelled wind, hidden from the keen eyes of the children.

The winds would always be rising and roiling like this. The waves told her so.

Her life would be exciting; she would see the world.

Tower

The Picker

The master felt chilled and he edged to the hearth at the great stone fireplace. He would rather be in the cellars where there were no draughts, but the chief preferred this round stone cell at the topmost of the high tower, with a narrow wooden stair to the roof where he made his observations, day and night. The master slipped his arms within the heavy woollen robe he wore and pulled the folds close. It was a sign of authority to wear a robe because it showed the wearer conducted business within walls, out of the winds. He looked down to admire the purple and gold weave, the finest to be procured in the League. He sighed. His high status couldn't raise warmth.

It wasn't only cold. Every day save for the finest in summer, he chilled in the damp air and sea winds that made a cold day bitter. *Bracing*, the jarls called it laughingly when they came to his chief for their assignments.

He looked up. He must be seen to be attentive to the chief, but his eyes wandered. The tapestries that hung around the walls had colourful scenes of mountains, forest and lakes and strong wooden towns at the water's edge, but the dim, trickling gaslight barely kept the darkness at bay.

He sniffed loudly. Maybe the chief would dismiss him.

Not likely. The chief was busy as usual this evening with cataloguing. On the desk was a stack of papers and notebooks. The master had observed that the chief found cataloguing a settling pastime.

Yet, the chief had been testy, and he knew the reason why.

Abruptly, the chief spoke. 'This setback is troublesome. I will not allow it to interfere with my project. You lost my most experienced and brightest forecaster,' he remarked acidly.

The master didn't comment that the chief had supported the girl's proposal that she should go on the raid in order to reassure the children once they had been snatched. They had travelled far into the League and it had made sense that the girl should be there to watch over the children on the long return voyage. He waited. The chief was distracted by one of the texts which he had procured while away and he hoped the chief would be pleased with them at least. Those scraps were scarce, although when they turned up only a little silver was necessary to procure them. Why did the chief want them? Why should anyone want to read bitter, rambling thoughts, protests and raving tirades by the Last People at the injustice of the Extinction, or about the struggles and misfortunes of the new folk?

They were dead, gone and good riddance to them.

'Where were you when she escaped?'

'In my cabin. A storm was rising.'

'Not even a high wind-force 7.'

'No, Chief. I retired.'

'Because you were seasick.'

'Yes, Chief, and I believed the boat's watch would prevent Zal ...'

'You must get her back. Take the snatch crew.' The chief raised a paper. 'Have you seen the report from Wallburgh?'

'Yes. There does seem to be an anomaly regarding Zal's capture by the Watch.'

'Undoubtedly. Look into it. Take sufficient silver to pay for the information you need. This could be the one we lost; do you realise that?'

'Yes, Chief.'

'You must leave today.'

The master nodded and waited.

'Our mission must prevail. The signs are there. It is imminent.'

The chief stood. 'Call my assistant.'

The master went over to a tapestry, pulled it aside and pushed open a heavy wooden door. A clerk stepped in hurriedly from a small anteroom.

'Take these in the crate to the archive, these for copying and leave these here. Shortly I shall make my tour of inspection,' the chief instructed.

Surveying the papers, the chief snatched the topmost from the archive pile, then sat heavily at the desk, absorbed in whatever was written. The master moved to look over his shoulder. It was only a short note in the old dialect and barely readable.

The master saw the assistant was uncertain and wary as to what to do.

'Take them!' barked the chief.

'Damn it!' The master started as the chief slammed the desk. He peered more closely, curious as to what had caused an outburst.

The master read slowly because the text had been scrawled almost illegibly.

The word came this morning and I hate it. I feel sick in my stomach. It was the fortune-teller once again. I do so want to live without this. I want it to leave us alone. But no, the

55

fortune-teller speaks, and I have time only to gather my bedroll and basket, then away we troop inland before the end of the day. I pray this time as before I will feel better afterwards, in a few days' time. Then there should be respite for a while, I must hope. But most likely not.

I have a moment to write, it is hard for us. We must rush. I know my feet will be wet cold, my clothes sodden. Hunger will paw at me. There. These selfish thoughts are better out. My small sister, my grandfather, will need my strength. I will not think of myself at all from now on.

I will leave these notes safe and dry in a pot in our shelter for who knows what we will find when, or if ever, we return here.

That would certainly interest the chief. However, it wouldn't reveal any more about how this 'fortune-teller' had known what was about to happen and in good time for people to take shelter. He backed away quietly leaving the chief to ponder the mystery.

Dockside

'Master,' called the skipper, and the master tied his raiment close before climbing the steps to the wheelhouse. A blow-force 4 they called it, but it may as well have been a storm by the way the small freighter rocked, even though it was tied-up at the quay. Nowhere was better for the master's nerves than a room within thick stone walls, yet here he was once again, aboard a barrel of a boat that rolled with every wave and gust.

He was master, like the master navigators or ship owners of old, which was the highest rank below only the chief himself, yet still he had to undertake chores such as this foray. He had the authority to instruct the jarls when his chief was busy, and they knew his words were as good as the chief's, but these jarls were no use to his chief on this errand. The jarls were untrustworthy, brash and arrogant, and might try to outwit even the chief.

And so, the task had fallen to him. Despite his rank of ship's master, he belonged in the mountains. They were his home. One day, he would plead to retreat there, and he hoped his chief would hear him. Until then, he followed the chief because there were deals, fortunes and ... a vision.

It was secure enough from prying townsfolk in the darkness of middle evening to climb onto the quayside to address the gathering, a few dim lamps held low by barely two-dozen folk. Yet that was all they needed; the chief had said. His balance was still unsteady from the sailing. He forced himself to look up. He had their willing attention. They were loyal, eager to take part. He spoke clearly because in this large, settled town of Wallburgh just as everywhere on Sealand there was a mix of folk who spoke many languages and dialects. Many incomers had landed here from the League towns and still more League folk came to seek a new start. Some had been forced from those settlements not aligned with the League and therefore had no protection from displacement by new settler folk. All had come seeking employment for their skills or were determined to make riches from trade. All had had to meld their languages with the popular dialect of the town. Here, they had recovered from their voyages, stayed put, and prospered. Some had put themselves under the protection of the chief because they had heard his message and were convinced of what was to come.

The storms.

The master waited a moment for their full attention.

'Fellow guardians of the survival, I bring greetings from the chief, our visionary.'

'Aye,' called the crowd softly.

'I remind you; you have chosen the right path. Do not stray. It is a gracious mystery that we have been chosen, and we accept our destiny. You are essential to the cause and will join with a host of survivors at the Great Upheaval! You will be the first in a new world!'

'Aye.'

'You all have your duties and instructions. You must follow them to the letter.'

They would lead the jarls to the town's stores when the time came – that was their use.

'The visionary bids you keep your resolve. At the Great Upheaval, there will be strange forces at work that will try to confuse and deceive us. The very firmament will prickle at your minds. You must stay true. Today and every day you must set your hearts and minds on the path we take – for survival.'

He searched their faces in the glimmer of lamplight. Their gaze did not fall under his stare.

'We shall survive!'

'Aye!'

'The visionary will guide us. Be ready for his word. Guardians, you have strength and wisdom. Together ... together, we shall survive!'

'Aye!'

'I have a new instruction direct from the visionary. Take heed; carry out these orders.'

He explained the action required from these townsfolk. It had to be done quickly. He needed to know the whereabouts of the actors from the report, where they might gather and how he might intercept them. He couldn't linger in this town or he himself might become the subject of a report from those damn watchmen.

'I will tell the visionary myself of your selfless endeavours. Go well, guardians!'

The small assembly dispersed, to climb the steep lanes of the walled town to their homes.

He wouldn't fail the chief.

Mess

Jin

Jin reclined in the rangers' mess in the corner by the window. He heard the gas lamp spitting above him, as it glowed over scraps of his writing heaped on his lap. It was comfortable there, reclined on some stuffed sacks. Handar had threatened to throw them out almost every day, but the filthy fleeces packed inside were dry and soft, and the muck droppings hardly smelled at all, so she had never got around to it and he was always relieved to see the sacks there still on his return from patrol.

He had begged the scraps of paper from the office, had taken faded old texts (with permission) that seemed unimportant from the archivist, or had torn off out-of-date news posters from the Burgh Hall noticeboard. He had loitered at the door to the printing press for the typesetter to refill his inkpot and snatched feathers from a crow carcass when out on patrol and trimmed them for his quills.

Tans, his corporal, whooped and laughed loudly at the card table. He looked up and smiled.

He wasn't supposed to write about the matter that he did. Folk should have better things to do than mull over the past. Anyway, for anyone that looked into it, the past was supposed to be a celebration of all his folk had achieved. What more was there to it than that? The rangers didn't prohibit his deliberations on folk history, so long as he kept to his own time, and besides, there was precious little of that so what harm could there be in it?

The first few points he knew well. There was the accepted account of the foundation of the new folk soon after the Extinction when the Last People had all died out: that a folk similar to but distinctly separate from the Last People had endured terribly but rallied at the trial. The testing times for the new folk were also their awakening. They were released from their chains of submission to the Last People by the hardship of the Extinction.

To him, that simply didn't sound right. How could two tribes, the Last People and the 'new folk', exist side by side but separate for so long?

Remember, the Extinction was absolute. The Last People, in their desperation to survive, sought only warmth, shelter and food. Whatever technical gadgets or great industries that had been useful to them in their existence failed or were no use at all in the years and the ravages of the Extinction. Their ways were lost as the last of the Last People died. The new folk that arose were few, scattered, desperate and on the brink of failure. However, in the first generations, barely scraping sustenance from one year to the next, they held onto their ideas and tested new skills, which they passed down by word of mouth to their youngsters who, in the lulls between the storms, when the short summer seasons were merciful, reworked the key technology that their parents had described.

They had only what they could remember in their minds. Those that could scribbled brief texts on scrolls, leaves of paper or vellum. Yet, those texts might have been contaminated with the poor judgement of the Last People, which is why the texts, those of the Last People and the new folk, were few and kept hidden out of sight and mind.

It had been a dark age, and no one can say how long it had lasted.

After travelling the seas in search of new land safe from the worst of the storms, many gatherings of new folk came together in the Great Herding. The rise of the new folk was a wonder, fabulous to recount in their stories. Their technologies were varied and marvellous. On Sealand, they cut peat from drained bog and dried it to feed their power station. Waste heat warmed their workshops. Gas derived from baking peat was distributed by a deep-buried network of pipes, for light in their homes. Scrap left over by the Last People, brought in by traders, was tipped into their peat-coke furnaces, then cast and worked into new artefacts. They used hydro-electric – the reservoir high on the fell – to power an arc furnace, which combined lime and coke into calcium carbide for use in their acetylene hand lamps. They had all they could wish for.

Most industry was based at the shipwrights' houses in the works' quarter, a fenced stretch on the shore of the sound with quays, cranes and warehouses.

There, of great service to them, was their gunpowder mill, driven by water wheel. The constituents of gunpowder – he knew well because he made the same with pestle and mortar – were charcoal from flotsam from the beaches and coppices in the inland, saltpetre from the nitriaries in the works' quarter, and brimstone, which was imported.

From the quarries, gunpowder-blasted rock was dressed by saw and chisel into heavy stone blocks for their buildings.

Rough stone, huge blocks, built their wall. It offered handholds and footholds for nimble child climbers, like Alfren.

Also at the shipwrights' quarter were the lime kilns. Limestone was brought from one of the islands and heated at high temperature by peat gas in the tall shaft kiln to make quicklime for binding mortar and render. When it was burning, he had seen fellows attending night and day to feed the kiln and barrow away the lime.

Although, he had heard the stonemasons say they prided themselves on the fit of their blocks, thus requiring least mortar, which made their buildings all the stronger to stand the winds.

There was so much he wanted to set down as a record on his scraps and tatters of paper. The folk tradition was word of mouth and apprenticeship. What if that were lost if a storm dispersed them once more? He had to write it down. It was high time books were commonplace: some for reference, as technical guides and histories, there to pass on if disaster struck.

DAY 1

Infirmary

Alfren

It was a blustery breeze-force 5 on a dreich morning. Alfren and Liffet wore dry, clean uniforms with newly waxed leather boots, and she thought how smart they must look. She was wearing her watchman's dark-grey wind suit because she couldn't afford a ranger's green storm suit, not yet, and didn't feel ready to wear one until she had earned it in some way. Liffet wore her outland field suit in navy, as worn by a scout in the militia, but without the red flashes on cuff and shoulder because a scout had to be unseen. Alfren was surprised Liffet had put on her uniform. She stole glances at her friend to try to read her expression. She hadn't dared to send messages about their *promotions*, because she might have given away her annoyance that her friend had upset their way of sharing everything that happened to one another. What else had Liffet concealed from her? Maybe she should say something, but really Liffet had kept secrets and should say something first.

They were still and would always be the best of friends, though. She was arm in arm with Liffet as they walked the lanes to the infirmary. Liffet was carrying a single carnation cadged from a neighbour who had a cold frame in their small garden.

'It was good news to hear you're a scout when Lieutenant Handar told me.'

'Thanks, Ally. I'd hoped you'd be pleased for me. Everyone knows because I have to wear this suit with a scout badge on my arm. I was worried for you, you know after you shot that raider.'

'Seems you're special.'

'That's nice to know. I thought there was nothing for me and I didn't know where I wanted to work. I thought I was odd.'

'Yes, I thought that too.'

She pushed back as Liffet shouldered her gently.

'I don't have to do much. Right now I'm learning technical stuff about signals, which is alright.' Liffet tugged at her. 'How about you? You're a ranger! Everyone wants to be a ranger.'

'Handar said you were her first pick to be a ranger, but the militia got you instead.'

'Really?'

'Yes, but then I told her, you get lost in your own backyard.'

Liffet laughed. 'Did you tell her you leave chalk marks when you go to the shop? Really though, do you think they suspect anything about how you and I, you know, send thoughts between us?'

'Of course not. How would they know?'

'They ask folk about us when they're assessing us, and some folk are observant, even though we do our best to go about unnoticed.'

'Well, it's silly stuff. It's just our play, nothing more.'

'Yes, alright,' said her friend. 'What're you going to ask the raider?'

'I want to see what she's like. I'd like to know where she's from and who the children are.'

The infirmary was in the centre of the burgh.

Alfren rapped a large brass knocker on a great wooden double door. A flap opened and she called out, 'Ranger and militiaman present. Warrant to enter!'

One half of the door was winched open slowly and Alfren stepped in. A porter led them along clean, dimly lit corridors to a guard seated at a desk before a barred, steel door.

'Got a chitty, please, mister,' said Liffet.

'Oh, have you?' said the guard, clearly ready to be difficult. 'What's that to me?'

Alfren nudged her friend.

'May we see the raider prisoner, please, sir?' Liffet asked.

The guard glanced at the chitty and raised his eyebrows when he saw the names and signatures – the topmost officers in the militia, or so Alfren had been told when she had collected it.

'Seems all correct. Don't go tormenting the prisoners. Watch that girl raider. You can't be too careful. Third on the left.'

The guard unlocked and opened the heavy steel door and stood aside to let them through. This was it, thought Alfren. Suddenly, being a ranger was real. Here were violent prisoners and captured raiders. She stepped into a ward containing a dozen beds, with curtains drawn for privacy between them. Some were closed off across the front. Two guards inside the door played cards at a table. They looked up and waved her on.

She paused at the first cubicle where a prisoner lay with bandaging around leg and chest. He was awake and looked up at them. 'Who the bloody hell are you?' he asked roughly.

'Never you mind,' said Liffet, firmly.

One of the guards hissed.

Alfren peeked around the closed curtain of the third cubicle where she saw the girl raider lying, eyes closed. Above, there was a window letting in grey light.

'Hello,' Alfren said, as she entered leaving Liffet standing guard.

The girl's eyes opened wide with alarm then she started with surprise and winced in pain. Alfren put her finger to her lips.

This was the girl she had shot alright – on the beach, in anguish, smeared with blood, coated with grit. Yet here in the dim light was the same girl, a couple of years older than Alfren, seventeen or eighteen. Her chest was bandaged.

'Please, be calm,' Alfren said softly. She held out Liffet's carnation, approached the bed slowly and laid the flower on the blanket.

'I'm Alfren,' she said.

The girl looked down and aside. 'Go away.'

'I shot you, I know. I'm sorry. I had to; I was doing my duty.'

Alfren waited.

'What's your name?'

She drew a stool to the bedside and sat.

'I'm here to help if I can. It's strange that you took the risk you did. To come ashore I mean, close to the watchtower.'

The girl hesitated. 'Zal is my name. Can you do something for me?'

'What is it?' Alfren asked.

'Get a message to my chief to say I'm fine. Post a message anywhere, and someone will find it. I'm not going to tell you anything. I made a mistake, and you should let me go.'

What chief? There must be many chiefs in the outland and all around the League too. It might be important to know which one, but just then all she wanted to know was why Zal had landed where she had.

'What were you going to do, from there at the beach?'

No reply. Zal looked away again.

'The militia is going to ask you too. Have they already?'

'No one's been,' said Zal.

They hadn't? Why not?

'I came here to see you myself because I wanted to check you're recovering,' Alfren said. 'You seem not to be a usual raider at all,' she suggested – a prompt for an explanation.

'You're not a usual Lander, are you?' retorted Zal. 'How did you see my boat? It was completely dark. I'd shielded the lamp and I rowed for the sound of waves breaking on shingle.'

Zal calmed but only for a moment.

'What have you done with the children?' she demanded. 'Where are they?' She paused. 'Can you get a message to the children,' she said softly, 'to tell them I'm thinking of them and I'd like to see them? Please? I will see them, won't I?'

Zal clutched the flower from the blanket.

'The children are being looked after, I'm sure,' said Alfren. She had to press Zal.

'Why were you there at the beach? Why did you do this? For whom?'

Zal took her time. As soon as she began to speak, Alfren knew she would dodge not tell.

'Questions like that you'll have to put to our chief. If you do, there'll be something in it for you.'

Alfren was flummoxed. How could she have thought she could question a raider and get answers?

'Wait,' she said. 'If you tell me, then I'll get a message to the children.'

Zal was silent. Alfren studied the girl's face.

'Are you a child smuggler? Is that why you won't talk?'

It was hopeless. Clearly Zal couldn't trust her and would have to be convinced she was on her side. Alfren would have to think it through and visit again.

She jumped at a clang of steel. She had heard the door to the ward crash open and a muted scuffle, just as Liffet whipped into the cubicle, drawing the curtain closed.

'Villains!' Liffet hissed.

Not possible! But Liffet was earnest. Alfren glanced around the cubicle, but there was no exit, not even the window that was high above, small and probably locked.

'How many?'

'Five, maybe more.'

There were muffled cries, then quiet.

They wheeled the bed aside, to give themselves more room in the cubicle.

Why villains, just at that moment? Had they come for one of the prisoners? Surely not for Zal?

'There's no way out,' came a fellow's sneering voice. 'Put down any weapons and we won't harm you.'

That was directed at them. Liffet sprang to Alfren's side and pulled out a knife just as the curtain swished open to reveal a brutal-looking gang.

Zal recoiled.

'Don't be rash, Liffet,' called out the sneering fellow.

He knows Liffet's name?

The fellow was slight and wore a heavy robe. Four hirelings with him looked like dock workers, or deckhands from a trader. Alfren was in what should be the safest of places, in the infirmary at the heart of Wallburgh. She and Liffet faced menacing brutes who intended to take what they wanted by force, and straightaway. She supposed that the guards had been restrained or knocked out. She and Liffet were on their own unless the prisoners on the ward could help or raise the alarm. Otherwise this gang might snatch, even kill them. For what?

The sneering fellow stepped forward and stared at her.

'Bind those others,' he instructed.

The two heaviest hirelings turned about; one drew a knife. The curtains veiled what was happening. She heard shouts and struggles.

'Leave them alone!' she screamed.

These thugs were real, the worst, and they were beasts. She was ready to fight. Liffet would be too.

The sneering fellow turned to her.

'You must be Alfren. Tell me, which one of you is the seer?'

Seer?

He searched their eyes.

'We want only the seer. Zal's done her job and brought us the seer. Which one of you is it? Is it you?' he demanded of Alfren.

Her? One to call out prophecies like the fortune-tellers at their stalls on the market street?

This was unreal. This outland fellow must be too muddled and disturbed for reason.

She saw him become agitated. She must act quickly, for this was a *raid*!

These were raiders!

'We have the signs. One of you is the seer. Maybe Zal knows.'

He flicked his head to the men.

'Bring them!' he snapped.

Liffet sprang forward in a crouch, knife at the ready and drew a second.

'You're a live one,' said the sneering fellow. 'Quick. We must leave,' he addressed his hirelings.

Alfren backed beside her friend, the better to fight off the hirelings together. She would draw them to fall onto Liffet's knives. Although the hirelings were big and clearly had great strength, the watchmen had told her she was quick and that might be enough maybe to topple one of them.

'Bring the three,' the sneering fellow said and turned away.

Liffet stepped forward pushing Alfren aside and facing one of the hirelings as he approached, the bed a barrier to the others behind them. The hirelings wore thick leather tunics for carrying sacks and barrels. With all Liffet's strength it was unlikely even a direct stab could pierce through, then enough only to maim. Alfren made ready to lunge for the hireling's trailing leg, to unbalance him, when ...

There was a scream. Alfren tumbled forward and fell, pinned to the floor. The bed and Zal were on top of her, thrown over by hirelings behind them. She struggled but strong hands fixed her wrists. She wriggled and kicked her legs. A hand gripped her hair and twisted her head. A sweet-smelling pad was held tight over her mouth and nose. She mustn't breathe; she held on until her chest heaved. Would she ever wake?

She felt drowsy. She was bundled up in a sack, carried roughly by strong arms. She heard gruff voices, smelt sea air and heard faint mewing, most likely Zal. She tested her bonds. She was strapped tightly.

'This one's come round,' said the hireling carrying her.

'Get her on the boat quickly, and if she calls out, keep her quiet,' ordered the sneering fellow.

'This one's out still,' said another hireling, sounding relieved.

'Could be her then?' mumbled the sneering fellow. 'Come along. Make haste,' he urged.

From the rumble of boats in the sound and gulls' cries, Alfren knew she was at the quay. The hireling carried her down a steep gangplank and manhandled her through a hatch into a stowage hold. She was laid on a hard deck. She heard a steel gate clang and lock.

A new hireling spoke next, a charge-hand maybe.

'No one goes near those three without permission from the Picker. Is that clear? I have the key. These girls stay locked in this cage.'

'Any silver on them?' asked one.

There was a punch. 'Leave off, I was only asking, Skipper!'

'Go near 'em and you go overboard.'

'Aye alright, skip, steady!'

'They're odd ones. You'd regret it, that's what the Picker says. Come along, let's lock them up before ... go on, shift yourselves!'

Alfren heard the hatch above close and the squeak of latches screwed up. Then she heard shuffling and grunting, and one said, 'Pass another screw here.' When they were done, there was a clang of a steel door and a mechanism squeaked as bolts slid home.

Alfren heard moaning.

Zal.

She could hear light breathing too: Liffet. Most likely Liffet had put up the greater struggle, taken more of the anaesthesia, and would be under for a while.

Until the other girls became conscious, Alfren would be on her own.

The drum of the heavy-oil engine sounded urgent. She heard calls and the boat shuddered, then heaved over. They were underway.

No one called her name from the quay. There was no crack of rifle fire or warning shot of cannon. She heard no cries, threats or orders barked.

Wasn't there someone to stop this? Surely the children had seen the raiders in the lanes and alerted the guard? Wouldn't an off-duty watchman see there was something wrong at the quay? Wouldn't there be a docker right then who suspected something amiss, racing south along to the militia barracks or north to the shipwrights' quarter, waving his arms to attract attention. Soon wouldn't there be a host of folk tracking the boat from the water's edge, all shouting and waving? Surely a harbour tug was in pursuit and she would hear its bell! Wouldn't she? It would be a little time only before the engine stilled, she heard a scuffle and shouts, and she felt the grip of the watchmen on her arms to lift and guide her up on deck. There would be hugs and exclamations from the brave pursuers and then laughs at the relief of rescue. All that was surely to come.

Suddenly, the engine grew louder. It was overwhelming. It was in her mind. Was this a dream? Her senses filled with pounding, clanging, hot oil, stifling fumes, cold sea air, harsh voices, yelling. Next to her, shouting angry bitter curses, was a little girl. She remembered; this was a nightmare from long ago when she was only a small child. She fell into a rhythm of shouting with the girl, one then the other. In the dark, under the sacks that covered them, they cursed and wailed the lostness only small children could feel. The two of them bumped into one another, then shuffled together, touching arm to arm, the barest warmth. There was just a little comfort. Her terror lessened and became panic and fear, and she altered her mind somehow. She heard screams, and they faded.

The pounding of the engine changed again. She heard it with her ears in the present, not in her dream. This was now. Not then.

Alfren remembered the nightmares she had when a little girl. Stuffy, hot, then scarily cold, loud and smelly ... with screaming too. Her recall minutes before had been exactly like that but it told her more. Those had been screams of panicked men. The nightmares made sense; they had been real. She had been six, bound, taken and trapped, home unreachable. Yes, she knew already the noise and smell of a boat like this because although she thought she had never been on one, actually she had ... once before.

She had been kidnapped.

She had been told little about it because folk couldn't have known what had happened. But it had been there all along in her memory ready to return one day, but only if it should happen again.

Right then.

How had she escaped when she was only six? No one escaped a kidnapping. They were gone forever.

Yet, not her and the other little girl.

A ranger had found them on a beach. That was all she had been told.

When it was over the vicar and her mum said she had been naughty, she had run away and got into a panic. It wasn't that at all. At last she knew what had happened, or some of it.

She had been here before.

She sat up and took a deep breath. From her mind the engine beat softened. The smells cleared. There were no screams.

She shivered with the release of memory and she felt a little better. Actually, she felt a little warmth returning, just enough.

What was also clear was a question: how ever she had escaped the first time, could she do it again? If only more of the memory would return.

She let go of her memory quickly because she had to turn to what was happening right then. There was nothing she could do because she was bound, hooded and locked up, but what did she know of her plight? The sneering fellow searched for a seer. He had taken the wrong girls, her and Liffet, yet despite being in error he knew their names and he knew they would be at the infirmary that day. On top of that, the hirelings had been chary of her and Liffet and in a hurry to lock them in the stowage hold yet the girls were fully restrained and no threat to them.

Seer or not, why go to all this trouble to kidnap them?

Memory

The boat rolled as it sailed into the sound.

Alfren closed her eyes and tried to settle. She needed to recover from the anaesthesia to clear her mind. There was no point in straining her bonds or shouting for help. She prayed that Liffet would awake without harm and the same for Zal. She supposed she should be relieved they were unharmed. They would have to escape before they were taken far from home.

She was in a fix, and an artful fellow had planned this.

A memory rose in her mind: an encounter on a beach two years earlier. It couldn't be any use to her, she thought, not there, trussed up as she was and trapped. She could understand why it came to mind but right then it was a distraction. She resolved to drive it away.

To divert herself, she tried to collect any detail she could from noise and movement. The boat was a small freighter going by how it bobbed through the waves, with a single heavy-oil reciprocating engine; it must be one of the many tramper traders built at the shipwrights in Wallburgh for navigating Sealand's islands.

She couldn't concentrate. It was no good. Resist as she did, the memory flooded her mind.

Let it play, then be done with it, she relented. It was nonsense. Really, she was just the same as anyone else – no different from anybody. The girl she had met that day long ago? A trickster. They all were: outlanders, raiders ... and islesfolk.

Beach

Alfren had gone wandering in the near outland for as long as she could remember, almost always with Liffet. She shot birds and rabbits, Liffet climbed to take eggs from roosts, then they sold their haul back in the burgh at the door to a pub – the Lost Sheep was best.

They had found climbs over the wall and hidden ways away from the burgh, but they had to be careful. There were guards of course and getting past them was tricky: they had to be quiet and quick. There were the watchtowers too, so they went out at dusk or dawn, sometimes in daytime but then when the haar, the sea mist, covered the land. At first, they learned the ways from listening to the older children and sharing map-sketches on chalkboards at school. When they found a better way, they kept it secret lest someone followed, got caught, and gave it away.

Sometimes, they went over on a fairly clear day. Only a few children attempted that. They had known it was daring, but they hadn't rushed and they had taken care to time their run during squalls of rain and gusts of wind. Of course, if the rain had cleared, they had had to wait for darkness to return.

It was rangers on their way to and from the outland they had to be careful to avoid.

She saw them just sometimes in the burgh, dressed for patrol, garbed against fierce winds and chilling, drenching rain. They carried light arms, knives and bows, not the heavy pikes and crossbows of militia. Some children, if they were cheeky, approached them for a dare to beg a treat, but any child that went over the wall avoided them. Wall-runners believed it bad luck to fall under the gaze of a ranger.

What was troubling was that, once, one of them had smiled as though he knew her. She had hidden for the rest of that day.

When she was older, on those days when she wanted to be with the waves, she liked to go over by herself. She had found favourite places to visit. South was best, about 7 miles away, beyond Muckle Voe.

She shuffled to sit upright. The memory was vivid in her mind and unstoppable.

It was a rare, fine day, the light wind was a drier-force 2, pushing pummel-force 3, early in her fourteenth year. She had settled in a rock cranny high on the hillside of Fairview, where she felt real warmth from the sun whenever the cloud parted. She had closed her eyes and leant back against dry stone.

She saw waves rippling through her mind: waves of sweeping winds, churning seas and folding cloud; other waves too – the slow waves of timeless hills, the thrum of seabirds in flight.

On this day like many others, she dreamed of flying, carried on the winds, there and everywhere, to explore the waves as far as she could see. She followed the waves and forgot time until she shifted her body and opened her eyes to a chill wind and a speck of rain. It was late and time to go. Below, she saw the haar welling from the sea. She would have to walk home in the mist, which was helpful because she wouldn't be seen, and part of the way at dusk too. She scooted down the hillside, entered the mist and decided to run along the beach because it would be quicker, even though if the haar cleared there was a risk of being seen and chased from a watchtower on a headland not far away.

As she approached the dunes her step faltered and, even though she willed herself to run, her legs took a few steps and then refused, and she felt forced into a crouch where she knew clearly in her mind she had to take her bow and nock an arrow. It was odd that she had bid her body to run, but some other part of her mind made her stop. She opened up her mind to an answer and one came readily: someone was nearby and hidden from her. How she knew, she didn't know. Why she decided to approach them and how she knew exactly where they were and from what side to appear, she didn't know. Yet she felt it was right.

She paused. This could be trouble and she might need help. Before she went any farther, she should let Liffet know. She focused her mind and recalled Liffet's own special waves, those waves she knew well. She had done so often, which wasn't to say it was easy. She had to find her friend's waves exactly and they changed as Liffet grew older, but she saw Liffet regularly and each time she checked the waves when face to face. It was easiest to find waves through character, which meant there were a whole lot of traits to choose from. Liffet's were straightforward: liveliness, curiosity, bravery, wit, sharpness, all in the right measure.

Liffet could be anywhere at all in and around Wallburgh, maybe over the wall too, it didn't seem to matter. When she filled her mind with Liffet's waves, such that Liffet was as good as right next to her, she sent her own inner waves of doubt, daring and urgency, plus the warmth of the sun to show the south, and the feel of sand underfoot to show the beach. It seemed to her the waves she sent were absorbed, as they didn't bounce back, and she knew Liffet would come. Only then did she creep around a dune and step onto the beach, where in the mist she saw raiders sitting in a huddle.

Four of them.

Faran

Faran remembered that day too and clearly. It came to mind in the present when she saw swirling and tumbling through patterns of blue at the times when the far-away girl's enjoyment of her waves was strongest.

Faran had been on a sailing with her uncle, father and brother and it had been her suggestion to rest a while after landing at the beach as the haar breezed over them. She had heard the girl approach but didn't tell them. When the girl appeared and surprised her family, she stayed them with a hand on her brother's leg to stop him rising, and a sharp 'Tshh' to draw their attention to her stern face. Still, they were ready to spring, but the girl had a bow and her family saw straightaway that the girl had levelled it at them and held steady.

Now the girl was there, Faran felt momentarily guilty. She ought to have told her family the real reason why she had wanted to go with them, but they would have said no and called off the landing. They were wary of her mind-reading and where it could lead and they wouldn't have wanted to encounter anyone, no matter what. They knew that because of what she saw in other folk's minds, she liked to come up with suggestions to make things better. They couldn't deny some were good ideas, but they had always told her it was too much, it could overwhelm folk and it was best to keep quiet. She had learned that folk didn't like being told the truth and having to deal with the change that followed.

There was the girl was standing before her, at long last. She was dressed in waxed smock and breeches, with short boots and gaiters. A belt held pouches and a knife. Strapped to the leg was a quiver, the cap dangling and a sheaf of finely fletched arrows showing.

Faran knew the girl had pluck but then, present before her, it was plain; the girl was strong – the result of the strange way those Sealand folk nurtured their young to play a role in their defence arrays.

Strange folk they were.

Faran knew the girl was uncertain at facing her family. Her folk weren't warriors, nonetheless Faran was sure the girl saw they were bright and quick, and they were too. They were seafarers, they knew the ways of Landers and raiders, and they knew how to avoid them, until today, surprised by this girl.

Faran could sense her uncle suspected her.

'Don't move,' the girl called with a wavering voice, and then more firmly, 'I will shoot, and I mean it. Who are you? Aren't you raiders?'

'No, lass,' Faran said. She met the girl's eyes and stood slowly, smiling. They were about the same age, she thought. It was fun to meet the girl, after all this time: the wave girl.

'We don't mean any harm. We'll be going soon. Don't be afraid. Don't shoot.'

'Stay!' the girl called.

Faran slapped her hand on her father's shoulder as he shuffled, ready to leap.

'Don't shoot,' Faran repeated. 'I know I can trust you. We're from the Western Isles. Do you know them? I've wanted to see Sealand for a long time. I've heard a lot about it.'

Faran nodded towards her family.

'We're good folk. They won't try anything.'

The girl relaxed her bow.

'You know how to shoot, don't you; I see it.'

'How do you defend yourself?' asked the girl.

'We don't. We don't have to fight all the time like you Sealanders do ... or so I hear.'

They stared into one another's eyes. She saw the girl was curious.

'I'll be alright, Dad,' she said and stepped towards the girl. 'Shall we talk for a little while?'

'Alright.'

They walked 50 yards along the beach and sat down on the sand where the girl could keep watch. Any farther and they would be lost in the mist.

'What's your name?' Faran asked.

'Alfren, of Wallburgh and Sealand.'

'I'm Faran, family Steersman. Did you call me?' she asked.

'What?'

'I heard you. I can hear you from a long way.'

'No, you can't.'

'Do you think you could hear me?' Faran asked. Alfren shook her head.

'Try.'

Alfren nodded her consent.

Faran held a feeling of friendship and, after a few moments, she saw Alfren's eyes soften and look up. Alfren must have heard her.

This was exciting. Faran had been able to hear others around her at home, but no one had ever heard her. Alfren nodded again.

'I could hear you well, Alfren, from time to time, and at first I didn't understand who you were and where you were from. There were clues. Sorry for listening; it's rude when you don't know that I did it. I heard bits, only your dreams of sailing on your waves – nothing else really.'

It was lie: Faran had heard much more, but she was good at lying because she knew how annoyed folk became when they knew she knew their minds.

'That's why I had to come here today. I begged my dad. That's him, with my brother and uncle.'

Alfren looked puzzled. Faran laughed.

'Yes, those are my family. I have a big family. What about you?'

Faran hadn't needed to ask. She knew just at that moment.

Alfren lived in her waves and nowhere else.

'An only child? No brothers or sisters?'

Alfren seemed to forget her qualms and looked at her questioningly.

Faran had guessed what would happen next. Building slowly in her mind, she saw a jumble of flashes and colour and felt waves of heat. They settled and she saw tones with a slower pace. They were familiar somehow. She took her time to make the waves clearer, then picked them apart and found they married up with feelings and sensations that changed into meaning. It was the delight of watching children at play.

'Oh! We have lots of children,' Faran said, surprised at how clear Alfren's query was. 'Well, as many as we want. We don't have too many, in case of bad years when we might not have enough to feed us all.

'They say Sealand is wealthy, did you know? But water is tainted by poisons washed from the air, and you live too close together and trading brings illness. Sorry.'

Faran stopped and looked out to sea. There was no better time to say it. It was important. She turned to Alfren.

'You're a seer, aren't you?' she stated. It was blunt, but that's how she was, and that's why she had got into trouble with folk and had been told firmly not to say anything, no matter how truthful. At that moment she had to be clear with Alfren because they didn't have long there on the beach.

'I've never met a seer before.'

Alfren looked alarmed.

'No, I won't tell. Didn't you know? Don't worry.'

She heard Alfren's question: the sense of being in the haar and knowing nothing else, of not knowing there would ever be sunshine.

'How can I know a seer when I've never met one?' Faran asked her. 'They're part of the lore of our folk. They've been with us before, in times long past. They foretold great storms and the like. They saved us.

'We don't have one. We have a rune master, who can foretell things but not everything. He told us it would be safe to sail here.'

Faran smiled, to reassure Alfren. 'I suppose you could see all sorts of things, just as you wish, when you become a seer.'

She should tell her.

'I heard you, and I believe you called me here when you dreamed of the winds. Maybe here isn't the best place for you. You could come to live with me. Right now, if you like.'

Alfren

Faran had wide-open eyes, friendly smiles, and a lilting voice that was *floaty*. She was confident too, kindly, and seemed a lot older, although the same age as her. Alfren looked over to the Steersman family. They hadn't stirred and only the brother kept his eyes on them. The other two looked around, clearly nervous at being ashore.

Alfren knew it wasn't possible she was a seer, which made Faran odd for saying so, although having peered into her mind, in all other respects Faran was really at ease and happy. Her homeland must be lovely.

Alfren knew she would like to go.

She noticed then that she became annoyed. She didn't want to be suspected of being a seer. It was true that she could judge the weather and send messages to Liffet —

and Faran too. That was all though. She could see storms just before they landed, but so could most folk, which was why they brought in washing and closed window shutters. Certainly, she couldn't see the big storms, although that was because there hadn't been any, except that one time years ago when she was nine.

'I can't leave with you. I have a friend, Liffet, and she's on her way.'

They had a short time to talk. Alfren spoke about the burgh, the wall, the Watch, her mother and Liffet. Faran spoke about folklore, family, and home islands.

'You like chemistry,' Faran observed. 'On our islands we know it's really important to drink clean water. I told our rune master that I'd like to train to be a physician, although he says it will take a lifetime!' Faran laughed. 'We're both of us interested in the welfare of our folk.'

Faran looked over at her family. Her brother waved.

'I must be going. We'll take our skiff out to our sloop out there in the haar. You can come to visit or stay anytime. Send me a message. You'll know how. Goodbye, Alfren.'

'Goodbye, Faran.'

Alfren felt a pang of regret as Faran left, so soon after they had met. She stood to watch as the islesfolk carried their skiff into the surf. The four of them jumped in, took oars and pulled strongly out to sea, gone in a moment into the haar. Too late, she waved.

She felt glad, almost relieved, to have met Faran, although immediately she tried to shut down her thoughts. They should be only for herself and not leaky, such that someone else could hear her – certainly not Faran, someone she had only just met and from a long way away.

She didn't want to be a seer.

With the skiff gone, she sat down, still annoyed. Had Faran tricked her? After a moment she smiled. Faran had been believable, and there had been no harm done. She sent a fond farewell and who knew, maybe Faran heard her, but most probably not.

Just to be on the safe side, she would be careful in future when she dreamed of following the wind waves over the sea.

First though, there was something else. There! There were footprints in the sand to follow. She darted into the dunes. Hidden in a dip she found a pile of small crates.

Whisky!

Alfren laughed. Those Western Isles folk were smugglers, nothing more. It was all a trick. She had fallen for it, but it was a good trick.

A seer!

Faran had made her seem special. Of course, she wasn't – no one was. It was one of the easiest tricks to play, to flatter folk into thinking they were special.

Liffet's dad liked whisky. She prised open a crate with her fingers and took a pot bottle wrapped in straw.

It was late.

She scurried along the beach and made for a track above the shoreline. She hadn't gone far when ahead she heard Liffet call out.

'That you, Ally? You alright?'

Alfren saw her friend appear though the mist and run to join her.

'Were you in trouble? I thought maybe a ranger had got you.'

'No. I ran into some smugglers.'

'Blimey!'

Alfren sent messages about her encounter. It was more revealing that way. She recalled the character of the new girl, Faran, and her own fascination with what Faran had told her about life on the Western Isles.

'She was nice though, wasn't she?' asked Liffet. 'Maybe it's the whisky that does it. Come on, it'll be dark soon.'

They set off on a quick walk and jog, Liffet leading the way.

Alfren felt caught. She wanted to be just like everyone else.

'Liffy, no more sending messages ... ever.'

'Ally, when you send, I hear it and it's no trouble. I don't mind. It's alright.'

Nonetheless, Faran had suggested her thoughts could be leaking out; who else might hear? Also, as she grew older, she had begun to consider it might be an odd thing to send messages, as no one else did.

'Come on,' called Liffet. 'It's getting cold. We should run.'

Cage

That was the memory. There couldn't be anything there to help with the plight they were in. Alfren sighed. *Seer?* That was twice she had encountered fellows that talked of seers. Both of them were fanciful, but the sneering man was as mad as Faran had been kindly.

The engine chugged and the tramper rolled. Blindfolded and covered by a sack, there was only darkness.

A sudden, sharp nudge jolted her mind! She gasped and bent forward. Straightaway she knew where that had come from.

She sent a feeling of annoyance to Liffet.

Wake up gently!

Liffet had awoken still struggling. Alfren softened, sent calm and waited for her to awaken fully. Liffet lay for a while, then wriggled to sit up.

'We're captured,' Alfren said. 'You're on a tramper, and you're going to have to get us off.'

Liffet didn't speak.

Zal groaned.

'Zal,' she spoke softly, 'be still. You're with us. Zal? Say something.'

'Pain,' Zal moaned.

Zal needed care. There was nothing Alfren could do.

'We're on a tramper and safe for the present. Try to make yourself comfortable. Who are these hirelings? Do you know them?'

Silence, then, 'The chief sent ...' Zal whimpered. 'They call him the vis—.' It was too much effort.

Zal was distressed.

If only there was something Alfren could do to make amends for shooting her and to help her ...

A memory came to her from the lanes of the burgh.

Once again, she tried to ignore it.

The memory wouldn't help. The plain matter was that they were there, dark and chilled in the stowage, rolling and turning, the engine thumping, bound and uncomfortable, destined for slavery.

Yet her memory was strong, and once again she could only let it run.

It was a fiercely windy day. She was old, a full eight years old, one of the bigger children. She was wandering the lanes with her gang on the lookout for blown-away debris to scavenge; or bottle or mug they could return for the ha'penny deposit; or something lost by someone they could hand in to the guard for even more, a penny perhaps. They bent into the wind blowing hard against them, when they came across a small boy in tears, standing in a doorway, all alone.

'What's the matter?' she asked. The boy turned away, distraught. He must have been made to stand outside. She reached out and put her hand on the boy's shoulder. He shook, but she knew he feigned to throw her off.

'It's alright,' she said. From her mind, she slipped a comforting blanket of waves around the little boy and her gang. The waves were her own welcoming and calming memories which she cast gently: a cosy fire; warm soup; a mother's hug.

The little boy stopped sobbing.

'Come and see our den?' she asked.

The boy turned, nose running, his eyes red and tear stained.

'Yes,' he said and nodded.

The gang gathered around him, and off they went.

She smiled at the memory, which faded. She was back in the hold.

It seemed to suggest she could help Zal.

No, I can't.

Helping the children when she was eight years old, fine; helping Zal with her pain ... impossible.

She opened her mind to Liffet's waves, to check on her friend. She heard a liveliness from her, which meant simply, *I can hear you.*

When very close, it was true Liffet could hear her thoughts, which was alright so long as they weren't private thoughts.

Still, as a mild reprimand for listening, she sent a feeling of brisk movement and release. *Shouldn't you be thinking about how to escape?*

In reply she heard compassion and mild exasperation: *Help her, you ninny.*

Her instant response was prim: *I shouldn't.*

And obstinacy: *Not possible.*

She heard Liffet's thoughts of exasperation and admonishment: *Yes, you can.*

She tried to form puzzlement, to say she didn't know how, but too late realised when sending that she had betrayed her own stubbornness.

I can't.

She half expected impatience and sharpness in reply and got it.

You flipping well can.

Annoyed but relenting, she searched and found her memory of herself at eight years old, who had innocently done what was right. In her mind she found the blanket she had created from kindly waves, surprised she found it so easily, and instantly she slipped it over Zal with comfort and reassurance, such as she could give in the bare cage in the cold of the stowage hold.

Would it dull fear and pain? It must have worked because instantly Zal's moans and whimpers lessened.

Liffet had been right to say she should try.

Zal dozed.

'Now what?' whispered Liffet, at the squeak of the door mechanism.

'It'll be alright,' Alfren replied. 'They're afraid of us, but I don't know why.'

'They want you. A seer, they said.'

I can't be.

They heard the door open with a clang, then a click of the lock to the gate of their cage.

'Go easy, lads. Steady.' It was the skipper's voice.

They pulled the sack from over her, then removed the blindfold. In the dim light, she saw there were two hirelings in the cage, the skipper at the gate and two behind in the stowage. They uncovered Liffet too, then lifted Zal roughly although without hurt, from the cage, shut the gate behind them, and carried her through the bulkhead door.

'You should look after her!' Alfren called. 'You should let us tend to her!'

The skipper eyed them. He seemed relieved he had accomplished what was a simple task.

'See, that went alright, lads,' he said, addressing the two hirelings behind him. 'Don't know what the Picker was worried about. If they're no use to him, we'll have these two at the slave market in a day or two and a couple of silver dollars for each of us, eh?'

He blustered, didn't he?

She reasoned the Picker was the name of the sneering fellow.

The more the skipper tried to intimidate her, the more she wanted to outsmart him. It occurred to her from nowhere that maybe there was another blanket, different from the one she had used on the children.

'You'd better look after her, or else you know what I might do,' she called, whatever it was they were be afraid she might do.

Fear could make folk confused and hasty. She found just a trace of his waves then willed them to inflame, like blowing on kindling in the grate, to make him more edgy.

He backed away.

'Right, lads, off you go.'

He was in haste to leave but checked himself. 'Hold on!'

He was trembling but managed to calm himself and looked at her again. He was shrewd. He could manage his fear, and he had realised something wasn't right.

He took one more step back, this time the better to assess what he saw.

'Come on, Skipper,' urged one of the hirelings impatiently.

'Key!' exclaimed the skipper. 'You left the key in the lock, you mophead.'

The skipper jumped forward, snatched the key from the gate and hurriedly the three of them backed out through the bulkhead door, which clanged shut and locked.

'Good one!' Liffet said.

Alfren sighed.

'How are you after that anaesthesia?' asked Liffet.

'Just a headache. What about you?'

'Me too. They're afraid of you, don't you get it? They're worried what a seer might do.'

Alfren regretted what she had done. She shouldn't make folk fearful. Where might that end?

'The skipper fellow was just nervous. That's why he forgot the key.'

Liffet shuffled and was quiet.

Liffet was wrong about her being a seer.

Zal's capture at the beach had started it all, but there was no way back and Alfren and Liffet were caught up in a game of a madman, the Picker, and it was serious.

Picker

Zal should receive aid from the hirelings, but Alfren shuddered to think what nursing they could give.

By the weak glow of a gas lamp fixed on the bulkhead, she took in the stowage. It was a small hold which could be accessed through the bulkhead door, that had no handwheel on their side; or through the hatch topside, which was the way the hirelings had let them down. New brass screw heads meant it was shut tight. They were imprisoned in their cage and there was no way to escape.

It was uncomfortable on the hard, wooden deck and it was no help to think what might become of them, so she fidgeted and thought of nothing, not even waves because she didn't want to invite her waves into the horrid stowage.

She heard the lock mechanism winding and the bulkhead door squeak open. This time the sneering fellow stepped in alone, bracing himself against the sway of the boat with one arm and, with the other, he held a pendant before him raised in view as he looked over them.

'Ally!' whispered Liffet warningly.

Alfren sent a brief quizzical wave, but there was no reply from her friend. Alfren let her gaze be drawn to the pendant, a simple chain holding a clear crystal. The fellow drew his hand back and forth to make it swing. His eyes flitted between the girls and the crystal.

'You are prisoners but will be treated well if you are compliant.'

'Where's Zal?' Alfren interrupted.

'We're attending to her. If she recovers, she will be tried and punished.'

'Who are you?' demanded Liffet.

'I am the first ship's master in the service of my chief, the visionary.'

'You're called the Picker, aren't you?' accused Liffet. 'A kidnapper and murderer, you are. Did you kill the infirmary guards?'

'We would have done had they the strength to fight us. Only we who are the strongest, who obey our chief, who see the future, will survive. As you will, if you do what we tell you.'

Survive?

'Oh, really?' countered Liffet defiantly. 'True survivors help one another.'

'Is that so?' sneered the Picker. 'Then you don't know your own history. The Extinction of the Last People was long ago, but still real today. The high storms will come again. As the chief tells us, the first few survivors of the Extinction were resourceful; those afterwards were ruthless. It was through their cunning that they survived, not cooperation.'

He kept pushing his hand to make the pendulum swing.

'You should let us go, then it might not be so bad for you,' said Liffet.

'The chief and the chosen are the only ones who seek to create a future. We take what we want because we must because the Extinction comes again. I expect deference and obedience,' he said. 'Insolence will be punished. You are the seer, are you not?' he declared, addressing Alfren. 'This girl Liffet is your loyal friend from infancy.'

'I'm no seer,' Alfren said, watching as the pendant swung. 'She's just militia.'

The pendulum swung to and fro as before.

Lightly she listened for a message from Liffet. She heard doubt and mocking to say, *he won't believe that, you twit.*

Instantly the Picker turned to the pendant. She saw it curve offline.

'Ah,' he murmured. 'I believe that emanated from this one. So, Liffet, you are the seer.'

'Me?' said Liffet. 'Actually, yes. I'll tell you something. I don't see much future for you if you carry on like this. Let us go and it might turn out better, how about that?'

The Picker looked between them.

'I believe I have who we want.' He pocketed the pendant. 'It's inconclusive as to which one of you is the seer,' he said. 'I can test thoroughly when we reach the keep. Whichever one of you is playing tricks, I will find out and you will be punished.'

Using both hands and arms for balance he left abruptly. The bulkhead door clanged.

Seer

'He's a mean sod, isn't he,' said Liffet. 'And what was all that about survival and storms, and the Extinction? What has that got to do with anything?'

'He's mad,' said Alfren. How far would the fellow go in his delusion? 'I don't want to go to some keep to be tested.'

She imagined it would be a remote stone tower, impossible to escape from.

'Liffy, that pendulum seemed to bend when you had a message for me. We shouldn't make it worse for ourselves. Let's not send messages. And another thing – I can't be a seer.'

'Right,' Liffet replied weakly.

'Not the sort they want, you know, into storms and survival.'

'No. Alright, look,' said Liffet, 'if he suspects me of being a seer, not you, then you might get a chance to break free.'

Alfren first? Why? That had always been Liffet's way. Whenever they had done something daring, Liffet had taken the greater risk.

Liffet sat back. 'How far to this keep, do you think? It could be days away.'

'I hope not,' Alfren replied. 'This is just a tramper; it's a coaster and not for the open sea.'

'Right.'

'It's probably somewhere on Sealand.'

'They said slave market.'

Were there slave markets on Sealand?

'A couple of days to somewhere. No more, I hope,' Alfren said.

'Far enough.'

Far from rescue.

Alfren thought things through. Would someone look for them? Would rangers chance on them? She couldn't count on that. It was Liffet who would have to find a way to escape, not her. On the other hand, it might be an idea to do whatever she could do to help rather than be wary of revealing the little ability she had to see waves.

'Liffy,' she said, cautiously, 'I could try something. I could see just a bit, perhaps.'

'You mean, be a seer?'

'Of course not. I mean, just see what I can.'

Alfren thought she should admit to herself how through her childhood Liffet had helped her when seeing had alarmed her by its intensity and clarity, when there was no one she dared ask to explain it, not even the vicar. Liffet had made it fun.

Alfren had a knack of knowing when to go over the wall, when the weather would be fair, when squalls and cold blasts of wind would blow. She had known when to stay in the shelter of the dens in the burgh because a high wind approached. She had picked up other signs, such as when there were few watchmen on the towers above the burgh or when they looked the other way; when it was alright to sneak a little peat, slip a fish from a box on the quay, run a penny-errand for one of the dock workers (a bottle of whisky, sometimes a sealed letter). Liffet had accepted and encouraged her, and anyway Alfren seemed to avoid trouble, and Liffet had never called her odd because of sending and waves.

Alfren remembered clearly how she had made children feel welcome to her gang, and in a sort of way that was what had happened when she met Liffet. Alfren had heard of a roving gang of wild children that were daring in their raids and, most alarming, didn't bother with dens because they were always on the move and found shelter wherever they happened to be. One day she felt something would happen, but she didn't know what, but it wasn't the storm-force 10 that howled over the church roof because she had seen that coming. Suddenly the wild gang blew into the church and ran amok, snatching toys, taking more than their share of food scraps and breaking into games. Her gang cried and ran to her, so she confronted the wild gang leader. Instantly they charged at one another in a fight: the new girl was fast but Alfren saw her moves and dodged. They wrestled on the floor, but the girl, although light, was stronger. Alfren writhed and kicked, but the girl landed a punch on her cheek. Alfren couldn't win, but she wouldn't concede. The girl twisted her arm and it really hurt. Without thinking, without trying, Alfren found the girl's waves and saw anger … and loneliness. Those waves were so strong. She felt sorry for the girl. Just as her twisted arm hurt too much to bear, Alfren sent a message that was one last try before she fell a defeated leader, her wards never to trust her again.

Be my friend.

The girl recoiled from her, shocked by the invitation. They both wiped away their tears and runny noses. She found the girl's waves again. The girl's hatred dissolved and instead was fear of loneliness.

Liffet was the girl; the girl who had shouted with her when kidnapped and terrified; the girl who had helped her, given her courage, enough to alter her mind somehow.

Liffet knew too. They were both surprised and disbelieving, then they had laughed with recognition and relief.

Liffet said sorry to the vicar, and Alfren told her it was alright to be rough and wild. Liffet became a regular at the church; they became firm friends from that day.

'Oh, alright,' said Liffet. 'Whatever you do'll be alright. What might you see?'

'Just the usual really: the wind and the direction we're going in. That's not being a seer, that's just seeing.'

No more than she had always done, but she had never had to do it like this before, in such a fix. Could she see when she really had to? Could she make herself *see*?

'Go on then,' said Liffet encouragingly.

Alfren wriggled to sit comfortably on the sack, tucked up her knees, rested her chin and closed her eyes. She floated away in her mind and began to feel the waves: shapes, colours and energies. She floated along to where she sensed great, long blue waves, wrapping around one another – the giant wind waves. She swooped away and saw the immense, slow, green waves of the tides, then the fast brilliant sun waves, and the heavy, tumbling waves of the seasons. She settled and listened carefully for the lightest, wispiest waves – the earth's magnetic field. All those told her the time, and the pattern of the winds told her where they might blow from next, and earth's magnetic field told her roughly where she was, although this was the first time she had been so far from Wallburgh and had searched those waves so closely.

She opened her eyes.

'Liffy, I found what I wanted.'

'I know, you let it out. I saw a bit for myself. You were gone for ages.'

'We've been travelling west, and a high wind is on its way. You know, I'd say this tramper is sure to slip in somewhere to tie up.'

Maybe it would take shelter close to a windward shore, find a safe mooring if there was one, or perhaps there was a small port. Maybe they had travelled farther than she thought and reached Landing, although not the farthest settlements she had heard of – Whitewick and Strand Holm.

'We haven't left Sealand,' Alfren said. 'We must escape, while we can. We can swim for it or take a rowing boat, or whatever they have on the foredeck that could float.'

'What about Zal? Shouldn't we take her too?'

'Yes. She may be able to walk.'

Liffet gazed at her. 'Ally, you know that Picker? He seems certain you're a seer.'

'I'm definitely not.'

'Probably you are.'

'It has to be someone else.'

'Don't you think they were waiting for us at the infirmary? It seemed to me they were, as they knew our names. They didn't just happen to be there when we turned up.'

'But why us?' asked Alfren.

'Did you tell anyone we were going to the infirmary to see Zal?'

'No, of course not. I asked Handar if we could go, and she said it wasn't up to the rangers but the militia and that's how I got the chitty. You know that.'

'Maybe somebody was looking out for us and got to know, then they followed us.'

'Why?'

'Because somehow they found out that you were the watchman who shot Zal,' said Liffet.

'And why would that be of any use to them?'

'Perhaps they were looking for someone who could shoot someone when it was completely dark.'

'I didn't.'

'Yes, you did.'

She had.

'Even if I did, so what?'

'It's a clue you might be a seer – a dimwit seer, but all the same ...'

'Shooting someone when it's dark doesn't make anyone a seer,' Alfren said crossly.

They fell silent.

It wasn't fair. Alright, she could do some special tricks, but a seer must be someone quite different. As Liffet said, anyone who knew about her tricks might be mistaken in thinking she was a seer, if they didn't know what a seer was really. Come to think of it, she didn't really know what a seer was supposed to be able to do either. No one on Sealand had ever known of one, had they?

In the gloom of the stowage, lit by a feeble gas lamp, Liffet looked at her and smiled earnestly.

'I'd say it's alright to be a seer, you know.'

'Liffy,' she replied firmly, 'let me think about it.'

'Oh, alright.'

Liffet was always kind and had never pressed her. She was grateful; her friend, above all, knew ... how she became annoyed sometimes.

There was a point in all this, though. Wasn't it about time that she faced up to those different ways that she had?

Hungry

Alfren turned to the prospect of escape.

'Liffy, what could you do if those hirelings come back?'

'My knife's still in my boot and a blade to cut our bindings is stuck in my cuff. I'm not sure we should free ourselves until we have a plan.'

Liffet was right.

Alfren continued. 'We should try to escape. They won't sail through the high wind, not at night. We've got a chance.'

No matter the urgency, their captors wouldn't risk foundering the boat in darkness on the many islets and skerries offshore.

Liffet had been waiting to say something. 'Ally, you know how they're wary of us? Maybe you have to do your thing where you sort of reassure them and then they'll come to see us anyway.'

Alfren thought about it. She didn't want to take that step but she would try, just this once.

'Anyway, I'm hungry,' Liffet appealed.

Alfren sighed and closed her eyes. It seemed the best way was to create a feeling of confidence and boldness, then add a sense of harmlessness to that. Then she dropped the feeling like a small stone in a pool at a burn so it made ripples that spread throughout the tramper, such as she could imagine it. She did this for a couple of minutes.

'I tried,' she said, 'but I don't expect it worked.'

Just then, the bulkhead door swung open with a clang and the skipper and two hirelings clambered through.

'Still here then,' a hireling jeered.

'You've been good girls,' said the skipper. 'You wouldn't make fools of us, would you? We can make you comfy. Here's food, water and blankets and, no tricks mind, we could also release your bindings.'

Just so they didn't change their mind, she sent waves of meekness. The hirelings went about their task roughly.

'Right, we'll leave you be,' said the skipper, who once again paused to double-check everything.

Just then, the Picker grabbled through the bulkhead door.

'Who was it?' he demanded.

'Ask nicely,' rebuked Liffet.

He glared at her.

'Proof, we have you.' He held the pendant aloft. It swung gently. 'It's stopped, of course,' he muttered.

'We're hungry,' said Liffet, 'that's all.'

'Good, I have what I need, I know it.'

He turned to the skipper.

'Next time you think it's a good idea to do something for these two, see me first,' he said sternly.

'Aye, sir.'

The hirelings left and the door clanged. In the gloom, the waiting began again.

Quietly, Liffet said, 'There, it worked. Well done, Ally.'

Alfren sighed. There were some things she could do. And she would have to admit that their imprisonment had been made bearable because the Picker, mad as he was, had decided one of them was the seer he sought.

Rectory

The Vicar

A gale-force 8 whistled and groaned over the rectory. Alone at his kitchen table, the vicar heard only faintly the knocker strike at the door. At any other time, he might be found sharing his home with destitute seamen, those that had been cheated of their earnings, or had been robbed by crew; or more likely, had been forced off their ship because of age or illness and were waiting for a ship to take them home. Or it might be a family recently arrived from the League - from Windcape, Tallcliffs, Brightnessbay, Torrent Gorge, Rallyroundpoint, Hopewick, Sanctuary Isle, Long Garth, or any of the other towns. He had never been off Sealand to visit them, but the descriptions he had heard told of farmed lands set in sheltered valleys or corries; mountain mining towns with great railways; and shipwrights in great sea cave workshops. There were houses chiselled into rock faces or built from stout timber, on stilts high above flood plains, or hidden by waterfalls. Some towns were far inland, away from pounding waves, such as Highcoomb, Worship and Thankful Peak, accessible by narrow paths and safe from raids. Despite these wondrous descriptions, folk came here to Wallburgh because they had heard of a great burgh set in an abundant sea. He listened and soon they told him of overlords and taxes, guild payments and regulations, fixed markets and duties to pay. They had escaped. They brought stories which he set down on paper for the record. He had to write down the stories no matter how trivial they seemed. They would inform the next folk what this age had been like in his burgh and throughout the League.

However, the good folk of the burgh although poor were charitable and soon homes were found for his charges. Alas, this evening there was no one to answer the door for him. It was late, around nine o'clock. He should have been abed, not burning mains gas to light his reading, but the reason he never retired early was simply because often at evening time folk's fears and imaginings arose and they came to his door, even in a gale.

The knocker struck again.

'Yes, yes!'

He unlocked the door and held it ajar.

In the darkness, the figure appeared to be dressed in an outland suit. Just to be safe, he closed the door a little and put his foot behind it.

'How can I help you?' he asked.

'Sir, Ranger Marine Jin at your service. I have a few questions. It's an urgent matter.'

That explained the dress: a ranger's storm suit.

'Ah, may I see your pass-gate, Ranger Jin?'

Jin reached inside his top pocket and produced a tin-plate token inlaid with a silver dollar, bound by closely-stitched leather. This was no forgery; the stamped letters were worn almost smooth and the leather edge was frayed.

'Do come in, Ranger Jin. You're most welcome.'

He led the way across the hall through the scullery to the kitchen where a peat fire burned in the iron stove. He turned in the dim light to see Jin unshoulder a rifle case and shed an outer jacket. Ranger Jin was slight, the better for crossing that dreadful outland, and young, the better for endurance, and with a smile and confidence way beyond his years.

The vicar supposed that Jin, being a ranger who had spent many nights in the outland, might feel almost uncomfortable in shelter of a home. He beckoned Jin to sit at the table, put the kettle on the stove and opened the grating to raise the heat, which were courtesies that all burghers showed their guests if they could afford the peat.

He was puzzled. Rangers were seen rarely in the burgh and to his knowledge they never made house calls. The militia brought him ranger finds – the lost and starving. Most likely this enquiry concerned someone to whom he had given sanctuary.

'How can I help?' he asked, reaching for the teapot.

'I believe you know Alfren of the burgh, Vicar?'

The question startled him. 'Yes, of course. I do. I know most of the children in the burgh. What is it?'

'I have to inform you that she was kidnapped today, in a raid on the infirmary.'

The vicar stood still. 'Alfren? The infirmary?'

'Raiders retrieved one of their own and we believe they took a third person, a militiaman trooper. They hurt three guards. It was a determined and planned raid.

'As you know Alfren well, you may be able to help with our enquiries. Can you tell us anything about her? Did she confide anything to you?'

The vicar sat at the table, teapot in hand. His mind raced to collate the details he had been told, to form some conception of the event, the raid.

'You're searching for her? I mean, rangers? Why?'

If asked, everyone praised the Watch, the militia and the guard; proud of the formal standing arrays protecting their burgh. On the other hand, although everyone knew of the rangers, he had heard little said about them but neither had anyone said anything against them in his hearing. That must be because they knew at heart that rangers like Jin faced real peril they couldn't bear to think about. They were their first line of defence, far off in the outland.

'Sir, she's a ranger. She signed up two days ago.'

The vicar held his breath. Then the truth of it became real to him when Jin nodded.

'Oh, that's a surprise; I did see Alfren earlier, only she played with the children for a short time and didn't speak to me except to say hello and goodbye.

'Ranger Jin, you know how it is once children are taken: that's it, they're gone. Now you're going to give chase?'

'Sir?' Jin prompted him.

'Of course, I will tell you what I can. Alfren knows the burgh and its dangers. I can't imagine how she could have allowed this to happen.'

The vicar rose to prepare the tea. 'I have known her well since the flood, oh, six years ago. Folk took refuge in the church that night. Some said they saw her raising the alarm and that has always been a puzzle to me. Why was she down at the esplanade in a storm in the middle of the night? Her mother was there too. They arrived in time to see the flood breach the sea wall.

'After that I opened the church to the children, to give them somewhere to go. Alfren came here most days. The other children liked her and looked up to her. Liffet was her best friend. They met here. I think it was Alfren who caught Liffet misbehaving, then there was a tussle, and you know how contrary children can be, they became close. I suggested Alfren should join the Watch when she was old enough. I was her sponsor. I thought some activity and time in the outland – in the Watch – would be good for her.'

He placed a mug of tea on the table for Jin.

'Thank you.'

'I can tell you she was glad to leave school. She was keen to ensure our water supply is clean. With that and the Watch, she was busy. Yet, let me say, she has always seemed a little introspective to me, engaged with imaginings. You're young too. Possibly you understand.'

'Did she appear troubled or had she been threatened, do you think?'

'No, not at all.'

'What about after the capture of the raider three days ago? You did know about that, didn't you?'

'No?'

What had Alfren been involved with?

The vicar made a connection.

'I might add, she seemed determined that children should have somewhere safe to go in daytime, at the church here or anywhere, somewhere safe from kidnap.'

'Why was that, do you think?'

'It was said that she had been kidnapped herself when young but had managed to escape.'

'Surely not.'

'It was hearsay, but you could look into it.'

The vicar shook his head.

Surge

Alfren

The engine had stopped and the tramper rolled. Alfren heard the wind wail over the boat deck. This must be the anchorage.

'What are you thinking, Ally?' Liffet asked.

'Bread and cheese weren't enough,' Alfren said. 'I'm hungry. Anyway, I'm trying to not think anything because of that stupid pendant.'

'It'll be hard going for us,' said Liffet. 'I mean, to outrun the hirelings.'

'This will be a gale-force 8,' Alfren replied.

A gale was the limit for folk in open land. If the two of them, three with Zal, managed to escape, they would struggle against the wind. Once far away they would have to find or make shelter at night for which they would need canvas to repel the rain, as well as food and blankets. There would be the escape and the gale: two perils. They would need much in their favour. But what would they encounter hereabouts? At worst they might find impassable mud and marsh.

She settled to wait.

Alfren knew the storm grading from school. A strong gale-force 9 wind would throw a fellow over and you had to be careful to avoid wind-borne debris that could cut you down. A storm-force 10 would lift you off your feet and you would be beyond rescue because no one would go out in extreme winds to help. The high storms above that brought damage and destruction. Rage-force 11 whipped up sea spray and swept it far inland. Folk had tried to crawl through a force 11, but only some had the good fortune to survive. A fury-force 12 brought a high sea swell and mountainous waves that flooded the coast. Some watchmen on the towers by the sea told of waking in their storm shelters – underground bunkers below the towers – to find sea spray washed down the entrance shaft in a flood. They had had to climb to the deckhouse in murderous wind. A destroy-force 13 was more than a storm. It was a tempest. It drove folk mad in only a short time as they waited inside their homes for the wind to sweep them away. Only the strongest buildings withstood a destroy storm, although all lost roofs.

Folklore told of a rip-force 14, which flattened much in its path. Even large stones were hurled as missiles, lifted by the force of wind, deluge and ice-stones.

Folk even spoke of a cutter-force 15. It was a short-lived high storm that tore up good farmland to leave a desert of subsoil on which they could grow no crops and graze no livestock.

For folk living on the coast, high storms of force 11 and above brought arching waves, vast plumes of spray and surge tides that, together with the winds and rains, caused great destruction and made recovery arduous. Yet, their living was made on the coast, it was where they belonged, where the catch from the sea made up for the shortfall when the harvest on land failed.

Her folk had survived the worst coastal storms because hills sheltered the burghs. All were built with massive, heavy, quarried blocks of stone to resist the blows of the wind.

Still, destruction came.

She remembered as a little girl the damage she had seen caused by a surge tide and crashing wave. She and her gang had been to see the power station in ruins. She remembered that the electric tram, which took the burghers to the shipwrights' quarter, had never run again along the esplanade because the replacement power station was too small to supply the current. She had been disappointed because she and her gang had enjoyed hopping on and off the tram and teasing the conductor.

She remembered that night then. She didn't resist this memory. She had been nine years old.

She awoke with a start, leapt from bed, and shouted, 'Mum, get up!' There was no time to light the gas lamp as she dressed quickly. 'Come on, Mum,' she shouted. 'There's a flood!' In the hallway, she and her mum put on storm coats and goggles. Together they unlocked and opened the house door, and a thump of wind blew them back. The wind crackled; it was so noisy; pellets of rain stung her face. Battered by the wind, she staggered down the lanes to the esplanade, and in dim streetlight saw waves spill over the sea wall and the sea wash up the main street.

'We must raise the alarm. Mum, let's go to the church. You can ring the bell.'

They turned, but Alfren couldn't make herself run. A huge sea swell was just moments away. It would slam into the burgh.

'Mum, we won't make it in time. Hold on, hold on!'

'What is it, Ally? You're right. We must get to the church,' her mum replied, panicking.

Alfren stopped. She knew she had to turn to her mind.

'I think I can ... Wait!'

She saw the vast wave of seawater, dark and unstoppable, approaching the sound where it would funnel and rise before heaving over the sea wall and flooding the lower streets of the burgh. She saw it and allowed it to fill her mind, then she flung it from her mind as forcefully as she could, folding to her knees with the energy it took. She couldn't be certain she had done enough. She was about to do the same again, but windows opened, and there were shouts. Folk came running out with coats over their nightdresses, carrying children and helping the elderly. The first of them saw the water in the street and shouted in alarm. She didn't have to send the sea surge a second time – folk had been roused. She turned her mind to a picture of the church and sent out a thought of refuge and gathering, until she heard someone shout, 'To the church, everyone!'

She had done it. She was exhausted and relieved.

She and her mum joined a throng of folk climbing the lanes up through the burgh. The first to the church had rung the bell, whereupon all the burghers rose to do what they could to help folk and salvage goods. The storm raged all night long; the flood subsided. Some said it had been a rage-force 11 or even a fury-force 12 yet, within the safety of the wall, folk hadn't experienced the worst of it.

Her mum took a friend, Gleth, and her family into their home, who stayed for a few weeks until the repairs on their home were made. That had been alright because there was a combined peat allowance for everybody, and the house was just about warm. There were more rations to eat too. The two children were a lot older than her, and together they played card games, which Alfren liked. She learned that there should have been three siblings but the youngest had disappeared when only eight years old. For a while she became their youngest sister. She didn't like being someone she wasn't, but she did quite like the attention they gave her and the fun they had.

She remembered that her mum had never asked her about how she knew. She hadn't wanted to talk about it anyway. Folk believed that someone had rushed to the church and rung the bell and they said *he* was a hero. Everyone had been saved because of *him*.

There in the tramper, she thought about it. Yes, it had been her.

'Ally, you're thinking too much again. I can hear bits.'

Damn! Alfren cursed.

'Do you have to listen, Liffy?'

'It's not me, it's you! Your memories are loud when you think about them and you send them out. I know. You're thinking of times when you used your sending.'

'No, I do that only with you.'

'Right-oh. We haven't got a good plan yet, have we?'

'No. Even if you could pick the locks to the gate, there's no handle to open the bulkhead door. Then how can we get around the hirelings? Maybe we have to sit tight until we think of something, or they get drunk, leave the door open and fall asleep.'

'Yes, we can hope, but that Picker doesn't seem like a tippler.'

The bulkhead door clanged open, and this time the skipper clambered through alone, holding up a gas lamp.

'You girls alright?' he asked.

'We're hungry,' Alfren said.

'So are we all. Better get used to it,' he said. 'Give me your slop pails.'

They put their pails by the cage gate. The skipper did everything slowly and carefully to avoid missing a step.

'Where are we going?' asked Liffet.

'Don't try that,' said the skipper. 'The Picker told me you could make me answer questions I shouldn't.'

'No, I won't,' Alfren said softly, as she found his waves in her mind.

'Where are we going?' she asked gently, as though it was no question at all.

'To the keep, of course.' He checked himself and spoke roughly. 'Now look, girls, I'm taking care of you, aren't I? So, none of your tricks.'

'Promise,' she said. 'It's just, is it far?'

'Of course not. Now, you be good and stay put while I take these out.'

'Yes, we'll be here,' she said.

Within a couple of minutes, he returned with the empty pails. As he clambered into the stowage, he swore: 'Blast it. I left this door wide open.'

'How can we escape?' Alfren said, 'and where to?'

'That's right, there's no chance,' said the skipper. 'This high wind will pass by morning and then if there's a fair sea we should reach the keep in a day, then I won't have to mind you two any longer.'

'Good,' she said, 'and we don't want to get you into trouble. Not worth it, is it?'

She had used a reassuring voice, such as she knew how.

'That's right,' said the skipper again.

'Thanks for watching out for us.' She tried to appeal to him. 'We can trust you. I'm glad we're not far from the keep. Can I say, I am worried that Liffy here could be in trouble because you think she's a seer.'

'Oh no, if she does what's expected of her, she won't be in trouble at all, and you'll be alright too.'

'It's good we understand that from you, Skipper. Surely we don't scare you?'

'No, well, we just have to go careful. Right, no more chatting. Get some sleep,' and the skipper clambered out.

'Has he left the door unlocked?' asked Liffet quietly.

'Yes.'

After a moment, the locking mechanism turned.

'No.'

'I didn't hear you sending to him,' said Liffet.

'I wasn't, otherwise that Picker would be along right away.'

'You know what I think, Ally?' asked Liffet brightly.

'No,' Alfren replied, annoyed because she could guess what her friend might say.

Liffet whispered. 'I think you found a way to send waves softly and directly, so they weren't leaky and everywhere, so the pendant won't swing because it's too far away.'

'It wasn't a send, just a voice, that's all, Liffy. Shall we sleep? Maybe a good idea about escape will come to us if we rest a little.'

'Yes, alright.'

Extinction

Jin

'Vicar, Alfren told me that you talked to her about the Extinction.'

'Yes?'

'It's not something we talk about generally,' Jin said sharply. He wanted to unsettle the vicar.

'Only the curious bring it up, that's true,' said the vicar.

'It's unfair to press views on anyone, especially a 15-year-old girl who is dependent on you.'

The vicar looked contrite but sat up to defend himself.

'My keen interest and views on the Extinction are my own, but I am entitled to share when someone is willing to listen. Alfren asked for explanations for pollution and, I grant you, some may say that's a different matter, but I believe they're the same thing. Besides, I trusted she would think about what I had to say and form her own opinion.'

It was a fair rebuke.

'Was the Extinction of interest to her?' Jin was nevertheless polite, which was ranger practice.

'She was – sorry, she *is* – developing an interest, I would say. She asked if I knew what was behind pollution. She believed she could provide clean drinking water. "Surely we can improve filtration," she said.'

Jin gathered his thoughts. His own interest was in the causes of the Extinction, and whatever it was that the few survivors had done to survive. Alfren, on the other hand, was concerned for folk in the present day.

He persevered. 'Sir, do you keep notes and the like, originating from the Extinction?'

'Yes,' the vicar replied quietly. There was no hesitation or denial; the vicar was honest. But keeping such texts could lead to trouble. Jin guessed folk were glad to hand them over to the vicar, the better to avoid a visit from the militia but also trusting that the texts might be preserved.

'I read them, from time to time. They're old, written by hand most of them. I've found little presented as fact and, so long after the Extinction, there's no corroboration possible. Unless, of course, someone could bring together all the texts, study them, put together a timeline and cross-reference the texts with one another. Then it may be possible to build up a history and from that, who knows, an explanation. But who has the resources for that?'

Jin couldn't divulge he had read many of the same because he had been researching a problem with a valve radio he was modifying, as some texts were technical in part.

Did the vicar question the Extinction? Did he belong to some scientific society that discussed it? Could they have become aware of Alfren and her 'interest'? He had to provoke the vicar again.

'Isn't it simple? The Extinction destroyed the Last People and their civilisation. We don't need to know how it occurred, not really, though pollution could certainly have been a cause. Whatever it was, something happened and now we live with unending storms. Those few that survived the Extinction years were a new folk, enough in number and expertise to establish settlements and form the League.

We know we live in the shadow of the Extinction, but that's all.'

It worked. The vicar was edging to cut in.

'What you say is true, but it's an oversimplification. First, let me say, there are a few who seek to understand why the Extinction happened and why we live as we do now, under the storms. I correspond with my contacts on Sealand, occasionally exchanging research and ideas. My personal view is that we are living through the Extinction, and it's not over. Alfren was drawn to the mystery of the Extinction. She wanted to know about 'waves', she said to me one day, and then she found chemistry at the laboratory where she wanted to find out about how energies interact. I think she knew she was setting forth on her life path. There, that may be relevant.'

Jin didn't have the time, but one day he would return for a list of those folk with whom the vicar corresponded.

The vicar seemed to be simply gullible and had been playing a dangerous game, for once an alternative view was put about - such as the vicar's - to folk that had endured until now without need for an explanation of the Extinction, who had only their fortitude and skills to support them, what would that lead to?

He could guess: loss of will; dependency on a figurehead who had a plan for them.

'Anything you say may be of help later.'

It seemed clear that someone had targeted one or all three of the victims and planned the kidnap carefully. All he could say was that Alfren was interested in a better future, not one to dwell on the past. Could it be that somebody wanted to exploit that? It had happened before, as he knew from the old texts. Some settlements formed after the Extinction had councils that defended them from tyranny. Some though, had been lost to warlords who had sought out folk with skills, captured them and forced them into service. Which of those had risen above others? Was it a warlord with a calling for survival who inspired his clan, who took the ones with skills and knowledge and coerced them in his service?

He thought again. His reverie inclined him to a view that the kidnappers had local knowledge and could be Sealanders or based on Sealand.

The vicar was watching him and spoke up. 'Marine Jin, before our times, our church was a meeting place. Nought was left to us from the Extinction that could explain why. The church was damaged. The new folk rebuilt it stronger than before for the benefit of any burgher or traveller – whoever needed shelter. When I undertook my commission as vicar, the contract was to take in anyone who desired sanctuary. So it is that I provide pastoral care for all folk. What I see are folk in the wash of the Extinction and the cruel events that took place. It defines us, even now. Folk need reassurance so that they may believe there is a future. Those few who believe in our future are the greatest gift to us.

'You will find Alfren, won't you?'

The vicar was a passionate man, misguided and idealistic, and just the sort Jin admired.

Snatchers

Alfren

Alfren lay awake listening to the whine of wind and whipping of rigging. She and Liffet couldn't sleep.

'I hope they've moored this tramper securely. If it slips its anchor this high wind will drive us onto rocks in no time at all and we'll never get out,' said Liffet.

Alfren thought for a moment. 'Liffy, that's brilliant!'

'I think not!' Liffet retorted.

'One minute.'

'What are you up to? Any chance I get a say before I'm fish feed?'

'Maybe I can get the skipper to open the door, if I can make him think that the tramper might slip its anchor and we'd be trapped.'

Liffet agreed. 'Worth a try.'

'Liffy, can you block out my send?'

She wanted no influence on Liffet even in the slightest.

Over the years, as they had exchanged their sends, Liffet had learned to close off her mind when she wanted. It had started when they played and scuffled. Alfren had been able to anticipate her friend who was fast and tricky, and Liffet in turn had learned that Alfren could hear her thoughts instantly.

To counter this, Liffet had tried not to think until the last moment, but that hadn't succeeded. Then, Liffet had tried to think of more than one move, to confuse Alfren, and that hadn't worked either. Then, Liffet had learned to shut out the world and yet still move through it by focusing only on movement and saw everything else as just objects. It wasn't really blocking out the world, just making it uninteresting. That had worked. They had felt it was important for Liffet to be able to do that but Alfren had never done the same.

Alfren turned to the message she wanted to send. It had to be quiet but carry just enough weight to make the skipper unable to put a thought out of his mind. She trickled worry for their safety, fear of being trapped, like a whisper. She didn't wait to hear the send absorbed, which would tell her the skipper had heard it; she had to trust the send had carried just enough and directly.

'Done,' she said. 'Did you hear?'

'Nothing,' Liffet replied.

She thought about it. Liffet was right. Maybe she could send softly or a long way, wide or directed.

They waited.

After a few minutes, she saw the door wheel turn. It had been unlocked.

Liffet sat up, reached into her boot and brought out a bent pin.

'Just a tick!'

Her friend picked the lock to the cage gate. The two of them crouched at the bulkhead door. The rumble of wind would mask any sound on opening. It was held in place only by its tight fit in the frame. It budged easily, and they swung it back and peered out. There was a passage to the stern with doors both sides, and at the end, no doubt was a galley and mess with steps up to the wheelhouse, where the hirelings would be on watch.

Alfren stole along the passage a short way to a door and nodded to Liffet. A key was in the lock, which was thoughtful of the skipper in that the door could be unlocked straightaway in an emergency. Surely Zal lay behind.

Liffet had been right about her sends. Hopefully, they had put their captors at ease and made them lax. It was new to her, and it had worked.

She unlocked and opened the cabin door and slipped inside while Liffet stood guard within the doorway. The cabin was narrow, and on one side Zal lay curled on a bunk. Alfren saw her injured arm was uppermost, the sling and bandage bloody. It was clear that escape at night into a storm with Zal wounded so was impossible. Foremost, Zal needed nursing.

It was hopeless. It wasn't fair. Just like them, Zal should have freedom, not fear, imprisonment and misery.

Zal turned, woken by her presence.

'I thought you might turn up, that you wouldn't forget me,' she whispered.

'We – I – wanted to say goodbye,' Alfren replied.

There was nothing Alfren could do. It was heartless leaving Zal with the raiders. 'Tell me where the keep is, and we'll find you.'

Zal shook her head. 'I don't know. They make sure we don't know. I escaped only the once from a boat, just as you're doing.'

Alfren was caught. How could she leave Zal to suffer and without nursing, and to an awful fate at the hands of the Picker?

Yet, she and Liffet should escape and save themselves. That had always been the way: decide how best to survive for yourself and go along with it. There was no one to say what was right or wrong or what was fair, not in the lanes of Wallburgh and certainly not out here in the outland in the clutches of raiders.

Perhaps, if she knew more about it, she might be able to find the keep?

'What's there?' Zal's eyes opened as she struggled to answer. Alfren supposed Zal was gathering her thoughts, but it was more than that. Zal's memory was so strong, the waves spilled over clearly and in a rush. Alfren knew in an instant what Zal was about to tell her. She exclaimed in surprise.

'Yes!'

Liffet caught her shoulders from behind. 'Quiet, you idiot!'

Alfren reeled from the message. She had seen it clearly. How could she not? She was not long a child herself.

'Oh my, that's ... We must ... Liffy!'

'Be quiet!' hissed her friend.

'Liffy, we've got to ...' This needed a decision.

'Zal,' she said hoarsely, 'we're staying with you. Right, Liffy, let's clean her up.'

Liffet entered and closed the door gently.

'Come on then,' said her friend firmly.

Liffet helped Zal to turn a little, then stripped the bloody sling, unwound the bandaging and wiped the wound, while Alfren soothed Zal who winced with pain.

'Right, I'm off to the galley,' whispered Liffet, 'for water and a clean cloth. Ally, what's this all about?'

Alfren took her eyes off Zal for a moment. She focused and sent a message directly, filled with what she had heard from Zal: the terror of being taken, the loss of parents, long days of hopelessness, sadness and fear.

'The evil, scheming snatchers!' hissed Liffet.

'Liffy,' Alfren whispered, 'what do you think? We could stay on the boat with Zal to look after her, then escape with her when we can and find clues to where the keep is.'

'Fair enough,' Liffet grimaced. 'All the same, let me know when and I'll stab them if you like.'

Alfren nodded. It was bravado, wasn't it?

'Back soon.' Liffet sneaked from the cabin.

Alfren knelt and rested her hand on Zal's shoulder. How strange it was that in only a few hours she had grown to respect a girl she barely knew. Zal had found a way to escape from the Picker with two kidnapped children, had fallen among the burghers of Wallburgh, unknown in their loyalties, but she hadn't come across anyone to trust. It was then, captive once more and with a painful injury, that Zal had opened up to her with the disclosure – about the lost children.

The wind moaned.

Liffet returned.

'Bit lucky there: no hirelings. Anyway, here's the kettle. It's still warm from the stove.' She set about cleaning Zal's wound.

'I'll tear a new sling from a sheet,' Alfren said.

'Let me, Ally.'

There was room for only one, so she stood back.

Liffet eased Zal to rest on her bunk and tidied the bedding. Alfren saw her friend hide morsels of food from the galley under the pillow.

'Clearer?' Liffet asked, turning to her.

'Yes ... Liffy?'

'Yes, and I agree: we stay until the next chance to get away, this time with Zal.'

They slipped from the cabin, locked the door and returned to their cage in the stowage, where Liffet padlocked the gate.

'I took these,' Liffet said, handing her oatcakes and cheese.

'A feast,' Alfren said.

'It is.'

Soon after, they heard hirelings shouting.

'Damn!' said Liffet. 'I've just remembered ... the kettle! I left it in Zal's cabin. Quick, lie down and pretend to be asleep.'

Alfren stuffed the last oatcake in her mouth just as the bulkhead door swung open and the skipper squeezed through. He shone his lamp at them.

'You're there!' he exclaimed. They squinted into the light. Alfren could say nothing, her mouth full.

'Where else, mister?' said Liffet. 'We're comfy here anyway.'

The skipper checked the gate to the cage.

'Yes, well ...' he said and made to leave the stowage. As he did, he turned to Liffet, as though to catch her out.

'Where's the kettle then?'

'I don't know!' Liffet replied sharply, then she suggested, 'Have you checked Zal's cabin?'

'Bugger!' cursed the skipper and left hurriedly.

They turned to one another.

'Are we mad?' asked Liffet lightly. 'Shouldn't we have run for it?'

'Yes, but we had to stay, didn't we?'

'So do you think it's possible that all the children – all the children that've been taken – are there at the keep?'

Texts

Jin

'The Extinction? Marine Jin, our own greed and waste overcame us. Yes, ours. The world climate is in turmoil, trying to find a new level. We need someone to tell us when it will end, or there could be madness among us.

'There may be worse to come: some folk talk of a second Extinction. We may miss the signs and it will destroy us, with all of us lost. I think we begin the survival with a partnership of thinkers, healers and guides – the gifted.'

The vicar tailed off nervously.

'Sir, if I may, could I see a sample of these texts?'

They were unlikely to be any different from the texts in the ranger library, but still Jin was curious.

'Oh, well … they are most valuable to me.'

'I won't ask to take them.'

The vicar left and returned carrying a casket. 'These are some of the earliest texts.' He took out a sheaf of papers. 'You'll see they're mixed, unclassified.'

Jin separated the papers on the table: a mixture of handwritten and printed notes and diary pages. He knew what they would say but made a show of reading one.

This is Year Five since we fled, and I won't keep my diary for much longer; there are no more pencils and paper. I miss my dad. Mum says he'll be home soon. I hope Mum's right. I haven't seen him all winter and I fear he might never return. He said he'd bring me books and cloth. I want not to think of him taking risks for me. I'll be happy if he comes home with nothing, just so long as he comes.

There's barely anything left in our food store after last year's poor harvest. I cleared the mouldy grain. It'll be better this year, I'm sure. I want not to have to go to live with the folk at Sandy Wick. They have enough for us, so they say, and could take us in, but I don't like them because they like rules so much. I love it here at North Crag. Over winter I built up a bigger wind-berm to shield the potato crop. I told my mum we're sure to have many lambs this year. We'll net more fish in the voe and I'll chase the seals away. I'll keep watch for raiders this summer; they'll take nothing from us.

The gale turned the shed over last night. That was a silly mistake; we should tie down everything.

Today wind's light, so I'll teach the young ones. We'll write and draw in the sand on the beach. Old Billy said he'd make sand boxes for us so we can write indoors when the wind's up ...

Jin put it down.

'As you say, vicar, awful times. The writer lived in a remote dwelling vulnerable to ...'

'We must never fall into these ways again,' said the vicar grimly. 'I think Alfren knew that.'

'If there's anything you think might help, please leave a message at the barracks.'

Jin left. It was good to be outside in the gale, away from the stifling heat of the rectory kitchen.

No, neither he nor Alfren were anything like the Last People.

DAY 2

Daughter

Alfren

The high wind gale-force 8 had passed by mid-morning and slackened to a strong breeze-force 6, which would mean choppy seas with white-capped waves and spray.

Alfren longed to see for herself.

It would be rough sailing as the boat would roll over wave tops.

They sat confined to their cage. She was bored and wanted to be underway.

Were they right to stay when they could have escaped? Of course. How much worse it must have been for the children kidnapped over the years.

Somehow, they would find them.

The skipper brought breakfast before noon. Didn't he trust the hirelings to do it? She considered he wasn't a very bad man. He was still bad, but he wasn't the leader, and maybe doing what he did because he was forced to in some way.

He addressed Liffet. 'I found the kettle and I saw that Zal's dressings had been changed. So, you knew.'

'Where else would the kettle be?' asked Liffet.

'Ah, but who took it?'

'You mean it wasn't Zal?'

The skipper had no patience with them. He must have had a sleepless night on watch. He turned to leave.

'Do you work for the keep, Skipper?' Alfren asked. He turned to reply, which meant he might have something to confess.

'No. Well, just the odd job. If I didn't, he would make life difficult, wouldn't he?'

'Who?'

'The chief, of course.'

'Is he a reiver?'

A robber-jarl raiding settlements and islands, taking sides in feuds and quarrels?

'You know too much already and if I told you anything it wouldn't be good for you. You'd be a danger to yourself and everybody else. So, keep quiet.'

'Yes, Skipper.'

'Do your pails need emptying?'

'Later. Will we get to the keep today?'

'I think not. It's a clear day, but a late start and wind and waves are against us.'

'We'll get sick here in this stowage, pitching up and down. Can't you put us aft?'

'I'll ask the Picker.'

She faltered while she thought quickly. 'Yes, you mean the Picker who takes the ones that have the foretelling? They're children, aren't they?' she asked.

'Children, yes,' said the skipper quietly. He seemed upset by that, then continued. 'I wasn't telling you anything I shouldn't, was I? The Picker said you could trick me, but you've not been bad at all.'

'Come on, mister!' exclaimed Liffet. 'Trick you how?'

'Like last night, cheeky youngster!'

'You've been too long at sea, mister,' replied Liffet. 'Mind, if you need a deckhand, I'll work my passage, just to go somewhere new. Never mind all this seer nonsense.'

'Well, you are so, the Picker says, and that puts a pretty price on your head. Right, I've had enough and we're about to put to sea.'

He seemed to waver between being firm with them and faltering kindness. Alfren could imagine that in the wheelhouse he would wonder if he had said too much.

'You've looked after us.'

'Is that because you have a daughter yourself?' asked Liffet.

That was a good guess!

'Yes, I do. Yes.' The skipper nodded sombrely. 'Right, no more questions,' he said awkwardly and left.

Alfren exchanged a look with Liffet. Could his daughter be one of the kidnapped children grown-up?

Soon after, Alfren heard the engine crank over and warm up. They heard shouts on deck as the crew swung the tramper around to release anchor, then more shouts from far off and she realised the tramper had been tethered to the shore, for additional lashing against the high wind during the night. The hull lurched in the waves and the engine raced to propel the tramper into the open sea.

Zal

The Picker struggled through the bulkhead door, stumbling across the stowage as the tramper heaved over, and gripped the cage against the pitching and rolling. He didn't hold his pendant Alfren noticed, because he needed both hands for support and besides surely, he wouldn't be able to observe the pendant in such a rough sea. Despite this, she didn't trust that her sends might pass undetected.

'You will be moved aft, cuffed and blindfolded.' He sounded garbled with seasickness. 'Frankly, Liffet, you appear to have potential and I would like to show you how well you could be treated, but if you attempt to influence us with your thoughts, or if either of you try to escape, I will have no hesitation in throwing this one, Alfren, overboard.'

Staggering because of a high wave, the Picker made for the door.

'I know you're frightened of me,' called Liffet. 'But you've been alright. Promise I won't scare you.'

The Picker turned to look at her severely.

Liffet added, 'We'd like to see Zal, to be sure she's alright.'

Almost tripping through the door, the Picker stumbled from the stowage.

'I think he pretends to sneer, but really, he's relieved and will allow us a bit of freedom ... I hope,' said Liffet.

'Right,' Alfren said, looking askance at her friend. 'Just now it was you who used your tone of voice on the Picker. Good one, Liffy.'

'But I didn't!'

'I heard you.'

'Oh, really? Right-oh.'

They waited once more.

Once again, the skipper entered the stowage and this time he released them from the cage, and made sure new bonds were tied securely but lightly about their wrists, their arms before them. He bound their ankles, which meant they could shuffle along the passage, but any attempt to climb the steps to the wheelhouse would be checked. He didn't bother with blindfolds.

Alfren guessed the Picker was in his cabin. The skipper told them they were allowed to sit with Zal or in the galley, as they wished.

'If I catch you with a knife, I will cut your throats myself,' he said warningly, but without menace.

They waddled to join Zal. Liffet padded cushions around her in her bunk, while Alfren found stale bread and treacle from the cupboards in the galley. In the small cabin, they wedged themselves against the bucking and wheeling of the tramper.

Zal smiled weakly. 'I suppose you want to know what this is all about. It was wrong what I did, and then I lost the children to your folk. You haven't lived at the keep, so you don't know what it's like. I went with the Picker to the League, far off. There were mountains, a League town – I think it was called Salvation – in a boat bigger than this. I went because I asked, and the chief let me. I said the children would be less frightened if I was there with them. After we kidnapped them, I saw how awful it was and so I escaped with them and rowed for shore. I didn't know where we were but I'd seen lights on land. Then you shot me, Alfren,' Zal said, resentful still. 'I had armour on because I knew about settled folk and their fear of raiders. I was going to tell someone all about the keep and ask for help, but no one came to see me, only you two, and first I had to test you weren't the chief's fellows. I was confused. It seemed to me my story didn't matter to Sealanders, and I was out of their way in the infirmary and forgotten. It was hopeless. We're on our way back to the keep and it'll go badly for me.'

'You were suspicious of me?' Alfren asked.

'Yes. Someone who could shoot like you! I thought you were most likely to be working for the chief. His informants and allies are anywhere and everywhere.'

'Why did he want you back so much that he sent the Picker for you?'

'I don't know. He never said, but I think the chief depended on me. I know nothing that could lead anyone to him though. I could have told the Sealanders about all the children, but I've no clue as to where the keep is or how far. It's a grand stone building, surrounded by sea, and folk there are forbidden to speak to me.

'Maybe the chief was cross with the Picker for losing me, that's all. Or maybe they came for you, Alfren.'

Zal looked at her. 'Are you a seer?'

'No, of course I'm not. Anyway, why are you looking for a seer?' Alfren asked. 'Any seer, or just one?'

'Not me. It's the chief, he's been looking for a seer for a long time. Surely, you know why.'

Alfren looked at Liffet and both gazed blankly at Zal.

'Oh, come on! Surely you do! How else will we survive without a seer?'

Watchtowers

Jin

'Lieutenant Handar and Marine Jin,' Handar said in introduction, her face dim in dawn light.

'Oh, aye,' said the harbour master curtly. 'We don't see rangers in the burgh. Are you on business or on the scrounge for something?'

'Business,' Handar replied patiently.

They were in the harbour tower at the quayside, in an observation room with a sweeping view of both approaches to the sound.

'Only, what with the taxes we pay for you lot, I'd hope you'd spend more time out there bringing these raiders to account. There's too much piracy and hostage-taking going on these days. The complaints I get from the traders ... well, let's hope you catch some of those blighters.'

The fellow's protest was a bluff, thought Jin. They were all the same, traders and raiders alike, and this harbour master could be in among them. Anyway, he was likely annoyed at being roused by the militia and ordered to his workplace early that morning.

'It's why we're here, Harbour Master,' Handar said.

The rangers had got word from the militia in the early

evening of the day before, which was too long after the kidnapping had taken place. They had swept the burgh, the lanes and the wall, rooftops and yards, and gone out to the shipwrights' quarter. They had searched Alfren's home and the water testing laboratory, asked questions in the pubs, searched the esplanade and fishing smacks. They had stopped all traffic from leaving the burgh gates and the harbour. Through the night they had watched the harbour, called in the guard and the Watch for reports, and taken a smack to search the sound. The Watch had searched the fell above the burgh by lamplight, all the ghylls and sheepfolds. Nothing.

'Sir,' Jin spoke up and took out a chalk pad, 'we'd like to take a look at the harbour log listing all vessels berthed here yesterday.'

'Oh, aye? It's the militia that do that,' said the harbour master stubbornly.

'I'd like to take a look myself, sir,' Jin said with forced politeness. He went on, 'Could you tell me if you noticed anything unusual yesterday? I mean folk in a hurry, a hasty departure? You might have heard there was a raid on the infirmary. It was serious.'

'Yes, alright,' said the harbour master. 'The log's here.' He indicated a desk with a ledger open on it.

'Any traders here yesterday?' Jin asked, scanning the log.

'No, it's end of the season, isn't it? I expect none before winter.'

'There are fishing boats listed here and supply boats for the islands. Did you have any suspicions?'

'No, it was a regular day. The forecast was for the high wind we had overnight, so boats stayed in harbour, most of them. Any that left couldn't have had far to go to safe haven.'

'That'll be why so few left yesterday – only six,' Jin said. 'Yet, I see destinations are not recorded, nor their port of origin or registration details, Harbour Master. Tell me, which of these supply boats do you see least, or are unknown to you?'

The harbour master studied the list, pointed to three and Jin made a note of them.

'Now you wouldn't be misleading us, would you?' Jin studied the harbour master's eyes and expression.

'No need to take that tone,' retorted the harbour master, looking nervously at both rangers.

'Might I ask you to maintain good records, for the next time rangers ask to inspect them? We'll take this log and keep it for a few days.'

As Jin walked with Handar to the barracks, she said wryly, 'It won't be the three he picked out then.'

'I doubt it, Han.'

'I've instructed Tans and Falt to check with the guard once again this morning; they were the crew on duty yesterday afternoon too. Then, they'll make discrete enquiries at the militia barracks. They might find out something I can't. It seems Alfren and the two others – if they're still together – aren't here in the burgh, unless well concealed. That means the likeliest escape was to the harbour. No one would take notice of outlanders carrying sacks or crates which concealed the girls. Given the dealers, brokers and journeymen types there, they wouldn't tell us if they saw something.'

'No, Han.'

Jin hadn't ever been on patrol in the burgh. No ranger had. They covered the outland. Already it was a revelation that, despite their vigilance, burghers were vulnerable to a raid on their infirmary; and down at the harbour, rangers could not count on the loyalties of the workers.

At the barracks, they joined the two other rangers who made up the search squad, in front of the great maps of the

Operations Room. One map showed in detail the large main island of Sealand, the largest island by far. The next showed the whole of the Sealand archipelago, and the near and far island clusters. There were half-a-dozen large islands, larger than Jin's native Furrow – Bell, Grazing, Northlight, Sentry, Great Stacks, Fairmoor. On the third wall was a map of the League, showing the widespread lands and trading ports, with Sealand the farthest outpost to the west and Rockshore the closest trading port.

'Jin, lead off,' said Handar.

'We have brief written reports from the infirmary and the militia, which tell us only who was kidnapped, who the casualties are, and the time of the raid. There are no witness reports because the guards are recovering from their injuries. Tans said that this morning she found out the militia have verbal accounts from a child who watched and followed a raider gang to the harbour. The child tried to raise the alarm but to no avail. Our assumption is that the captives were taken to a boat which departed immediately – a Sealand tramper we believe, because no traders were in the harbour.'

He turned to the map.

'The tramper took refuge from the storm overnight, and even today in the high sea state it may remain at anchor, 50 miles distant at most. Six boats left harbour yesterday. We might presume Marine Alfren was in a seventh, unrecorded boat. We should find out where all were headed. Did they leave the sound to the south or north?'

He sat down, troubled that they had no time to examine the motive for such a daring raid. It was clear that one or more of the captives had a high value, and it was odd that while in captivity, the militia had let slip that no one had interviewed the girl raider. He stared at the maps on the wall.

'Rangers,' said Handar, 'this is day two, the first day after the raid. I will make a request to the militia to repeat our search of all boats and buildings at the harbour. Tans,' she addressed the young woman ranger, 'have a look around too.

'Falt,' she addressed her sergeant. 'See what you can find at the infirmary, but first come with me to see the militia. We must press them to tell us everything.

'Jin, go to the watchtowers above the burgh. Anything else?'

No. He was itching to be outside.

'Rangers, away,' she ordered.

It was eight o'clock. The wind buffeted Jin as he strode up the steep lanes leading from the barracks to the little-used West Gate. This opened directly to the steep hillsides above the burgh to the line of three watchtowers, each 1½ to 2 miles apart. They had been built for their sweeping views over and far beyond the burgh.

He enjoyed the climb and the chilling breeze. He took a path to the first, northernmost watchtower, Angler. It was windier high on the fellside. Up on the deck, he looked down on the shipwrights' quarter and the highway leading north. Directly to the east was the burgh girdled by its wall, then the sound, and Whaleback across the water, then to the south stretched Sealand's coastline. To the west and north rose moorland and hills over which raiders had streamed in the past.

He saw from the logbook that the watchmen had no record of boats in the sound, although he had expected this because this watchtower was there to survey the northern approach to the burgh. There had been scheduled motor transports and a few horse-drawn carts, horse-riders and bicycles, but nothing of note. It was possible the raiders had taken Alfren and the militiaman that way, he thought, but they would have had to stand scrutiny by guards at the gate.

At night, the gates were closed and guarded, and during the gale, escape would have been nigh impossible.

He descended from the tower, waved goodbye to the watchmen far aloft and trotted to the next watchtower, Barb, which had a larger deck as well as a grand view of the burgh and the sound. As he had hoped, the log detailed harbour movements and boat features, such as forward cabin (a fishing boat) and aft cabin (a supply boat), and added details such as masts, rigging and colour. He was glad of that and told the watchmen so.

The weather continued fair as he jogged along to the last of the three watchtowers, Cod. From the deck, as well as the sound, he took in the southern tip of Whaleback and the southern hills of Sealand. The logbook listed only those boats that had been seen heading along the southern approach, which corroborated details of boats from the middle watchtower.

He ran down the hillside to enter the burgh through the South Gate. He had learned which directions the boats had taken.

Strike

Alfren

'The chief is brutal, you know,' explained Zal. 'He has ruined folk and cast them out. When he gets really annoyed, he sells them off to slavers. When he wants to know something, he keeps folk captive until they tell. He's got it worked out. He's made alliances with all the raider jarls and their squads. He has contacts and influence in all the League towns. He's wealthy and pays hirelings who flock to him. They're his hirelings on this tramper, except the skipper. Maybe it's the skipper's own boat and he's been pressed into this. The hirelings don't care what they do so long as they get their silver. They're the worst.

'The keep is a stronghold, and we're kept inside all the time. It can't be far, because otherwise how else could he send letters to his clients and dispatch his hirelings straightaway when they're called for. If the Picker knew I was telling you this, he'd be angry. In any case, he'll make an example of me before the children and frighten them to do his bidding.'

Zal turned her head away from them. She would say no more for a while.

It seemed to Alfren that Zal must believe there was no escape: if she tried, punishment awaited; if she did escape, there was nowhere to go; no one would take her in; the chief would find her anyway.

There was a knock and the skipper pulled open the door to the cabin, bracing himself in the opening. The boat heaved, twisted and swirled.

'Back to the cage for the night, girls. There's good anchorage just ahead.'

'Why, Skipper?' asked Liffet.

'Headwind and sea state,' he said. He meant their progress had been slow. On top of the late start that morning, that meant they wouldn't reach the keep. This was the girls' last chance to escape.

They would have to trust Zal was better.

'You can take some stew from the galley,' the skipper said gruffly.

Alfren nodded and glanced at Liffet. Also in their favour, it was likely the Picker was weary from hours of passage by sea and might believe his task almost done and so relax the watch over them.

She shuffled to the galley with the slops pail from the cabin. Two of the hirelings were there. One was a lad in his teens, not much older than her, and the other a fellow in his twenties. She held up the pail.

'Can I throw it?' she asked.

The hireling nodded his head towards the steps. He was ready to laugh at her attempt to climb while bound and carrying a pail. She took a line hung on the bulkhead and tied one end to the pail handle and the other to her belt. She jumped, then hopped from one step to the next. When her head cleared the hatch, she saw it was a fine, windy day, clear with no rain. In the wheelhouse the skipper had his back to her, and she guessed the other two hirelings were forward watching for submerged rocks, guiding the skipper as he steered the tramper close to the coast. She raised herself onto the deck, pulled up the pail and emptied it over the stern on the landward side, then filled and rinsed it with seawater. The rocky coast was steep, slippery with slime and seaweed, and above that, steep hillside – impossible for Zal.

The tramper was about to enter a cove. The skipper saw her and shouted at her to go below. She raised the pail to signal the reason for her being topside and, as she did, she found what she was looking for: there in the wheelhouse, a bow and quiver of harpoon arrows to hook seals and porpoises, and on the deck forward of the wheelhouse she saw the stern of a rowing boat to ferry folk to shore and transfer supplies. She lowered the pail through the hatch and hopped down.

The hireling stuck out his leg as though to trip her.

'Just a minute, if no one wants you how about the lad here asks the chief,' he laughed, and turned to the lad. 'She's a bit scrawny but I bet she's a good worker. It's time you had a slave or two and started out on your own garth, away from the keep.'

She knew the hireling meant a farm smallholding on a remote island which she supposed was the sort of home that many hirelings came from.

'She'll do nicely for you, lad. You can be free of service to the chief, you'll make more silver that way.'

The hireling laughed at her. 'Good lad, isn't he. He'll treat you right, better than you deserve. There, that'll be a good deal for you. Go on,' and he dropped his leg and nodded her away.

She cast her eyes down, retrieved her pail, careful to keep the line coiled, then shuffled back to the cabin.

The sea calmed – the tramper had entered the cove.

'Liffy, the hireling in the galley is a brash sort and won't suspect us. Could you bring some stew and bread?'

'He won't give me any trouble.'

'Don't set them off, just be quick.'

'Right-oh!' her friend said brightly.

The hirelings were strong and scuffling with them could ruin the girls' chance of escape. Alfren had to think straight. In a couple of hours it would be dusk, which would cover their flight.

She roused Zal and checked the dressing, then bound her arm tightly to her chest. Zal looked at her enquiringly.

'We should go,' Alfren said. 'When we get to Wallburgh, the rangers will listen to us and we'll do what we can to locate the keep. That's the plan.'

She would rely on her training and make her best effort to escape. The trick would be to deal with each hireling one at a time, and to get to the harpoon bow first.

Liffet returned with a plate of stew, she helped Zal to sit up, and the girls gorged themselves. 'I teased them a bit, got them going,' said Liffet.

'What?'

'They'll be too busy having a laugh to see what we're doing.'

'Right.'

She would have to trust Liffet's instinct in a fight. She explained her plan. It was simple and risky, but it was all they could do.

'Liffy, it's up to you. Don't hesitate.'

Liffet retrieved her stub knife from her boot and cut through her bindings.

They waited. After a short while, the door to the cabin swung out and the skipper called. 'Right, out you come.'

Alfren was nearest Zal, who lay with her eyes closed.

'Could you check her temperature, please, Skipper?'

'What do I know?' he asked.

'Please, think of your daughter,' she said. It was wrong but they had to escape. She saw him hesitate, but he didn't refuse.

He entered the cabin and bent over the bunk. Immediately Liffet jumped on his back and she pricked his throat with her knife. Her legs wrapped his upper body and clamped his arms to his sides..

'Move or say a word, Skipper, and this knife goes in, and I want to kill you, really I do, but Ally here says you've been decent with us, but she did say I could kill you if I wanted to, and I do, because I'm a mad seer girl, so get on the deck.'

Clearly, he was surprised at the strength and bitterness of Liffet's strike.-He collapsed heavily by the bunk. Quickly Alfren pulled his hands together behind his back, then with Liffet she used the line from the pail and some bedding as a restraint and gag.

Liffet crouched over the skipper.

'Ally, it's a mistake not to kill him. He's a raider and kidnapper.'

For the first time in her life Alfren wasn't certain what her friend meant: did Liffet want to scare the skipper or actually follow through with her threat?

'Liffy, let's go.'

'What about the Picker?'

'I hope he stays where he is.'

Still in her bonds, Alfren shuffled along the passage to the galley.

'Didn't you hear him? The skipper needs help with Zal,' she said to the hireling. He leaned forward to peer along the passage.

'You stay here, lad,' he said. 'Watch her.'

Immediately the hireling entered the passageway, she turned to the lad. She had to hold him back somehow. She had an idea straightaway.

Quietly she said, 'You didn't laugh at me just now, you didn't see me as your slave.'

She held his gaze, smiled gently, and in her mind found

a thin bond to him. She meant to send waves to make her appear helpless, but instead they were mixed: part coy and submissive; part haughty. That was odd. They weren't the waves she had intended, and she had no idea if they would work. She turned to the galley, took a knife and cut through her bindings. The lad was indecisive. She freed herself. He seemed foggy. Whatever she had done had worked, hopefully for just long enough.

She saw that in the passageway the hireling had hesitated to open the cabin door and looked toward the stowage, as if to check there first. Thankfully, he pulled open the door and rushed in when he saw the skipper. Liffet, knife in hand, leapt behind him into the cabin and Alfren heard a pained howl. Had Liffet wounded and subdued him?

Harpoon

Alfren had to move quickly. The lad watched as she climbed the ladder, but he didn't call out. Through the hatch and on deck, she swung around to the wheelhouse. A hireling saw her straightaway but hesitated. He must have heard the cries from below. He shouted to his mate on the fore-deck and then sprang towards her, arms wide and menacing. He was a big, heavy-set fellow. Alfren waved her knife to delay him. The hireling had probably been in many fights whereas this was her first. Only terrible things would happen if she failed and the girls were unable to escape. She had to succeed, and she had to move fast. The hireling stepped forward as if to send her tumbling over the gunwale or back down the steps to the galley below.

Do what they taught in training for the Watch: fight hard.

The hireling had made a mistake. He could easily overpower her, but instead he took a step back because he must have judged how purposeful she was. He reached for a pike pole hooked on the outside of the wheelhouse. It was heavy and fearsome looking, for clawing or spiking large fish, or wresting floating debris from the sea. She knew she had to move before the pike swung round at her. She lunged. The hireling saw and kicked out, but her timing and aim were good.

With one hand grasping the handle and the other pushing on the butt, she jabbed the knife through his woven trouser leg above the boot, into the calf. The hireling yelped, lost his balance and fell towards her, hitting out as he did. She dodged and sprang into the wheelhouse to grab the bow. From the quiver she snatched a harpoon. It was heavy, flightless, barbed and for short range only. She looked up to see the second hireling making for his mate, so she ducked and slipped around the other side of the wheelhouse to the foredeck. The second hireling saw her and turned to chase. Quickly she strung the bow, nocked the harpoon and stood firm just as he approached. He pulled back, his sight on the harpoon pointed at him.

'You're a scrap of a girl, and you daren't,' he called.

Immediately she raised the bow and leaned into it. He should recognise the poise of a bowman and her strong draw on the bow. She had only a moment to hold the strain before she had to release. Her aim was steady. He stepped back. She relaxed a little but kept aim.

'Take your mate forward. Do it now,' she hissed. 'Move or I'll have your blood.' She meant it. She had found her voice, just as Liffet had.

The hireling growled and hastened to lift his mate from the wheelhouse. She followed. As they hobbled forward, she called down to the galley for Liffet. There was no reply. She looked up through the wheelhouse window to see the second hireling prop his injured mate on the gunwale and turn, intent on stealing up on her. She stepped to the side of the wheelhouse, raised her bow, aimed and leant into it again. The hireling called out, 'No!' The harpoon thudded and pierced his shoulder. He spun and fell with a cry. She called to the heavy hireling.

'Go all the way forward or you're next. Move!'

She dropped her bow and slid down the steps into the

galley, to the gloom of the lower deck.

'There you are. Do join us,' the Picker gloated.

The lad was standing uselessly in the galley. The Picker held Liffet in the narrow passageway.

'As you see, you've lost. Your friend, the seer, will die by my hand unless you do as I say.'

She faced Liffet. The Picker held a knife at her friend's throat.

'Lad,' called the Picker, 'tie her wrists.'

The lad fumbled on the deck of the galley to collect ropes that had bound her a minute earlier. From Zal's cabin, the stabbed hireling beside the skipper called out for help.

'Deck hands!' shouted the Picker, calling to the hirelings topside.

'They're not coming,' she said. She held out her arms to the lad to show she was being compliant with the Picker's instruction. She focused on Liffet and found her friend easily.

The Picker sneered. 'There's nothing the seer can do, not this time. The apparatus in my cabin has shown no indication of thought waves.'

'You can't measure waves,' she said.

'All energies can be measured, even the mildest. Lad, hurry up.'

'Can you detect what she is sending now?'

'She isn't. You're fooling. You will be punished as she is made to watch.'

'She is sending. If you could detect thought, then you would know what will happen next.'

'What!'

She had distracted the Picker. He yelped in pain, released Liffet, and turned to see Zal, arm raised with knife in hand. Liffet pushed back hard. The Picker fell backwards and Liffet pushed away his knife arm. The Picker yelled again and turned to see Zal beside him. He writhed in agony, for Zal held Liffet's small knife which had punctured his hip.

'Zal, are you alright?' asked Liffet.

Zal groaned. 'Help me up.'

'Let's get Zal topside,' Alfren called. She and Liffet kicked and stamped on the flailing legs and arms of the Picker and hireling as they lifted Zal and brought her to the galley.

'Lad, up on deck,' she instructed, and he climbed the steps sullenly.

'You too, Liffy. Mind, there are two hirelings forward.'

Hurriedly, she fashioned a harness from bindings to fit around Zal's waist and legs. Liffet dropped a rope and she tied it to the harness.

'Take in,' she called. Liffet and the lad hoisted Zal aloft, as she guided her from below.

She turned to check on the Picker and hireling. They were struggling to right themselves and release the skipper. The Picker glared at her.

'I'll tear out your eyes, damn you!' he snarled.

More threats! She took a heavy pan from beside the stove, and with a grunt, threw it with all her strength. The Picker turned away from the missile, which struck him on his arm. It seemed to make the Picker and hireling more violent and desperate to chase. They would fight until they were too hurt to move ... or dead.

She heard shouts from above. She grabbed the stew pot – they would need it – and raced up the steps. She saw Zal slumped in the wheelhouse and Liffet on the foredeck. The lad had hold of the pike pole and was steering Liffet towards the two hirelings. Liffet was unarmed, and the lad was vengeful. Alfren took the harpoon bow and slipped around the other side of the wheelhouse.

'That's enough,' she called out to him. The lad was crying bitterly.

'Get back, you witch,' he sobbed. 'I'll slit this one wide open if you raise that bow. You won't trick me!'

'That's it, son,' called the heavy hireling with the leg wound. 'Bring her to me.'

The lad jabbed the pike pole and Liffet shuffled back.

'Save yourself, Ally!' called Liffet.

The lad jabbed again, distraught. His was quick and caught Liffet, who fell over clutching her arm.

'Ally, now!' Liffet called.

The lad was trembling. He pointed the pike pole at Liffet's chest. He had only to stumble ...

Much filled Alfren's mind in that moment. She heard Liffet's call and found her waves. She felt the waves in the winds that whirled over the deck, and she breathed a deep breath and felt enormous energy. These hirelings might wound her friend, torment Zal, and surely beat her if they caught her.

In an instant, she sent out a searing shriek of intense waves, bitter and angry.

She saw Liffet twitch and slump.

No! What had happened?

The lad dropped the pike and reached to cover his head. He stood, reeled and staggered, cried out with pain and doubled over the gunwale. The hirelings curled up on the deck, heads covered by arms. At this, she found some other part of her mind that said, simply, *Stop*. She broke off her shriek.

She recovered, shocked by what she had done with her mind. She shouldered her bow, slipped the harpoon in a loop in her webbing and leapt across the deck. She dragged Liffet to the wheelhouse, as the hirelings righted themselves.

She knelt beside her friend.

'Come on, Liffy. Come on, please,' she called.

There was nothing: no waves, nothing, but Liffet was breathing. Liffet opened her eyes and looked blank.

Alfren saw Zal, standing with effort, holding onto the wheelhouse. 'Leave her to me,' Zal said. 'I've barred the hatch to the galley.'

The hirelings below couldn't get out that way, not for a while. Zal knelt and cradled Liffet's head and shoulders.

Alfren stood, hefted her bow and nocked an arrow. She saw the lad help the two hirelings to rest against the gunwale. He was young, strong and quick-witted, fast too, so she needed to keep a distance.

Could the girls lock all the hirelings in the hold? Could the girls fathom how to sail the boat? These hirelings were resourceful and strong. There would be no safety from them if the girls stayed on the tramper.

They would have to flee as far as they could from these raiders.

Rowing Boat

'Drop the shore boat in the water,' Alfren called to the lad.

'No,' he shouted bitterly.

She drew the bow with her arms - rather than lean and push into it - which meant she drew with less force but still enough to injure at short range, and she aimed at the lad. She saw the others shrink from her.

The first hireling, the lad's father with an injured leg, called out, 'Do as she says, son.'

She relaxed her draw.

'Dad?'

'Go on.'

Rigging the davit arm, used for lifting goods into the hold, the lad upended the rowing boat and made ready to winch it over the side.

She reckoned the hirelings would hurl any missile they could find as the girls rowed away, so called out, 'Put in the pike.'

The lad complied.

'And the oars.'

He unfastened the oars that were strapped to the wheelhouse.

She needed Liffet but there were no waves.

Come on, Liffy!

No waves at all.

In desperation, she searched the waves of all the folk she knew. Maybe Liffet had moved a little, somewhere else, among them.

There was an answer; it was faint. It said simply, *Alfren?*

She was surprised. She recognised those waves – waves from a long time ago.

After so long, why now?

The waves were faint and seemed to rise then fall away, as though recreating waves that used to be.

Faran!

She wanted to send but there was no time. Yet, she must send to say she had heard. She sent a memory of the gladness that, really, she knew she had felt on meeting Faran that day at the beach.

Will find you soon.

In the action of their escape, she was relieved to find a friend.

The lad looked at her. Her bow was down. She had stalled while she went with the waves.

'Two tarps,' she called, 'from the hold, and sacking too. Go!'

The lad hesitated. She hefted the bow. 'I could put you down and get them myself!'

He unlatched the hatch to the hold and descended.

The hirelings could give chase. How to disable the tramper? An idea occurred to her.

The flue from the galley stove was bracketed to the side of the wheelhouse. Wisps of smoke whisked from the top in the wind. She shouldered her bow. Sprinting to the wheelhouse, she took sacking and a pail, then stretched over the side to scoop up seawater. She sprang onto the gunwale and lifted everything onto the wheelhouse roof, then climbed to stand on the roof. Reaching up she poured the pail of water down the flue to gush into the galley stove, and quickly stuffed the sacking into the open end.

As she jumped down, she heard a *bang* and hoped the stove had cracked open, spilling hot coals into the galley. A fire might not catch, she thought, but the fumes should drive the hirelings below away from the aft hatch. If it did catch, they would shift to put out the fire rather than chase after the girls. She rushed to check on her friends. Liffet sat up, dazed and blank. *Whatever could be the matter?*

'Liffy? Liffy, in the boat. You have to row. Liffy?'

Liffet nodded and stood up.

'Take Zal.'

Liffet turned with blank eyes to help Zal stand.

Alfren watched as the lad loaded the boat with tarpaulins and sacks.

'This side,' she called, meaning the lad should lower the boat on the seaward side of the tramper. She meant to leave the cove for the sea, not to row ashore. The two hirelings she had injured watched but were no threat. She could tell the lad was looking for a chance and weighing up whether or not she would loose a harpoon.

She would, instantly.

She wanted the lad out of the way but couldn't call on Liffet to bind and hobble him.

'Get in the hold,' she told him.

'That's enough, witch. I'll do nothing more.'

There was another *bang* below deck. Smoke welled from the hatch to the galley. Fire had caught and, most likely, a gas lamp had exploded. The tramper would be ablaze soon. She heard hammering from the forward hatch to the stowage. The hirelings below were working to escape and she had little time.

If she loosed a harpoon to cripple the lad, the only able fellow from six would be the skipper. If only the skipper was able to fight the fire, could he prevent the boat from sinking? If not, the hirelings might have to swim for shore in bitterly cold sea. They might drown.

Why was she thinking of their lives?

'Does your dad want a harpoon in his one good leg?' she shouted, so that the first hireling could hear her.

'Son, do as she says, and hurry!' his father told him.

The lad cursed at her, turned and jumped down into the hold. She followed to close and secure the hatch but didn't lock it. The hirelings would be able to release him easily.

She spoke to the lad's father sitting on the gunwale together with the second hireling looking miserable and in pain from the arrow in his shoulder.

'That's a harpoon,' she said, nodding to the second. 'It won't pull out. You'll have to push it through. I aimed to miss artery and bone, so it should go through easily.

'You've only minutes to put out the fire. As soon as we're well clear, release your son. I've seen a pump and hoses to fight the fire in the wheelhouse.

'If you give chase, I'll put a harpoon through your heart. Just yours, I promise you. Tell me you've heard me.'

'Aye.'

She wheeled about, but the hireling called after her.

'Lassie, I know you. *You're* the seer.

'Only a madman goes after the seer.'

Liffet's eyes had regained some sparkle, she was alert and looking around, but there were no replies; Alfren couldn't find her friend's waves.

First into the shore boat they lowered Zal who slumped onto the sacks and tarps in the stern. Liffet jumped down next, set the oars into the rowlocks and sat ready on the thwart.

Alfren risked a return to the wheelhouse. Thick smoke bellowed from the aft hatch. She took the stew pot and whatever else remained there and put everything into a sack. She looked around. The hirelings waited as she had instructed.

The water in the cove was choppy. No one observed them from the heights.

The hammering at the forward hatch was heavy. She must hasten to get away.

She jumped down into the shore boat, released the tether to the tramper and took her place next to Liffet. They dipped their oars in unison and pulled away.

Alfren was concerned lest there was an explosion of the tramper's fuel tank. The hirelings should hurry to save themselves. She looked behind her to see the sea state beyond the cove and, seeing whitecaps, she called to Liffet to pause rowing. They spent a few minutes rigging one tarp over the stern where Zal lay covered with sacking for comfort, the other over the bow. These would prevent the boat taking on water. They left a gap in the middle where they would sit to row.

Alfren took a last look at the tramper. It was ablaze, flames showing at the wheelhouse. She saw that the lad had wrenched open the hatch to the stowage and the skipper had climbed out.

They rowed, pulling hard against the wind running across the mouth of the cove, where waves crashed over rocks on both sides. They had to work together as, for all their strength, they were two slight girls in a heavy boat pitted against a heaving sea. As soon as they were clear of the cove, they allowed the boat to turn before the wind and run eastwards along the coast the tramper had passed shortly before. The coastline was steep with exposed rock on the water line, where waves poured and spilled in plumes of spray. There were narrow inlets and caves, sea stacks, headlands and cliffs, but no suitable landing.

It was hard. The boat pitched steeply up and down. Oars clashed with waves, which broke their stroke but always they recovered and fell in time together.

No matter where they were, it was freedom from the tramper.

Night

It was dusk and half-light when Alfren saw calmer water around a headland. They turned the boat across the wind and rowed with fading strength until they entered a bay in the lee of the wind, a relief from the high waves at sea. She saw a shingle beach between rock outcrops, and a gentle swell rather than spilling surf that rolled onto the beach. Landing would be easy but getting there would be hazardous. Water swirled over submerged rocks on the approach, a barrier to the sea's waves. Patiently, they picked a course along a channel, working as one to propel and steer the boat with their oars. In dim light, they ran the boat onto the shingle. They jumped out to tie off higher up the beach.

It was an ebb tide: the water was receding, and it would soon be slack water.

'We should spend the night in the boat,' Alfren suggested.

Liffet nodded her agreement. The beach shelved too steeply for the girls to pull the boat higher. It would float again at dawn on the flood tide. They retied the tarpaulins to cover the boat, to keep out wind and rain, then climbed in and made Zal comfortable. In a flask Alfren had taken from the wheelhouse there was just a little beer. They shared cold stew from the pot.

In darkness, Alfren climbed out to walk the beach and looked out to sea for lamps on boats. There would be none surely. The sea state was rough, and no one sailed at night close to shore. It had been a desperate escape, but they had done it. She had shrieked in her mind and that had tormented the hirelings terribly. Could she control herself if something like that happened again? Had she hurt Liffet in some way? She had to put that aside. What mattered was survival. That was all that mattered.

She decided to catch some sleep before taking watch. She climbed back into the boat and made herself as comfortable as could be, with Zal between her and Liffet for warmth.

They were free.

This was farther than Alfren had ever been from home. All she knew for certain was there was no watchtower, no safe place of refuge, not on the west of Sealand.

Not out there in the badland.

Kidnap

Jin

At the barracks, the ranger squad assembled in the operations room at midday.

Handar said. 'There's no update from the militia with regard to their search of the harbour. They assure me they will be thorough.'

She looked over her squad. 'Falt, your report on our visit to the militia barracks and infirmary?'

Falt was a trim fellow with a grey-stubble beard. He sat with his feet up on a chair. When Jin had first met his sergeant, he had thought him rude to officers because he was slow to answer, but later he had realised Falt's attitude was first-rate.

'Nought of great use,' said Falt. 'The militia records of kidnappings made available to me were sparse. At the infirmary there was no one who saw what happened and those I asked clammed up, telling me they'd told the militia everything. I found a service door I suspect was the exit they took. It was locked securely. Just as in the outland burghs, Handar, I'd say we're looking at folk who don't know who to trust, even rangers. The militia disclosed more than they intended when they released the report of a child who'd witnessed the kidnap. It corroborates what we can guess: that the kidnappers fled the burgh by boat.'

As usual, thought Jin, Falt seemed weary of the insolence of folk. His sergeant was alright though: thorough and knowledgeable.

'This was well-coordinated,' Falt concluded. 'It had silver behind it to hire the best raiders. That's all.'

'Good. Tans?' asked Handar.

'I asked around at the harbour and found that one of the trampers simply took on fuel. It was the only one without a load schedule and none of the dockers went near it as it was moored at the end of the quay out of the way. One docker remembered it was riding high in the water, it contained no cargo and not enough ballast, so it would make slow progress and would have to shelter in a storm. Also, he saw a fellow on deck dressed in robes, so perhaps the boat was running an errand for one of the chieftains.'

Tans referred to settlements on Sealand where they knew the chiefs made silver in illegal trade and blackmail. His first candidate would be Chief Barl on the small isle of Redstone to the north, or Jarl Wull on the barren Isle of Moss away to the west. Rangers could make allowances for these folk so long as they didn't get greedy and kept the peace in their land.

'Jin?'

'I've compared notes with Tans already. From the Watch logs, the tramper headed south out of the sound. It's not one that the harbour master listed or picked out, but I doubt we'll get anything further from him.'

'Agreed,' Handar said, 'and right now it won't be worth our while. These raiders were daring. It was a daylight raid by their best. They've thrown down a challenge and the chase is on.'

Handar stood to point to the great map. 'This boat was not set up to go far, so we'll pursue on land and split up:

two go south along the chain of watchtowers to Tornsea lighthouse; two go west, taking the camp and supplies. We must find where they anchored during the storm overnight, who gave assistance and whether they disembarked to travel overland. To the west, on the road to Landing, there are no settlements. It's rough, hilly and sodden. Even so, if there were folk on shore, they may have seen the boat along its route. I think we can cover good ground today and tomorrow. Our objective is here, at Landing. I'll send a ketch to follow by sea. If we come across scavengers, we're likely to be outnumbered so arm up, but I want you light to travel fast. Understood?'

'Ma'am,' they replied.

'Good. We'll leave at two o'clock.'

She paused to look at the squad members. Handar was a skilled leader, Jin thought, and one of those skills was the ability to read the slightest hesitation.

'Jin, there's something on your mind; yours too, Falt.'

'Ma'am,' Jin said, 'a couple of things. I interviewed the vicar here and it seems possible he had unwittingly alerted these kidnappers to our Alfren. I've got to come out and say it. From what I heard from this same vicar, Alfren seems to have had extraordinary intuition, almost premonition really. His story was that she'd raised the alarm over the Great Flood six years ago. Also, she seems to have a connection with other children that goes beyond the empathic.'

'Yes,' said Handar. Jin was taken aback that Handar acknowledged this coolly.

'So, it seems too much a coincidence that the raid to release the captive raider also resulted in the kidnap of Alfren,' he added.

There was silence. Handar nodded at Falt.

'Folks, I have a story to tell you,' Falt said. 'Nine years ago, I was on duty one night when a telegraph called for me to attend the watchtower on Muckle Voe. The watchmen had heard pitiful cries for help, they said. When I arrived, I heard nothing, so I thought they'd been drinking and then, seeping into my mind, I heard crying too, just as they'd described, and it got louder. I followed the crying out and around the voe for a long way, until I came across a bundle on the beach. Tied up inside were two girls. One of them was our Alfren.

'The point is, I didn't hear her crying out aloud. It was in my head. I had to follow the cry; it wouldn't let me go. When I found her, it stopped. Without those cries for help, no one would have found the girls for days, and they would have perished from cold. I carried them both back to the watchtower. It was a fair way to carry two girls, but I couldn't leave one or the other. It was like I was being told what to do: "Take the both of us."' Falt grimaced. 'I'm damn glad I heard the cries.

'I didn't discuss this with other rangers. Well, only with the boss here, who was on detachment then. We decided, for Alfren's safety, not to report anything. Anyone could have intercepted a report and passed it on. We wanted no one to know. We've watched her ever since and despite being careful, I think she knew we did.

'I believe the girls had been kidnapped and Alfren sent her cries to my mind somehow, and loudly too. I suppose the same had driven the kidnappers mad. I guess they pleaded with her and she told them, in the same way she influenced me, to carry them both ashore, to let them both go. That's why they abandoned the girls.'

'Blimey!' Jin chorused with Tans.

'So, you know another reason why we're going after her,' said Handar. 'We don't want her to fall into the hands of anyone who might have plans for her. It would make it worse for her and suddenly our small band of rangers could have a lot more to deal with besides a few raiders. We want to find Alfren because she's one of us. I'm not bothered about premonition or anything else; that's for Alfren to sort out and one day she may be able to tell us what's going on. Any questions?'

Jin and Tans shook their heads.

'Rangers, away.'

Shingle Beach

Alfren

Sleep did not come.

She was responsible for all the mayhem that day. What wouldn't she do to survive?

She remembered the watchmen had told her many times that Landers survived only because their determination was greater than the raiders' intent to take all they had and displace them. That meant a lot to her then.

She could have maimed or killed the hirelings outright, all of them. She hadn't; she had wanted to save them almost as much as she had wanted to escape from them. She had wounded them the least she could, hadn't she?

The tramper had been safe from wild seas in the cove and, if it had started to sink, the hirelings could have grounded it or swum for shore. Hadn't she thought of all that and hadn't she weighed all risks, to the girls and the hirelings?

Really, she had done horrible things, yet she felt nothing but contempt for the hirelings, their evil ways and their raiding life.

Hadn't she to be ruthless to save folk, even to save folk from themselves? Was this what would be expected of her as a ranger? Jin and Handar had tried to tell her something about it, but she hadn't listened.

And another matter. She should take a moment to allow that, actually, she was a seer although not one to depend on in any way, certainly she couldn't be the one that the chief thought necessary for 'survival'.

Also, it just wasn't possible children could assist the chief in his scheme. Yet, the good news was the children were there at the keep.

She tried to sleep but part of her mind nagged at her.

Storms.

She had seen fortune-tellers in the burgh, some from Sealand, some came with the traders. They set up stalls in the market street and cried out that the end-of-time was coming; that folk-kind had only a few years and would then be swept from the world; that folk should make ready, as only those prepared for the ending would be chosen – the ones deemed fit to survive. The burghers went to see them to have their fortunes told, their palms read, their ailments diagnosed, and bought charms and perfumed salves. She remembered them as a child when they had seemed scary.

A seer, though, must be someone who could see what might bring about the end; not only a storm, maybe disease or famine or invasion. That wasn't her. Not her at all.

It might be a storm. There were floods in living memory as well as high storms at rage-force 11 and fury-force 12 but only exceptionally. Fortune-tellers on the market street called out that high storms at destroy-force 13 and rip-force 14 were certain – even cutter-force 15. When one such came, the land would be devastated, and it would be too difficult to start again. Any survivors would cling to life for a few short years then perish. All folk lost forever.

That wasn't possible. It might happen, but not any time soon.

All that mattered was to find a way home. Zal was sickening because of her injury. Liffet was in a daze. Both needed food, warmth and care.

South

Jin

In places the telegraph line ran alongside the track that Jin and Handar followed on their ponies. Farther along, beyond the voe, they passed the first of the several farmsteads that would mark their way to Tornsea lighthouse at Farewell. Standing guard on their way were the watchtowers separated by many miles, but at any point Jin could see one of them, before or behind him.

He had never been to this settled part of Sealand before, so he observed what he could as they trotted by in their hurry. A farmstead was an occupied stone tower surrounded by small fields with walls of heaped stone and rubble to shelter cattle and crops from winds. Other field walls were built higher and wider with a low tunnel between an outer and inner wall, which were typical all over Sealand, where livestock filed to safety at dusk every evening. Within some fields were mazes of walls to baffle the winds further, so the crops weren't flattened, just as on his home Furrow. One farmstead lay close to the track. He saw the planticrubs – the small stone enclosures close to the tower where the cabbage crop would be left in the ground into winter.

He supposed this way was where Alfren had come as a child on her runs over the wall.

He and Handar wanted to be certain to see the written watchtower logs for themselves rather than telegraph each watchtower and ask for news of the tramper. They had agreed that each pair would call at alternate watchtowers and that way leapfrog the other to the lighthouse. Whenever they caught up, they could share news.

Landers had built their watchtowers off the track, on islets on the shore, accessible only at low tide, or on rocky bluffs high on the hillsides, which were steep and tricky to climb, or on piles sunk into bog and wetland, where detailed local knowledge was required for safe paths of approach. Jin and Handar hastened to those nearest the track, which weaved with the coastline.

It had taken too long. They conferred and agreed to press on into the evening, riding by lamplight, and took rest in a watchtower a few hours for a start at dawn.

DAY 3

Black

Alfren

Alfren awoke with a jump and wanted to spring up, snatch her bow and leap from the boat.

For what? The boat rocked on the rising tide. She heard nothing above the waves rolling the shingle and wind blowing over canvas. Beside her, Zal was warm and uncomfortable and slept fitfully, which was as well as could be.

Liffet lay still, but awake.

It was the middle of the night. The dark hid their boat and Alfren was glad of that.

She had settled, but thoughts had returned.

The hireling, father to the lad, had said she was a seer. He had been told that, but he couldn't know really.

She thought most probably what she did was what a few girls and boys had done through all time, so it wasn't so well known, and it might all go away when she was older, which is why no one talked about it because it had been forgotten.

She was nearly sixteen years old. Would she miss sending to Liffet and seeing the waves? She would. Did she want to lose that ability when she was older? No.

She decided to rise and scout around before dawn.

Gently, she got up.

'I'm going to pull the boat up the beach, Liffy.'

She covered the girls with her own sacking, slipped from the boat, tied down the covers, and pulled all she could on the tether rope. It was high tide. The wind was fresh and chilling, the kind of cold, bitter weather her watchman's wind suit had been made for.

It was good that it was a strong breeze-force 6 still. Surely scavengers stayed in their shelters, especially at night. The girls should be left alone.

On the narrow, shingle beach between rock outcrops, there was a black darkness with no speck of light anywhere. She walked up the shingle and climbed a low rock to stand on deep grass.

She sighed. She would have to admit she was different. Folk didn't just walk around in the black dark of night. They put out their arms, shuffled and stumbled. They didn't hop up onto a rock. They couldn't even see the rock, let alone the beach, the sea and the hills behind. But she had always been able to see in darkness, although she had never needed to do it much.

Now, she could see more easily and farther in the dark.

She hoped one day, once she was back in the burgh, she could ask say Handar to help find someone who knew about why she was different and could explain it and help her understand.

She scanned her surroundings and saw no threat. She made a plan. First, the girls should set up camp by the beach. They would find natural shelter and construct a hide, build a fire from driftwood and go hunting. She would send the boat out at low tide and scuttle it so that it couldn't be spied by anyone passing and give away their whereabouts. They would revive Zal and set off for Wallburgh.

That didn't seem right.

She wanted to find the keep and rescue the children. It had to be soon. It was urgent.

Why couldn't it wait? Wouldn't it have to wait until after they had reached Wallburgh?

She couldn't decide what was best. Surely it was to find a way home? But the children!

Better she should find the waves. They would help her understand. She floated off among them just as she had always done.

Something big and heavy slammed into her mind. She fell and clutched the grass. It slammed again. It was like receiving a punch to her head and then being sat on, although it didn't hurt. She was off-balance and upside down. 'I hear it,' she said in her mind, groping for a sense of it, appealing for it to let her go. It was a maelstrom of waves, pummelling her, spinning her, then pounding her, as if to knock all sense from her.

She gripped the grass. The waves whipped her around, catching and tossing her like a fish in a net. Under the weight of them, she couldn't breathe, she was dizzy. She would have to let go to be hurled into the wind.

Just as suddenly, the weight faded.

Her mind was free. Chill, dark night returned. Sea waves lapped on the shingle and wind brushed her land.

What that had been, she had no idea. She didn't want it to come back, but if she pretended it hadn't happened then it might.

She released the grass from her clutch.

All was upright again.

What had happened? It was a mighty tremor; she hadn't seen it coming and it had knocked her over. They had been waves, but what sort she didn't know, and there had been no message in them. None at all.

But there were ripples still. She waited for them to settle.

The waves had been strong. If she had dared to demand, 'Stop!' they might have become stronger and never gone away.

What could she do?

Hadn't it always worked when she allowed the waves? Although she had never been lifted and thrown like that. Could she let a few through? She would have to try.

She prepared her mind to welcome the waves and sent a message, she wasn't sure where, asking them to be gentle. A wave trickled through. It was a bit loud and that was it, only that and no more.

What had she been worried about? There it was. What did it say? She looked carefully at the wave she held in her mind, and the answer dismayed her.

She jumped down from the rock and stamped her feet on the shingle.

She had seen urgency and pleading that only children could convey.

'So, that's it? I have to go? That means there's no time to go back to Wallburgh. Is that right? Don't slam me again.'

The new waves had urged her to press on. The children were there, and there was only so much time left. But why was it urgent?

What about Zal?

Could she leave Zal and Liffy to look for help? No. They had all to stay together.

The girls couldn't trust anyone they came across in the badland as they could betray them to chief.

There might be a search party looking for the tramper she had set alight and the crew she had marooned, and they might chance upon the girls too.

What to do?

The first step was clear: right here, she must make the girls comfortable.

She rested, sat on her rock outcrop on a tuft of dry grass, looking out to sea. She faced south, she settled, and she waited in the cold air for dawn. She found Liffet in her mind: they were faint waves, enough to tell her that Liffet was recovering, although slowly. She was thankful. Liffet's mind could be awake or dreaming, she wasn't sure, but she expected that Liffet had withdrawn, to better focus on her recovery. Her friend trusted her to do the right thing and to watch over the girls.

Alfren let waves wash over her; those waves full of colour, depth and energy, from all directions, from sea and air, earth and magnetism, from folk ... from fire.

Why fire?

If only the wind could carry my thoughts, then I could summon help.

Wind, fire.

It didn't make sense.

Alfren curled up on the grass and slept the short sleep that was worth many hours. She awoke as the darkness was on the cusp of becoming a patchwork of dark shadows. It was about six o'clock, for sunrise was half past six.

Time to get up and do some work.

Morning

Alfren's search around the narrow shingle beach revealed a dry sandy patch in a corner of bedrock above the high-water mark. They should rig a hide there. She gathered handfuls of dry moss and collected driftwood.

The tide was ebbing, the boat stranded.

Alfren roused Liffet and they removed one of the tarpaulin covers from the boat. Zal was awake and wanted to try to get up. At the hide, Alfren and Liffet arranged the tarp first as a groundsheet and then tied off to rock belays and pegs they drove into cracks to form a tent, using the pike pole from the tramper to frame it. It was hardly different from a children's makeshift den in the burgh.

Liffet was alert and energetic but didn't speak as she layered grass, kindling and driftwood against the bedrock and lit a fire with a spark from a tinderbox salvaged from the wheelhouse of the tramper. Alfren nodded to herself. Liffet could light a fire anywhere.

Zal walked from the boat with their support to the shelter and slumped by the fire, on a mattress of sacking and dry grass. Liffet set about removing her bloody dressing and tending to her wounds.

It was daylight. Alfren returned to the boat and removed

the coastal navigation chart that she had recovered from the wheelhouse of the tramper and opened it on the thwart. They were to the west of Sealand, not far from the burgh of Landing, some 20 miles west in a direct line. Even allowing for the hills, bogs, burns and sea inlets the actual distance shouldn't be more than 30 miles, and taking care to look out for scavengers, she could run there in a day. She should pick a way along the coast. There was a track a long way inland that ran from Wallburgh to Landing. If she happened upon it, she would take it.

The sea chart showed only few features of the land. Hereabouts was uninhabited and barren.

Some part of her mind prompted her to open the chart fully. She set it on the shingle using stones to weight the sides and corners. Sixty miles directly to the east was Wallburgh. To the south-east was the Tail of Sealand, the long mull that reached down to Farewell.

At the western edge of the chart was an arrow with a note stating 200 nautical miles to the Western Isles – Faran's home – over 300 nautical miles away from Wallburgh, where they had met for the first and only time.

Alfren was thoughtful as she folded the map and hid under the tarp as a rain squall passed over. It would be a grey, chill, rainy day, not a day for Zal to be outside even if she could walk. She reckoned a force 4, gusting 5.

She fought back maddening thoughts.

Wind. Fire.

She should hunt or fish. They needed fresh water. She should be on watch for scavengers or beachcombing for firewood.

She checked all was well with the girls in the hide, then took her bow and a canteen and left to find clean water. Perhaps there would be a burn just along the coast.

After a few paces along the shingle beach, she felt she

was losing her balance. Something in her mind was calling for attention.

She dropped her bow and canteen and bent over. Her mind was woozy. When she righted herself, she felt a stabbing pain in her head.

'Aargh,' she clenched her teeth. *Whatever it is, not now,* she thought.

She made to pick up her bow but couldn't focus. She staggered.

'Alright,' she said to herself. 'Damn it! Let it run.'

She knelt on the shingle and crouched over.

There was nothing. Her mind was empty.

Fire, wind.

From nowhere, the faintest thought fluttered like a thread held aloft in the wind.

Faran.

Her memory of meeting the smuggler returned clear as day.

Fire

Now was the right time to send to Faran and not when back in Wallburgh.

Do it now, when we need help, Alfren thought.

Faran had told her to send and had said she would know how.

She didn't.

She hadn't seen Faran for nearly three years. Faran's waves had been faint anyway and they must have changed completely. What had Faran done so that on the tramper in the cove Alfren had heard her?

'Do as my mind tells me. Just do it! Let my mind run!' Alfren murmured.

She opened her mind to waves. What if she was slammed again?

Nothing happened.

She found waves from the girls in the hide. There was almost a blank where Liffet should be. Zal's were changing, unsettled.

'Faran,' she whispered, uselessly. 'Faran, where are you?'

'You will know how,' Faran had said.

'Then know,' she said to herself.

Fire, wind.

She could try.

Alfren ran to the head of the beach to check that there was no sign of scavengers. She saw a runnel some distance away where there was sure to be a burn. Crouching low, she sprinted. She knelt to take a sip. It tasted clear but that was no certainty it wasn't polluted. She filled her canteen with clear water, then slipped back to the beach and into the hide. She gave Liffet the canteen. She took away the empty stew pot and a square of sacking, gathered a scoop of sand and scrambled to a rock pool where she cleaned the stew pot using the sand as an abrasive. She returned to the hide, rinsed the pot, poured in a measure of water and set the pot on the fire, intending that Zal could sip warm water for comfort. She stoked the fire with driftwood, and from the fire, she took a burning stick. The end would be hot, so she held it with her folded glove.

Then she returned to the beach where she knelt once more.

She saw vast waves all together and was relieved to see them: enormous, fathomless, endless.

She opened her eyes to the charred, smoking stick. A lick of flame spat in the wind. A light rain began, and the stick hissed as a drop landed on the glowing ember. She looked for Faran's waves as best she could from what she remembered and carried on searching in those few waves where she expected Faran to be. She opened her eyes to waft the smouldering stick. Once again, flame seeped out. Did the flame lift the waves somehow? She waited, searching.

Faintly, new waves appeared, which were nearly the same as the ones she sought. She latched onto them, so close it could be only Faran. She followed the waves as they drifted; there was a little extra patience one moment, a little more passion to be of service, more confidence and independence too. She had certainly never seen waves shift like that before. This was Faran.

Relieved to find her, she sent to Faran's new waves showing simply what she could see: patterns of land and sky, rain, cold, a weak fire, lostness and Zal's wave, which just then she knew could only be illness. Finally, she sent the urgency of the big new waves that had slammed her.

Alfren waited. It seemed her message was absorbed. She waited, chilled to her bones in the damp wind from the exertion of sending, open and focused on Faran's waves. Eventually, a reply came, sung in a faint, high wind-whistle. The meaning wasn't plain to her. Gently, she replayed it. It wasn't an answer to the waves she had sent; it had something to do with only her.

Suddenly, she shouted loudly with a push of anger. Something had burst. It was sudden and helped a lot. She felt clean inside. 'I'm not a crazy girl,' she gasped. Faran sent an understanding of the conflict Alfren had felt, which was annoyance at being different on the one hand, and on the other, drawn to her mind waves and all that they revealed. Faran accepted who she was – not a seer, but a girl who floated among the waves.

She breathed deeply and coughed heavily. She blew her nose. She wafted the stick she held and felt a little warmth from the blackened end. Faran was nearly gone.

There was the faintest message: 'Keep the fire burning. I shall come.'

Alfren raised herself to see Liffet watching from the hide, who approached.

'Zal explained it,' Liffet said simply.

'What?' Alfren asked.

'She's heard about you. They know.'

'Know what?'

'Figure it out, Ally.'

Liffet sat alongside her.

She didn't want to think about what Liffet had said. 'Just tell me, Liffy.'

Liffet looked far away to the sea and didn't answer at once. 'I didn't take any notice of how difficult it's been for you.'

'What?'

Liffet made no sense.

'I should've been a better friend.'

There was no point telling Liffet how much she had counted on her friendship. Her friend didn't need praise or gratitude.

'Liffy, how're you?'

'Very odd: I can't think.'

'Help will be here soon.'

'We need food.'

'Can you stand watch?'

'Yes.'

Sea

Rain fell. Alfren tilted her face and felt raindrops mix with the mucus running from her nose. She had questions about her own nature, but she felt ready to face them in her own time.

She was cold. Warmth would come with cleansing. She stripped off where she stood and ran naked into the sharp, grey-cold sea, washing her body and splashing her face. She felt refreshed. She called Liffet, who had climbed above the beach on watch, and they pushed off the boat. She rowed out a little way, and with a struggle heaved it over so it flooded and sank. The sea was bitingly cold, and she swam ashore briskly. Alfren picked her way up the beach back to her clothes and brushed the seawater off herself. Her feet were ice-cold on the stones. She dressed and felt warmed.

'I am me,' she said to herself with satisfaction. 'That's who I am.'

She left Liffet on watch to pick along the coastline, returning with mussels and oysters which the girls toasted on the fire. She had found some large shrimp too in rock pools which they baked in hot embers. It rained and the wind blew bitterly. In their hide it felt snug. She went out again and brought down a hare, the first ever time she had shot one. She butchered it and they put it in the pot to stew and kept the hind legs for roasting.

She was concerned for Zal. There may be infection. Liffet had kept the wound clean. Alfren took soiled bandages to wash in the burn, then wandered farther off for a couple of miles to look for driftwood. She saw no one, no dwelling, not even a track. She searched out to sea. Three boats passed far off through the day. Rain would obscure their view of the coast and anyway she didn't want them to see her.

Whenever she had a moment, she thought of the message from Faran. There was an alignment to sending. With Liffet it had always needed a search, and it had been easier at some times and less so at others. Both had to be inclined to share their waves at the same time. With Faran, this alignment needed preparation. Alfren had to assume that Faran was fully occupied.

Faran would come, but Alfren didn't know when. Zal was sick and the hirelings might be searching for the girls right then. The girls were vulnerable.

The following day, she would have to patrol farther off.

Tornsea

Jin

At dawn, by lamplight, Jin and Handar were in pursuit once more, their ponies trotting along and leaping over landslides and fallen rocks as the track became poorly maintained farther along the peninsula.

By eight o'clock, they had crossed the ayre, a stretch of dunes and beach, and climbed the headland to Tornsea lighthouse to consult the keeper. Hiding from the strong breeze-force 6 behind the parapet, high above the sea, waves breaking on rocks below, they took a moment to rest.

They had confirmed the course of the tramper, which had rounded the headland and turned west.

Following a suggestion from the keeper, they took a short cut, the sooner to meet up with Tans and Falt. A tricky, steep path led down and along the west side of the peninsula to Whirl Bay, a wide expanse of sand bars and channels exposed at low tide. They crossed the sands. Jin was mindful that the tide had turned and was flooding, pushed by the wind. They took care not to be caught by quicksand and deep, filling channels. The ponies sunk well above their fetlocks up to their knees on occasion, then Handar had pulled, and he pushed to coax them out of sucking mud. Whenever visibility improved between rain squalls, Jin took bearings on features of the bay. They were on track.

On the west side of the bay, they climbed out three hours ahead of high tide. Jin turned to see the flood covering the bay.

Life was like that; his best effort was just enough to keep ahead of trouble.

Long might that continue.

They entered an area of low hills and wind-bent scrub. Progress was slow as they wound their way up to higher land of treeless bog before they came upon the track from Wallburgh to Landing. It was early afternoon when they met Tans and Falt camped by a burn.

Jin felt impatient. They should press on.

Long Voe Ferry

Certainly, a precarious life, Jin thought: one desperate raider band on the run with no silver for payment and the solitary ferryman might have to fight or surrender. However, Jin nodded to himself in appreciation when he saw the arrangement to haul the ferry. His ranger squad stood on the east side of the loch where there was a pulley and chain set into great stone blocks. At a wave from Handar, the ferry pontoon was floated across and they and their ponies embarked. The ferry was unmanned. Jin took in what he could see on the far shore. The ferryman's fortification included the winding house, from which the chain towed the pontoon, and a curtain wall high enough to deter scaling by attackers. There was a short wharf for berthing supply boats, but even at high tide he could see it was silted up.

The ferry was winched across the loch into a dock enclosed by stone walls and a closed gate. Once inside, a portcullis lowered behind them. They were trapped. The ferryman stepped out of a small door, wearing a telescope on a belt, he noticed. The ferryman would have seen while they waited on the far bank that the passengers were East Sealanders and military too, and most likely recognised they were rangers because of their storm suits and were therefore safe to approach in person.

'That'll be—'

'I'll make out a requisition,' interrupted Handar. 'How much is payable?'

'It'll be ten shillings: two bob each horse,' said the ferryman. 'A piece of paper is no good to me, sirs.'

'You'll be reimbursed when you present it at the ranger barracks in Wallburgh,' said Handar.

'When do you see I will have the time to go to Wallburgh, if you don't mind my asking?' complained the ferryman.

'When you go to make your annual return and pay your taxes, of course. Now, make way for rangers in hot pursuit.'

'Oh, right,' said the ferryman, realising there was to be no discussion. 'I'll open the west gate then, shall I?'

The ferryman closed the small door behind him and soon after the land gate swung forward. The squad made ready to lead their ponies through, but Jin had seen Handar nod to him.

He approached the ferryman. 'Sir, before we leave, I have questions.'

'Oh, aye?'

'First, may I watch you enter this transaction in your ledger?'

The ferryman shrugged and led him through the small door to a dark room with only an arrow slit that looked out onto the dock.

'All there, see,' said the ferryman, pointing to his ledger. 'The customs check every few months. Has to be correct, see.'

'Here,' Jin said. 'Two nights ago, there was a tramper at anchor here, isn't that right?'

'It's what it says,' said the ferryman guardedly.

'Can you describe it?'

'Just a tramper; no interest to the customs.'

The ferryman was nervous.

'Did anyone transfer to or from the boat?'

'Just, you know, for lodging.'

'No payment made to you?' Jin asked.

'No. Well, turns out no, not for a berth, it was just at anchor, see.'

'Yet tethered to the wharf because of the storm?'

'Yes,' admitted the ferryman, 'with just a couple of lines to secure it.'

The ferryman was quieter, as if that would hide the details Jin was seeking.

'Can you expect to receive payment?'

The ferryman stalled. 'Not sure. It's on account.'

'Are you beholden to them?'

It was often better to be direct, to bring the matter in the open, to save the suspect his embarrassment. To add weight, Jin stared at the ferryman.

'Can't say,' the ferryman mumbled.

'Would you prefer to provide an answer in Wallburgh?'

The ferryman cleared his throat. 'I do it as a favour, see. Everyone does a little. We don't want to get in their way.'

The ferryman shuffled. There was a long silence that Jin left open, which told the ferryman he wouldn't leave until he had a satisfactory answer.

'They tell us about the storm to come. Out here, we'll know when. That's all I know. Wallburgh does nothing for us, with respect to you, sirs, and will leave us to fend for ourselves when it comes.'

It must be a scare such that folk did favours, hedging against being left out. So many folk in this Land worried they were in danger and could be open to being duped.

'What storm?'

'I'd have a chance, do you see, down here by the voe. I can't sleep some nights thinking about the flood to come with the storm. I bunk at the top of the winding house, but that's no good, not in a great storm surge, is it?'

'How do you know who to help on their way?'

'I don't. Well, I know who's on business and who's friendly – there to help us.'

'Who are they, and where are they from?'

'No one tells. I don't ask.'

'Did you see a fellow in robes?'

'Only for a moment.'

'Who is he?'

'All I know is he's one of those who're going to help us.'

'Have you have seen this fellow and this tramper before?'

'Yes.'

'Are you aware they're kidnappers?'

The ferryman shook his head.

'We don't allow that,' Jin said. 'We'd like to know who these folk are, so we'll be back this way. Please find out what you can. They bring trouble just as we should be pulling together. Understood?'

'Very well,' said the ferryman, not convinced.

No matter. They had a trail to follow.

As they continued on their way, Jin recounted the interview to his squad. Tans and Falt had heard similar stories from folk they had met on the track from Wallburgh. The rangers parted company: Tans and Falt continued on the track towards Landing; Jin and Handar turned off to follow the coastline. There would be no path.

Their ponies faltered in soft moss and deep heather, and they dismounted to lead them. They moved hurriedly, turning around steep slopes and deep gullies. Sweeping rain squalls were bitter. There were no dwellings, no farmsteads and they crossed no tracks. It was land to hide in, Jin thought. No one would see a tramper putting in here. He and Handar would have to check the coast thoroughly.

At dusk, he mused that the chance of finding Alfren here may be slim and that they should cut the search and make direct for Landing, ask questions there and take the ranger ketch to the island settlements to continue.

He took a long look around. No movement. No one followed or spied. They found a patch of damp but not boggy ground by a burn under the shelter of a crag. It would be a cold, rainy night in the open.

Jin took first watch. He found a seat on the crag and wrapped himself in his cape against the bitter wind. As darkness fell, he saw only dark-grey clouds, green-brown high lands and slate-grey sea specked with white tops. There was no lamplight on land, no lights out at sea.

It was the third day since the kidnapping.

He reached deep into a pocket and took out an old watch made by the Last People. They had worn them on their wrist in those far-off times. He wound the watch. It was broken. It amused him to think that the Last People liked to know the time by reading a watch. He knew the day and the time from the tides, sun and moon. On occasion, he read the time on the great clocks kept at Wallburgh. There was an upright case in the barracks with a clock face and a pendulum wound up by the ranger on timekeeper duty. He felt the glass with his thumb. It was heavily scratched and the face obscured. Only in sunlight could he make out the numbers. The long hand had dropped off. One day he would find a good lamp and a big magnifying glass and unscrew the back to take the mechanism apart. He didn't want to do that anytime soon. He wanted to keep this watch as it was. It was his link through the Extinction to the Last People.

He wished he could understand what led them to their undoing.

DAY 4

Fever

Alfren

Alfren was in a melancholy when she awoke. If she hadn't shot Zal and if she hadn't been curious to see her in infirmary, then she wouldn't be in this mess.

Seer?

Hardly.

Once again, she rose in the dark to await the dawn. It was colder. The wind had swung around and dropped a little to breeze-force 5, and above there was deep cloud. She pulled her hood tight. It was high water, five o'clock, and at least an hour until light broke. Liffet was revived and Faran was on the way, she who was training to be a physician and able to help Zal ... hopefully.

They were hungry but they had eaten. Food Alfren had brought in had been fresh and hot from the fire.

She had to press on to where the children were held at the keep wherever that might be. There was an urgency she didn't know the reason for.

In her mind, she floated on the waves. It was only after she had begun that she realised that was where she had gone. It was peaceful there in the dark, the sound of the water rolling the shingle, the wind running around the rocks and through the grass with a low hum as it passed over the hillside above. The waves were peaceful too. She floated among them more easily than she had done before and welcomed them then more than ever.

A wave floated across her mind that was familiar: a wave within waves.

Liffet's.

Alfren had spent much time looking for her friend's topmost waves but not seen this – Liffet's *self-wave*, a wave she realised she had known forever.

Since they were kidnapped as small children.

That was it!

She realised she must have shrieked then too.

How had the kidnappers reacted? Somehow, it had worked, and they had been freed. Or had Liffet been hurt then too? Anyway, hadn't Liffet mended? Whatever the cause, her friend was the calm one and she was the cross one, the bossy one.

'Damn it, Alfren!' she said to herself. At the cove, Liffet's mind had reeled from her shriek. Her friend had been overwhelmed, she was dazed.

What about Zal? Maybe Zal had been outwith the focus of her shriek?

Liffet had known all this when she had joined her on the beach the day before, but hadn't recovered enough to talk it through, not just then.

Something came to Alfren and at first she pushed away because it might be another truth that she would have to admit to. It was like a loss – something she could have had but had denied herself. Faran had invited her to run away to the Western Isles. If she had gone, she would have been free, welcomed into a big family, accepted by the rune master. She had turned down the offer.

What if she had accepted?

No watchmen.

No mad vicar and Extinction.

No reservoir and water testing.

No rangers.

Wouldn't she have missed all that?

Although right then and there she would rather be on the Western Isles bottling whisky to smuggle around the League.

She and Faran could have been fine friends.

All her life she had been frightened to tell adults anything about the waves, rightly too, because some madman on a quest for a seer might have found her sooner. Yet, on the Western Isles, all could have been different.

It was quiet. She checked Faran's waves, fleeting, faint as they were – and found a simple message, a sense of reassurance. The waves were brief and so she let them roll around her mind. She believed she was right: Faran was coming.

She wished she knew when.

Liffet appeared from the hide carrying the stew pot and climbed the rock to sit with her. Neither said anything. They looked out to sea. Liffet turned to her. 'It's Zal. We can't wait. I'll go.'

Go for help?

Liffet rose to fetch water.

Alfren went to sit in the hide; she stirred the fire, releasing a dim, warm glow. Zal's eyes opened. 'Alfren, Liffet's better,' she said in a hoarse whisper.

'Yes, she is,' Alfren replied. 'Not you though, Zal.'

'Alfren, infection has started. I won't live. You and Liffet must go. Leave me. You know what to do – release the children.'

Alfren leant closer to Zal. 'No, Zal, please hold on. You can live! Please!'

Zal weakened and closed her eyes.

Alfren watched Zal's breath struggle, her heart race, the pain sting and writhe.

This was all her doing. She must have been mad to take Zal off the tramper.

'You've really, really got to do something,' she said to herself.

'Liffy?' she called to her friend who had returned from the burn. It was light, shortly after half past six. There were still thirteen hours of daylight, with low tide at eleven o'clock. The wind would be a breeze-force 5, with rain and mist. It would be damp and chill.

They went to sit on the shingle.

'No,' said Alfren firmly. She had heard Liffet's message.

'Yes,' Liffet insisted. 'I'll go.'

'No. Faran will be here soon – I hope – but I don't know when and you're better than me at nursing Zal. She draws on your strength I think.'

'Do you know what?'

'What?'

'You're even bossier now you're a marine in the rangers.'

Alfren tried to suppress a smile – she had her old friend back.

Alfren went to forage and hunt. She tasted seaweed, but it needed soaking in fresh water, so she found a pool up the hillside a short way. She skewered a large cod with a harpoon and line attached to it; she was pleased with that. She returned a little wet from the rain and fingers chilled from the wind.

'Brilliant,' said Liffet. 'That'll be tasty. Zal, look, she'll bring a whale home next.'

Zal moaned and smiled weakly.

'I'm just going outside to fillet it and we'll cook on a hot stone, eh?'

They stood on the beach.

'I'm worried too,' Alfren admitted.

'What if there's medication on the tramper? If it's still afloat, that is,' Liffet asked. 'Maybe silver-in-water or a herb mix – honey for the wound if nothing else. Garlic I can press and then apply the oil.'

'Yes, and we could find out what happened to the hirelings. They may come after us. I won't be long. I'll be back by half-tide, at two o'clock. Look, Liffy, if there's nothing, I could go on to Landing. Whatever I decide, Liffy, promise me ...'

'Yes, I know. We won't wait for you should Faran land here. Ally. I heard. You have to go for the children. I'll be waiting for you to reach me, so no need to flipping shriek. I'll come.'

'Alright.'

'Come on. Let's get you food before you go.'

Cove

The wind continued a fresh breeze-force 5. It had swung around so that the wind wasn't always against Alfren as she walked, trotted or ran wherever the way was firm. To help with her whereabouts she had torn a strip from the navigation chart which showed the coast from the shingle beach to the burgh of Landing and beyond. It was folded and dry inside her smock.

She crossed high, steep, soggy land, just as it was above Wallburgh, and climbed higher still, seeking an easier way. She was in the mist and glad it concealed her from scavengers, although when she dropped low between hills where the mist cleared, she checked for sign of them. It would be a terrible mistake to be spotted.

The wind was relentless and wet; she wore her wind suit close to stay dry. She took several gulps of water from the burns she crossed. She felt at ease, probably because she was on track to find the missing children. She hoped she wouldn't receive a slam when she turned back with medication for Zal.

She counted her steps just as every watchman should, which told her how far and for how long she had walked. That made it ten o'clock. Although she cheated just a bit as she knew the way much as a bird did, she supposed, homing on its nest over a long migration and it was only a little bit odd that she did that she told herself. Also, she sensed the sun and its angle through thick cloud, which confirmed the time. That wasn't odd at all – anyone should be able to sense the sun high behind thick cloud if they applied themselves to it.

She reached the right spot and descended. She crouched when, just below the mist, she had a view down the hillside to the sea. She ran to the land's edge to look over. The cove was shaped like a half-moon.

She was dismayed to see a camp far below. Also, she could see the mast and prow of the tramper above water. From its position, she guessed the hirelings had allowed the wind and tide to drive the tramper onto rocks from where they had jumped ashore.

Had they salvaged any medication?

The west side of the cove was a steep slope to the camp. She slipped her way down and they saw her as she approached. They appeared unarmed but she was concerned lest they had a crossbow. She hefted her bow, nocked a harpoon and continued.

The camp was a single tent on a rock shelf. The hireling Liffet had stabbed stood as though to run at her.

'Come to kill us, girl?' he challenged.

The skipper emerged and called him back. He stepped forward and looked at her sadly. 'We were good to you girls. Look what you did to us.'

They should never have kidnapped her.

'Where's the lad?' she asked.

'Gone.'

That was no answer. She was in a hurry.

'Bring out your medication and dressings. I have need of them.'

A sneering voice called out. 'Give yourself up!' The Picker

hobbled from the tent. 'It's just a matter of time before we have you again.'

'The medication, or I will shoot and make it painful.'

She flicked her bow.

'We should've chucked her over,' said the hireling. 'It was you, Skipper. You were soft on them. That's never been our way. Not with Sealanders.'

The Picker stared at her.

'Yes, I see,' he said. 'This one's soft on Zal.'

Did he intend to needle her? This must be his way; to upset folk.

'How is she?' he grimaced. 'Shot her, didn't you? That's the way we do it.'

She bristled. Zal had suffered so much.

'You're the one we want,' said the Picker. 'It was you all along. The lad told me you shrieked in our minds. You're the seer, as I thought.'

He preened and threw out his arms.

'I know what you want, girl. You care too much. You betray your weakness. You're soft.' He spoke meanly. 'Come with us. We have the children you want.'

How could she think of going with the Picker? She must return to Liffet and Zal. Suddenly she feared more for them. How had she believed it allowable to leave them? Yet they hadn't asked her to stay.

'Medication, I said.' Her voice was weak. 'First, the medication,' she repeated firmly. 'What do you have? Skipper, bring what you have.'

'There's nothing, girl. Can't you see? We're four fellows with wounds that would fester,' the skipper replied.

Any medication had been used up. She hadn't thought of that.

There should be no delay. She needed to cover her tracks and run back to her friends, but with nothing. Should she go back all the same and lead them to a safer place? Or run on to Landing? Her mind became foggy. How long must the girls wait for Faran? She forced herself to think straight. It may be days. No, it would be soon, she was sure. Think. Because of her appearance before them, the hirelings would know the girls were hiding not far away. The lad might return by boat that day with help. The hirelings would search for the girls immediately. She had made a trap for herself.

It was confusing, but it shouldn't be.

'If I agree to come with you, mister Picker, when should I return to this cove in time to board your boat?'

There, she had asked.

'If I tell you, you would lead your Sealanders to us.'

'True, I could. None nearby though.'

'Then who are they?' asked the Picker, in alarm.

She stepped back and away lest that was a trick to distract her. She swung round – he was right – to see a half-dozen figures high above on the hillside.

A scavenger band, their cloaks wrapped close, a laden pony, and quick to spring their attack.

The hirelings were vulnerable prey. The scavengers had begun their charge down the hillside. There would be no appeal to them, no escape for her. They might kill and strip her and the hirelings for only a petty haul. She was the only one fit and ready to fight. She saw two scavengers fall back from the race, to stand guard and prevent flight. They carried crossbows, which from above and afar had a greater range than her bow and heavy harpoons. But their running crew mates screened her from them. She seized her opportunity and ran up the steep slope to a rock step. Four scavengers charged to reach her before she could shoot. She followed her drill: picked her spot, raised her bow, leaned into it and the tension in the string cut like wire into her leather finger tab. Facing up slope, in wind and wet mist, she picked out her target. She loosed, and the harpoon flew long, rising up the slope, to hit the leg of a crossbowman. The second harpoon did the same, just as the first scavenger bore down on her. He carried a long pike; the second, an axe. She lowered her bow and rolled to one side as the scavengers tripped and fell down the rock step. Before they could pick themselves up and snatch at her, she sprinted up the slope leaving them behind. She had to be quick. She heard cries from the hirelings but didn't look back. They would have to fend for themselves. She raced to the crossbowmen, who were reeling with pain. Her harpoons had only pierced soft flesh, although the wounds would be painful enough to cripple them. She wrested their crossbows and threw them out of reach, then turned to face two scavengers who had pursued her up the slope. They stopped, breathing heavily, as she raised her bow again.

'Drop your arms. No second warning' she called. If they didn't understand her words, they could see the intent on her face. They glanced at their crossbowmen; she would inflict the same pain on them. They must fear abandonment more than a wound itself if they became a burden and no use to their mates. They threw short swords and knives on the steep grass slope.

'Down to the camp,' she flicked her bow. After they had turned, she flung the crossbows and weapons down into the cove but retained two fine-looking knives for herself and strapped them to her chest and hip. She hurried to follow.

At the camp, the scavengers held the hirelings at bay. The pikeman was their leader who jabbed at the Picker.

'Strong girl,' he said. 'This one your boss? Yield or we kill him.'

This was a stand-off and it was daunting that she faced desperate and ruthless scavengers.

She had the advantage of a bow on higher ground. This was her land. She found strength from that.

'Put down your pike and I'll let you go.'

'I kill him first.'

'Then I'll kill you anyway.'

The pikeman shifted nervously. 'You let me go?'

'Yes. I'll follow you. If you go west towards Landing, you live; east to Wallburgh, you die. Take your wounded and make sure you look after them well. You can take everything from the camp. Deal?'

'No trick?'

'See this uniform I'm wearing? I give my word. Deal?'

The pikeman nodded. 'You big boss. Deal.'

She watched as the scavengers, wary of her, stripped the camp and took what silver they found on the hirelings in only minutes and made off up the hill carrying their haul. They had to believe she would follow them through the mist. Though unarmed and with the burden of two wounded crossbowmen, if they turned east and stumbled on the hide at the shingle beach, still they could overpower Liffet.

She recalled the action only moments before. She had come dreadfully close to being caught by the pike and had been only an arm's length from being grabbed. This was what it was like to be a ranger, was it?

The Picker and the hirelings were silent.

'I saved you,' she stated. 'Those were scavengers who kill for their haul.'

'You did, aye,' said the skipper. He looked at her questioningly. 'You could have felled them by driving them mad.'

A mind-shriek?

'Why didn't you?'

That would have been quicker and more certain than arrows and knives, if only she had known how she did it.

'Do you want to hear it again?' she asked.

'No, no,' conceded the skipper. 'You're right, lass. You saved us.'

'If I agree to go with you when rescue arrives, when should I return here?'

She put it to them a second time. Would she really go with them?

'Today. Not long,' said the Picker.

The lad must have raised the alarm yesterday or that morning, she thought. Would the rescue come from the keep? Or maybe from Landing?

'The deal is you won't search for Zal.'

The Picker nodded slightly. She thought of a bluff.

'I know enough to bring forces to bear on the keep, to gain entry. Instead, to save time, I would go only to meet with your chief and negotiate the release of the children you've kidnapped, without harm to them or me.'

No doubt the chief held a strong keep and paid hirelings well in silver to defend it but, however well he paid them, wouldn't they run off if the militia appeared below the walls? In turn, the chief would reckon that the militia would not leave the burghs for if they did, that would leave them vulnerable to attack from his hirelings.

Surely the Picker had worked this out. Certainly, he would doubt she could raise the militia.

Hadn't Wallburgh given up the girls for lost? Wasn't she on her own?

'We will negotiate, of course,' said the Picker slyly. She saw the skipper shake his head.

She replayed her plan. She had to trust her friends more than ever; trust that Faran would come and the two girls would leave with her. The hirelings reckoned without her ability to guide Liffet to wherever she was, if that was still possible, and Faran too, hopefully. On her way to the keep, she could send to Liffet who could raise the alarm at Landing. There was an unmanned ranger station there, equipped with a radio set. Liffet had done a signals course ... well, part of it.

The Picker taunted. 'What about Zal? Dying, isn't she? Would you leave her when we could help?'

'The deal is I come with you and you leave Zal alone.'

'My, you reckon on the children before Zal, do you? Maybe you want to take Zal's place, is that it? The chief respected Zal. She was an advisor to him. Didn't she tell you? Jealous of Zal, are you? Yes, I see. Alfren, the new saviour of the children,' he said.

She made no reply. The Picker was persistent, probing to get a reaction. She had to be tough. He would be sure to touch on something sensitive to her at some point but only if she let him.

If she set off to return to the shingle beach, she would arrive late in the afternoon at high tide, not at the time she had told Liffet to expect her. She had nothing to take for Zal and no news for them. She had no time to return to the cove if she were to go with the Picker and ensure they turned for the keep and kept to the deal to not search for Zal.

It seemed easier to decide than it should have been.

'You should take what shelter you can now your tent has gone.'

She turned to climb the steep slope to a rock face where she could watch the hirelings and hide from the wind, then thought otherwise and climbed into the mist, and ran when the slope eased. She caught up with the scavengers. The two ponies carried their wounded and were making their way neither east nor west, but north. She accepted that – Liffet was safe from them. She turned away without them seeing her and returned to the cove to take up watch.

She hoped that her plan was sound and she relaxed as she waited, roaming the waves to look for anything amiss. She found Liffet's self-wave. It was much stronger.

She straightened up and smiled. Liffet had no message ready for her. Instead, she had a brief experience of what Liffet could see: wind, sea spray and the thrill of passing over wave tops. Had she imagined it? Did it mean Liffet and Zal were safe? She dared hope.

She sent only a simple message: joy at making contact with Liffet again; warmth for Zal. She waited, but nothing. Then, she searched for Faran's waves where happily there was a message: reassurance, as she had received before. Could she be deceiving herself? Wasn't that just a memory of Faran's previous messages?

Was she imagining her friends were safe? Or had the girls departed without her, just as she had insisted?

Exposed to the afternoon's bitter-cold wind and under a passing squall, she breathed in. She could be sure of only one thing, that there were five hirelings before her who hated her.

She sent a last message to both girls, this time about the winds. Liffet had always understood her wind signs easily. That day the wind would rise to high wind-force 7, increasing to gale-force 8 overnight, with the chance of a rogue wave. Whether or not it would be received this time, she couldn't know. She sent calm, meaning 'find safe haven'.

She sat back. She was cold and hungry, weary too, facing hirelings and certain captivity.

What she wanted right then was a hot lamb stew with dumplings, a jug of beer, followed by a rowdy singsong in the best of the watchmen's pubs, the Bald Lady in Wallburgh. A tot of whisky too, to warm her throat and settle her stomach; there was always a watchman with a small flask to share, and nobody in the pub told tales to the customs.

The slam hit her hard. She reeled in her mind and braced her legs as she felt her balance up-end. It was a hurly-burly of waves, waves bright and flashing with spitting lightning, smothering her senses. They writhed and twisted, heaved her over and snapped and grabbed at her, throwing her mercilessly. She had no way to stop them, so she called out, 'Yes, yes.' At that, the slam stopped suddenly. She saw the hirelings alert to her. If this was madness, they would be concerned for themselves.

Once more she went carefully to her memory of the slam and allowed a message: it was the same and plain to read – the children; it was urgent. She had wished herself at home and had received a slam for thinking of something other than her goal.

The hireling on watch called out. She raised herself to see a tramper crash through waves towards the cove. The hirelings began their descent from their camp, just 100 feet above the sea. She waited at the top and watched. There was no doubt she would go, yet she had no idea where the journey would take her. This could be foolish. She should turn about and run for Landing. She had to trust ... in what? Had she deceived herself that her friends were safe and that the slam was directing her to the children? She was crazy most likely.

She watched the tramper enter the cove. From afar, she saw clearly the lad was on deck. He would resent finding her there. Would he attack her? Wasn't the tramper a trap? 'Don't say that,' she said to herself. 'Don't lose courage. If you do, you might get a slam and you mustn't allow that again before these hirelings.' She skittered down to join them on the rock shore and approached the Picker.

'I would be grateful if you would prepare a cabin for me with water to wash, and food and drink.'

The Picker appeared to give way. She made an offering.

'There'll be a storm this evening; you'll be seasick,' she added.

The Picker nodded. 'Time?' he asked.

She had never been precise with the time of her foretelling before. She could be, couldn't she?

'One moment.'

From observation of the sea level and high-water line, she knew it was half past two in the afternoon, but best to confirm that by the height of the sun she saw through the cloud, which was easier. She found the wind waves straightaway: she had always enjoyed them the most because these waves were the ones she could ride on, tumble through and follow like a chase, sometimes pushed along, sometimes falling, but always safe. She could jump off anytime she wanted, but often she hadn't known when to stop. The fun was that they took her everywhere. She knew them well, knew their patterns and knew the time right then, so she paced through them instead of racing off. Measuring her pace carefully against sunset at half past seven and low tide at half past nine that evening, she stated, 'The high wind will rise from six o'clock and will run from nine o'clock this evening, all night and all-day tomorrow.'

She didn't say that the wind would drive a surge at high tide the following morning at six o'clock, because she didn't want to tell the Picker more than was necessary, and she didn't want to show off either.

'Very well. Skipper, Landing,' ordered the Picker.

They would berth there to wait out the high wind and take on supplies, she supposed. She unstrung and shouldered her bow and returned the harpoon to the quiver at her back. She checked her new small knife at her chest and the longer knife at her hip, the ones she had taken from the scavengers. They were sheathed and clasped so they wouldn't slip out, nor could they be wrested from her without a struggle.

This was her last opportunity to turn and run.

She saw the hirelings glance at her. They were a sorry squad.

She and the Picker climbed into a shore boat.

The Picker

The master was keen to return to the keep; he and this wretched crew needed stitches, remedies, and dressings on their wounds. Yet, the seer had chosen to go with them. He was relieved at that. He had done something to lure her back. Maybe, like him, she was attracted to the mystery of the chief. He would say nothing more for fear of breaking the enchantment.

His place was with the chief from then on. The seer would be brought into his chief's service and there would be no need for more of these ridiculous expeditions. His assignment was almost done and, as master, he could look forward to attendance as counsel to the chief each day.

The seer had betrayed her ability through her mind-shriek, her foretelling of the strength and time of landfall of a high wind, her silent communication with her friend, and even the influences she had over the weak minds of the crew, not forgetting her skill with the bow and her hardiness out in this bleak land. He had had suspicions about her eyesight too – like an owl it seemed. Her weakness was her fondness for her folk. It was wasteful but it wasn't unheard of for the strong to throw themselves into the service of their settlement. She would have to be handled carefully, as he couldn't expect to lock her up, or not for long.

He should congratulate himself. It wasn't altogether by his design, but he would deliver the seer to his chief who would overlook all that hadn't gone to plan.

Alfren

Two hirelings rowed them to the tramper. The lad took Alfren's arm to lift her aboard; he was definitely strong. He looked sourly in her eyes. A hireling in the wheelhouse indicated she should go below. Instead, she went forward to inspect the deck and pulled open the hatch to the hold. There was nothing below but stone ballast. The hatch to the stowage was fastened shut. She unlatched it and peered in. There were only lobster creels. She went below and searched the cabins and stores, until she found a small cabin similar to the one Zal had occupied. There was no porthole, not in any of the cabins.

'This one's fine,' she called to the Picker.

She approached him in the galley. 'Remember. I'm not your captive. I'm going to negotiate with your chief.'

She had some advantage: the hirelings were wary of her and she had fought and outwitted them. Perhaps her good fortune would continue, though there would be many hurdles to clear before she found a way to free the children. It occurred to her that what she had learned about escape from a tramper might not help much at the keep. She would find it completely different there. The hirelings might keep their distance from her, which would help, but she should have a plan.

She tried not to think about being alone.

Once she was in her cabin, the lad brought her water, bread, smoked fish, cheese, and a pail of water. It was fine food and must be from Landing. She closed the door, tied a light cord from the handle to the bunk bed to secure it shut, washed herself with a flannel, and then ate from her plate. The tramper was underway, rising with each wave and crashing into the next, rolling back and forth, high from side to side, through the rising, rough sea.

Sloop

Faran

Faran enjoyed being at sea, although she was invited to go only occasionally when she had a free day, and really, she didn't have the time when there were folk to nurse. The best part of being at sea was being away from those patients with their fretful minds. She had learned to ignore all their maddening voices and, with care, be open only to the fellow she was nursing right then, but her family had told her she shouldn't even do that and should stop reading minds altogether. They never believed her when she said she had, but that was because she would say something soon afterwards that she couldn't have known otherwise, and she couldn't stop chatting because how else could she rid herself of all those thoughts?

The mind she couldn't ignore was the one which, when it was strongest, brought fascinating dreams and insight into new energies – Alfren of Wallburgh, the Sealander.

She sat in the cockpit with her brother who was taking his turn as steersman. The wind and sea spray seemed to clear her mind, which was a relief to her.

She was still amazed that after she had called her family together at home and told them what she knew, and after

223

her father had had a brief consultation with their rune master, her family had approved of the trip. What was more, they had been allowed a ration of fuel and had put to sea immediately.

It was doubly surprising because there was little fuel. It was only to be used for running the League towns (for evasion of their fast cutters), or in the Sealand inlets where pirates laid in wait, and then only to use in an emergency. They were going only to the south end of Sealand, which was largely uninhabited, but it was better to have it and it was clear the rune master thought they might need it.

It was new to her to search for the fire raised by Alfren, but it had seemed likely it would work. In truth when a fellow's mind was as strong as Alfren's at those times she was with her waves so intensely, she could find her by a sense of warmth. Not actual warmth but a closeness of minds, hers and Alfren's. She couldn't describe how exactly, and she had done it once to find Alfren that time three years earlier although ever since it had worked when she wanted to find her brother or family, and then she had never had to look far.

Somehow, she and Alfren had by chance found a way when Alfren had focused on fire and had fixed a bond to the fire that Faran could follow. She wasn't the sort to dwell on how she knew. It was fun just to see what happened.

She told her brother they were in the right place as they crossed a large bay, and her father scanned the shoreline for a landing while her uncle started up the turbine. Then her uncle called to her and she helped furl the main sail. She would have known if she had read his mind that they were aiming for a lightning-quick landing to collect the girls, Alfren and the other one who was ill – poisoned actually. They shouldn't delay, not on this shore. Scavengers could rally there in a flash.

The turbine was noisy and the fumes reeked, yet with it in service her uncle could turn the sloop on a sixpence and counter any tide or current. He dropped anchor and steered to pull it deep into the sandy bed of the bay. They already had their skiff in the water, towed behind. Faran drew it alongside and the men lowered themselves in. She was about to follow when her father called, 'No,' but her brother appealed. Her brother and father rowed, she steered, and her uncle at the prow signalled the direction. They ran onto the shingle beach and jumped ashore.

She led them to a shelter concealed under a rock outcrop, a wisp of smoke curling from a vent. It was too quiet. But as she approached, a girl flew from the tent, knife in hand. Faran held up both hands as the girl called, 'Thank daisy, you're here.'

Faran entered the tent and assessed the ill girl lying there, her life ebbing. From her shoulder bag she took a bottle and syringe. The knife girl held back her arm and Faran explained, 'It's an antibiotic.' It might be too late. She gave the injection. Her family cleared the camp and extinguished the fire, then they lifted the girl onto a stretcher, strapped her securely, and hastened to the boat. All were aboard. She waved to her brother on guard at the head of the beach. He rushed to push off the boat and leapt in. They were away after just a few minutes and out of range of the shore. She turned to attend to the girl, but her father caught her arm and pointed.

There, above the beach, a scavenger band.

The knife girl introduced herself as Liffet. There was a moment to sit back as her uncle and brother rowed, so Liffet explained that Alfren had gone for aid but, more than that, had an urgent quest. Faran knew about that: she had read turmoil in the seer.

It was interesting to be with Liffet. Faran read so much energy it made her want to laugh.

She noticed her uncle wanted to be underway from these treacherous shores where a pirate could intercept them at any moment.

Wasn't it easier to read minds all the time? There were times when it was best.

The five of them lifted the ill girl who was called Zal onto the sloop and down into the cabin. As Faran and Liffet made Zal comfortable, the turbine propelled the sloop around to release the anchor and then to slip from the bay. The loud whine fell away. Then they were under sail once again.

The girls stripped and washed Zal, cleaned and bandaged wounds, dressed her in a nightdress and wrapped her in bedclothes.

Faran left Liffet to wash and waited for her in the galley. When Liffet appeared, she drank a large glass of beer, followed by hot tea and then ate a bowl of fish stew with a hunk of dark bread.

'Faran, you have no idea how good this tastes.'

'Good. We'll let Zal rest a while, then let's see if she'll eat.'

'Thank you for coming for us.'

'We came as quickly as we could. My uncle knows this coast.'

'How did you find us?'

'Alfren held a fire; it worked.'

Why should she say more?

'Alfren is a seer, don't you think?' Liffet asked. 'They were looking for her.'

'Yes. Though Alfren is right in what she thinks, I'd say. All seers are different and she's like none before.'

'How do you know about seers? We don't really, not real ones, not where we're from.'

'It's in our lore and before that in the texts of the Last

People. It's everywhere if you know where to look, they say. Only a few search, but most don't.'

'Why not?'

'Then they would have to face the truth. Our rune master says folk-kind has never been good at that.'

'What truth?'

'The Extinction.'

Liffet looked surprised. 'I'm not sure Ally could say what to do to survive an Extinction.'

Faran didn't reply. She had been told over and over again it wasn't her place to put the truth to folk. Folk were stubborn however intelligent they were and they learned only when faced with peril.

She smiled at Liffet. She hoped they might become friends.

Liffet left to tend to Zal; Faran climbed out to sit in the cockpit.

When, later, Liffet joined her, they were far offshore.

'I don't see land, where are we?'

'Out at sea, to avoid pirates.'

'Oh, Alfren ...' said Liffet.

'I hear too,' Faran replied.

Liffet nodded. 'Gale-force 8.'

'Oh, is that what those shapes mean?'

Faran held a feeling of encouragement for Alfren, but whether it was received or not, she couldn't know.

'Is she safe?' Faran asked.

'With the hirelings, I think. I get messages from her: they're not as clear as they were but that's because I've changed a bit.'

Faran spoke to her uncle to warn him about the high wind and he altered course. Certain that Liffet wouldn't understand their dialect, she explained, 'We'll put in at

Landing. Better for Zal, don't you think?'

Zal needed to rest in the calm water of a harbour rather than out at sea in a storm.

'Yes.' Liffet nodded.

Scavenger

Jin

Jin and Handar picked their way along the coast. The day before he had felt keen to cover ground and head west. Today he noticed, he was determined to search well. It would be careless if they missed something.

From afar, at a small bay, he saw a tumbledown, abandoned village with a smashed stone jetty and a narrow esplanade collapsed in places. They rode their ponies along the main street, cracked and overgrown with heather and gorse.

It was clear why the village was in ruins. It was low-lying; storm surges had raised floods. He remembered one of the first texts he had read, from a time early in the Extinction: on a fine day, the Last People had been surprised by a sea surge that had capsized boats in the harbour, dashed them against the sea wall or carried them inland. The storm that raised the surge must have been far out at sea. The writer was probably one of only a few who survived.

They led their ponies farther along rocky coastline and climbed high above cliffs and sea stacks on steep slopes of thick grass and heather. The mist obscured the view he would have wished for. By mid-afternoon, they crossed

lower land with a gentler slope to the sea, riven by several burns. They came across a wide bay, with inlets and rock outcrops. Their progress slowed as they searched the ragged coastline. For a moment they halted, and Handar took out her telescope.

'Two miles off and they've seen us,' she said, not that he and Handar were trying to be stealthy. It could only be a scavenger gang. 'They know who we are and are making away.'

'Let's hope they stay on the move,' he replied. If Alfren was there, he hoped to drive the scavengers past her.

They resumed their search.

Just as he prepared to cross a burn, he called out, 'Han!'

He had spotted seaweed soaking in a freshwater pool. Handar, who patrolled higher up, descended to join him.

'I'll take your pony,' she said, leaving him free to explore the rocks at the land's edge. After 100 yards, he called again: there was a narrow, shingle beach that required a search. Once on the beach, he saw, concealed in a corner on fine sand, traces of a hide. He called Handar to join him.

'They left in a hurry: the fire pit is warm; sacking is bloodied. Good place to hide. This could have been only them, Han.'

He climbed above the beach. It was near half tide – two o'clock in the afternoon.

'Shore boat there, sunk below low water,' he pointed out. 'It looks like they were not captive at this point.'

'We've missed something, Jin,' Handar said.

They returned to search the hide.

'If it was in fact our girls ...' said Handar.

'The militiaman is a scout.'

There were large pebbles around the extinguished fire. Jin turned over a couple, then flipped the third one from the left to reveal scratches on the underside. He picked it up.

'3-LAZ. That's obvious,' he said. 'The third day; three of them, their initials.'

He reached for the fourth pebble and turned it over. '4-LZ-R-WI. Alfren had left the beach. R could mean raider, recce or rescue, but where or who is WI?'

Handar summarized. 'Scout Liffet and the girl raider have gone, taken off the beach within the last hour by friendly folk I hope, and I say that because there was time to scratch the message. Alfren must've gone for help, or she had some good reason to leave, perhaps to distract a scavenger gang. We may be only a short distance behind her. Let's be going, Jin.'

'Could she have gone inland to take the track?' Jin asked as he adjusted the girth on his pony.

'Possibly. That shore boat came from somewhere. We'll follow the coast a little farther. Ready?'

From the last recorded sighting of the tramper the day before at the ferry crossing, to hot embers on a shingle beach, they had made progress. Jin put his hand on his rifle case, strapped to the pannier on his pony. They were close, weren't they?

It was too early to say. There could be as much land to cross again with meaner folk than the harbour master and ferryman. They should be prepared for the worst. He wanted to believe the signs were good, but a good ranger knew more disappointment than reward. He must stay resolute.

He allowed his thoughts to stray. The militia had failed all other kidnapped children. The persistence of raiders and fickleness of burghers meant no one knew who sided with whom. He would not allow it to get worse. There had to be a point where the ripples from the Extinction no longer mattered and folk could turn to a better future.

As for Alfren, those abilities of hers that he suspected rather marked her out. It would be best to find ways to conceal them otherwise her days of freedom may be short.

All the same, Jin felt recharged by the evidence on the beach. It gave him hope. It was cold, yet the wind was his inspiration, fresh and bringing change.

'Alright, Jin?'

'Yes, Han, ready,' he responded.

They continued westwards, high above the sea, riding fast and recklessly because this had turned into a chase. After two hours, Jin was inclined to ride past a curved edge over the sea, no doubt sheer above ragged rocks; however, he checked and saw a fair, sheltered cove, a deep-water natural haven. He was astonished to see a sunken tramper, the mast poking above the high tide, the same as the description he had for the one that left Wallburgh. They dismounted and descended to an obvious shelf above the only possible path to the shore. There they found flattened tufts of grass and heavy stones for weighting tarpaulin – evidence of a camp. Handar reported crossbows and weapons at the base of a grass slope too steep to descend. When Jin turned to look back up the slope to check on the ponies, he saw letters chalked on a rock step. A-KEEP. They took a last close look around and climbed onto their ponies.

'This is where she came from the shingle beach, Han,' Jin said. 'She was here this afternoon too. There had been an accident or commotion of some kind here at the cove, perhaps as recent as today.'

'Yes, the camp suggests the raiders were here awaiting rescue. It's four o'clock. Alright, it'll be dark when we get to Landing in ... let's say five hours. We should meet Tans and Falt on the track just outside the burgh.'

Jin brought out his pocket barometer from a pack on the pony. He had paid a trader a whole sovereign for it, all his savings, when the trader ran aground on Furrow. Other rangers, Falt especially, had admired it. It was old like the broken watch he carried in his pocket, and from before the Extinction, but this device worked still.

'Temperature is 6°C and pressure is falling. It's 29 inches.'

The wind was freshening, perhaps a high wind-force 7 later. Rain showers had swept over them all day and just then a heavier squall passed.

The coast would become too hilly and wild further west, Handar said, so they went north. They followed a burn where the ground was boggy and contoured around steep hillsides, before crossing a watershed to the head of the next valley.

They were only an hour from the cove when they found a camp, a tarpaulin tent, in a ghyll. There was no one on guard and two small ponies were hobbled and they grazed.

Scavengers.

Carefully they descended into the ghyll, any sound drowned by wind and waterfall. They followed procedure. Jin unsheathed his rifle and rested it on the saddle of his pony, aiming at the camp. Handar went forward with her pony as a shield and called out.

'Rangers at large! Be warned! Firing weapon at hand. Show yourself!'

There was nothing. They waited. The waterfalls rumbled. The air was calm. The tent rippled. A scavenger appeared from the canvas, startled to see their uniform storm suits.

'Don't kill! We go west! Landing!'

Handar held up her hands to show she was unarmed. She gestured to the scavenger he should step away from the camp shelter. She peered in.

'Bring out the wounded.'

The scavengers carried out two of their own suffering arrow wounds to their thighs, and laid them by the burn in the rain. Handar took a surgical kit from her pony's saddlebag. She instructed the scavengers to strip the wounded and lay them on their sides. She gave both of them anaesthetic. For the first, she cleaned the wound with alcohol and the shaft of the arrow – it was a harpoon! She pushed the arrow through, then cleaned, stitched and dressed the wound. She did the same to the second. She gave the scavengers clean bandages. She was practised and quick: the procedures took only a half hour.

There was only one person he knew who could shoot two scavengers accurately in the same place high on the leg. Handar, too.

'Ranger?' she asked the scavengers.

'Girl? Yes,' replied the leader. 'She with raiders. She likes them not.'

'Where is she?'

The leader shrugged.

'Listen,' said Handar, slowly so the leader would understand. 'Go to Landing. Surrender there. Go west, yes? I will assume responsibility for you. Look, Landing, yes?'

'I know,' said the leader, looking up at Jin's rifle.

'Safe. Landing!' said Handar firmly.

'Landing,' said the leader. 'Deal?'

She looked nonplussed.

'Yes, deal.'

They were quick to pack up and move on.

'Landing, Jin. As quick as we can!'

'And then to find the keep?'

'First to raise the alarm: we know for certain we're on the trail of Alfren and there's a raider kidnap gang on our land.'

They rode urgently. An hour later, they reached the track where they met Tans and Falt camped at a ruin. They stopped for a few minutes while the pair broke camp.

Jin studied the ruin. There were thick stone walls that gave respite from the wind. Long ago, folk had built it well yet there on the track it was remote. Perhaps it had once been a halt station between Landing and Wallburgh, a refuge to wait out the worst weather. Maybe someone had lived out here long ago during the Extinction, far from a polluted coast, far from towns crowded with diseased folk?

The ranger squad took out their goggles and buttoned up their storm suits. They would be sure to head into a high wind-force 7, with heavy rain. Jin patted his pony's neck and swung up into the saddle. In these conditions and left to themselves, the ponies would group together in a paddock, turn their tails to the wind and stand it out. Here, out in the badland, his pony shook its head and with a little encouragement turned into the wind and trotted on willingly. Tucked under his hood, Jin watched his pony's step, guiding the pony as he could.

'Who were those that had survived the Extinction?' he asked himself. Were they the ones who could endure a high wind-force 7, on saddled ponies, running from scavengers perhaps? Or were they the ones who had built solid stone shelters far from others? Were they scavengers themselves, who hunted in packs and took every last item they could because it gave them that little advantage, something to keep them warm, something to barter? Did the Extinction come down to that? Was he descended from pack-hunters? Was that why everything known about the Last People had been lost, because only the meanest, most brutal folk survived?

He caught himself before he toppled in a strong gust. They trotted and cantered where the track was firm and well made. Their ponies were tough and would rest when they reached Landing.

In the badland, as East Sealanders called it, storms made landfall from the west. It was wild out here. Folk kept to their fastnesses and didn't mix as they did in the east. Sea lochs, voes and poor tracks around the steep coastline meant folk on the move were vulnerable to scavengers and pirates.

Rangers prowled the land to keep raiders in check. Jin had patrolled many islands, but his squad visited them only in summer and just once in a season. An annual visit was enough to keep folk together because they knew to expect rangers who would come with news from the burghs. Each year though, when he visited the brochs and crannogs, he found some overrun or abandoned – folk had left and gone who knew where. Some he saw again: they told him they had been starving and sought charity from a neighbouring settlement, where they earned their keep by raiding, which was better than slavery.

A heavy squall of rain and whipping blows of wind drenched the riders. Ordinarily they would turn off to find a little shelter from the worst, but this was a hot pursuit – earlier that day they had been only minutes behind the girls.

Handar was right: rangers would accept Alfren for who she was; someone with the promise of becoming a good ranger, who folk could see as fair and understanding. Those folk would look forward to seeing her each summer when she patrolled the islands.

Landing

By mid-evening, in the last of the light, they spied Landing through grey rain, a dark shadow against a grey sea loch, an impressive walled burgh. A curtain wall stood on high rock above the sea. Just the sight of it would deter an attack. Jin had heard folk say the first to make landfall after the Extinction had built Landing, when they had found this bluff overlooking a deep natural harbour. Once settled they had built a steep funicular railway to connect the two, which had been the largest single engineering achievement of a new age. A wonder to folk was the massive breakwater curved across the harbour to create a narrow entrance, over which chains had been slung to prevent surprise raids from the sea. Folk said Landing was an impregnable fortification. It had to be. Out west, there were no watchtowers, no telegraph line linking the burgh to the east.

There was, however, a radio at the ranger base and Handar had said she would request reinforcements from Wallburgh. They approached the burgh gate across a short wooden drawbridge over a deep gully. The gate was closed, which was as they had expected to find it. A guard called from an arrow slit in the wall and Handar replied: 'Rangers, open up.'

There was a delay, and the call came, 'Identify yourselves.'

Jin would have pointed his rifle through the slit and asked for the opportunity to discuss his identity at their pleasure.

'Ranger squad as notified by post to the guard, please confirm.'

The weekly post should have arrived: the coded and sealed letter had been posted with the departure of a caravan of traders and travellers from Wallburgh. Usually rangers passed into burghs without question. They stood in the rain until after a few minutes the gate opened and they entered a barbican, an enclosed yard, before a heavy, second gate that closed off the passage into the burgh.

A guard sergeant received them. They dismounted and Handar saluted. Jin stood alongside her. She was polite although she outranked the guard.

'We require admission to the ranger base,' she declared.

'Yes, ma'am. Sorry, ma'am. Bad news for you: thieves broke into the base. It happened today.'

'I see. Allow us through and we'll assess the damage.'

The sergeant checked that the guard had closed the outer gate before he rapped on the great main gate and called for it to open. Handar allowed Jin, Tans and Falt through first. Jin turned to stay at her side. They waited for the sergeant to retrieve the keys to the ranger base, which the guard to Landing held securely.

On receiving them, Handar asked, 'Where was the guard for the base, Sergeant?'

The sergeant's eyes darted, then settled to the left, deciding an edited version of the truth was best.

'All were on watch on the walls, on lookout for a missing tramper. Word was there were important folk on board. Shipwrecked, I heard, and a rescue brought them in today.'

'Thank you, Sergeant,' Handar responded as though it was no matter.

They walked a short way along the main street as far as the main square. Jin noticed there was no guard in the centre at a raised cross although one should always be posted there. A narrow alley led to the base, which was the old treasury building. Three separate locks to the steel door had been wrenched open and someone had fixed a wooden plank across the door to deter anyone from entering. The barred window was intact. Falt unlocked and opened a large steel door to the side, which led along a ginnel to a courtyard and stables.

Darkness had fallen. Jin and Falt attended to the ponies. Tans lit a carbide lamp, drew her knife, unlocked the rear door to the base and entered, while Jin checked over the peat-gas generator, which was housed in a stable. Falt followed Handar into the base and a moment later reappeared. 'All clear.'

Jin cranked and started the generator. Electric light glowed in the yard and from the door to the base. He entered and at the first door to the radio room he saw thieves had forced their way in.

'I have to ask, is a repair possible?' said Handar.

'No,' he said bitterly. The radio was smashed: wanton destruction of a purposeful, functioning object. Sealanders didn't have the skills to make new radios, only to repair them. It was a big loss.

'Spares in the cellar won't fix this,' he said. 'If they were thieves, why didn't they take it? Why smash it?'

'The safe is untouched,' said Tans. 'Code books and silver all there.'

'Clearly, they weren't thieves. Lock up and let's head down to the harbour,' Handar ordered. 'I want to know who's there. Quietly. I want to be unobserved.'

Jin grabbed some rations and refilled his canteen.

Falt had visited Landing many times, so led them along the back lanes to the funicular top station where a small rail car was waiting in its docking bay. The squad held carbide lamps that sputtered in the strong wind. In the darkness, no one challenged them as they descended the steep steps alongside the funicular rails. Jin estimated it was 200 feet to the base station and quay. There were many boats of all kinds tied up in the harbour, most with a carbide lamp atop the wheelhouse or swaying to and fro on the mast high above deck. The squad huddled at the corner of the base station. Handar pointed out the ranger ketch.

Handar called to the squad, above the wind roar. 'We could search every one of these boats as there's a chance Alfren is aboard one of them. I'm supposing that she went with the raider party willingly, so we'll hold back. It's no coincidence that prior to our arrival today the base radio was destroyed. Let's find out what's going on and be discreet about it. Best we show ourselves only when we know more. Tans, let our sailors know we're here and take watch from the ketch and Jin, take watch from the quay. You'll be relieved at midnight.'

Jin watched Tans stroll over to the ketch. At the quayside she picked up a mooring rope and climbed down out of sight. It was half-tide, which would make the time nine o'clock. He decided the best vantage point would be the roof of the funicular base station, so he climbed the steps a short way alongside, clipped his lamp to his belt, jumped on the handrail and reached to pull himself up. There was a parapet on the flat roof, which gave some shelter. He took a folding stool from his backpack and an oil cloth cape, which he wrapped over and around himself.

The wind howled and the boats rocked. Sheets of rain sluiced the quay. Jin wiped drops from his brow and eyes. The few gas lamps on the boats cast hardly any light. It was a quarter moon, but they would be unlikely to glimpse it. Jin had a feeling the high wind bringing thick cloud would run for a day and more. Once he had settled, he didn't mind the wait. A few folk dashed to the funicular station and the car ran, easing away with a clunk and after a few minutes, with a whooshing noise, the second car arrived on the parallel track from the top station. He wished he could climb down off the roof to watch it.

Suddenly, he felt a presence. He released his cape and spun around brandishing his knife. A girl stood on the roof behind him holding a lamp in one hand and a flask in the other.

'Are you Jin?' she asked.

'Blimey, yes. You gave me a start.'

'Yes, windy, isn't it. Tans said you might like some soup.'

'What? Yes, I would. Perfect.'

The girl was dressed in an outland field suit from the militia, much like his own storm suit, and she had a badge on her arm he recognised.

'Are you ...?'

'Liffet, yes. Or no — Scout Liffet of the Wallburgh militia, Sealand, that's what I'm supposed to say. Drink it quickly, before it goes cold. It's from the Western Isles. It's got whisky in it. It's delicious, so if you don't want it ...'

'I do, thanks.'

Jin reached out and took the flask. Liffet crouched by him, and Jin arranged the cape around them both.

'What are you watching for?' she asked.

'You, among others.'

He made a connection. 'WI? Western Isles? On the stone?'

'I didn't know what else to write.'

'I'm relieved to see you.'

'Why?'

'We've been searching for you for the past three days. Where's Alfren, do you know?'

'See the top of that tramper wheelhouse? One, two ...'

she counted, 'seven vessels along from the mooring cleat next to the big freighter?'

'Yes?'

'There.'

'Crikey! Why don't we go in and get her?'

'She says not to.'

'You've spoken to her?'

'No.'

He smiled to himself.

'Please explain, Scout Liffet.'

'You can call me Liffet.'

'You say you've spoken to her?'

'Not exactly.'

'Then how?'

'I can't say.'

'Why?'

'You shouldn't know.'

'Is it like telepathy?'

'I don't know what that is.'

'Have you got a plan?' he asked.

'Sort of. We should have a chat.'

'When?'

'When you've finished your soup.'

'Did you come from a boat?'

'Yes.'

It all had come together and there he was, part of it all, and everyone involved was in this small burgh.

'Which boat?'

'The one from the Western Isles, of course.'

She was light and humorous.

'That would be which one?'

'It's a sloop, a nice one, tied up to the ranger ketch. Can you fix the radio?'

'How do you know about the radio?'

'You ask a lot of questions, don't you, Jin? The ranger sailors checked on the base today.'

'Of course. Alright. How do you know I fix radios?'

'Alfren told me. You spoke to her at the barracks, remember?'

Jin smiled. Liffet crouched close.

'I can't fix it. It's smashed.'

He thought about what he had seen along the coast. 'It's been a tough couple of days for you.'

'Yes. At first we thought they had us forever and we'd become slaves or something.'

'How did you escape?'

'Ally tricked them.'

He sighed. Liffet gave the briefest answers.

'You're right, that soup was fabulous. Shall we—?'

'Tans is here.'

He turned to see Tans climb onto the roof and then pull a girl up after her. The four of them sat in a huddle. Jin lit his gas lamp so there was a faint glow, enough to see each other's faces.

'Welcome everyone,' he said. 'Shouldn't we gather in a shelter?'

'Alfren will be here in a moment,' said Tans, 'and we should make sure she isn't seen talking to us. Jin, this is Faran.'

He greeted the new girl. 'How do you do.'

'Merry meet,' Faran replied brightly.

'You must be from the Western Isles. Thanks for the soup.'

'My brother made it; too much whisky for me.'

'How's the girl raider?'

'He means Zal,' Liffet explained to Faran and turned to him. 'She's poorly and resting. She's had antibiotics and food. We wait.'

Behind Tans he saw a figure climb onto the roof to join them.

'Liffy, Faran!'

It was Alfren! What the story would be regards escape and the sunken tramper, he couldn't fathom, but Alfren had rejoined them all and in good health and spirit too.

Alfren

'Let's keep low everyone,' called the new ranger, a corporal.

Alfren was beaming at seeing her friends. Faran had grown in three years, but her full smile and bright eyes hadn't changed. Liffet was back to normal, full of energy and sharp-witted.

'Jin! Did you follow us? Thank you,' Alfren gushed.

She had thought she and the girls were lost. Yet here was not one but two rangers together in the same place!

'Yes, and great to see you, Alfren. Handar's here too.'

Handar? Had they all come to look for her?

'Marine Alfren, I'm Corporal Tans; you're in my squad as of right now. Everyone,' and the group of them leant in to listen, 'we've found the girls which was our objective. Jin and I know little about what's happened. Alfren, explain.'

Alfren had to make her report right there?

'The raiders were waiting for us at the infirmary, Tans. They have informants in Wallburgh. They're crazy. They said I'm a seer and wanted to take me to their chief who they call the visionary. He has his base at the keep, which I guess is within a day of here. We escaped. You know about the tramper, the camp on the beach and rescue by a Western Isles sloop that was passing by.' She hoped she wouldn't be questioned on that, but Jin's eyes opened in wonder at such good fortune.

She continued, 'I decided to go with the raiders because they've kidnapped our children over the years, and I felt

compelled to find them. Tans, this is difficult to explain: I felt an urge to find them and I know I must find them, very soon.'

She turned to Jin. He might understand. 'Jin, I don't know why, but when I try to think of something else, I get a slam in my mind and I lose balance. I suppose I might sound mad.'

'Yes, well, not as mad as us should we do nothing about it,' replied Jin.

Just what she needed to hear!

'Alfren, you're entitled to propose an extension to the patrol,' said Tans. 'You have a case based on the missing children. Go on.'

'I told the raiders that I would go willingly to see the chief to negotiate. They'll take me to their keep, and I expect to find the children there.'

'Why does this chief kidnap children?' asked Jin.

'Zal hasn't told us fully. It's something to do with his name, the *visionary*. He's crazy enough to believe children can help him predict the future. The point is, this chief believes there're a big storms to come.'

'Well, high storms do pass, from time to time,' said Jin, 'and of a strength to worry folk. This chief has, cleverly and quietly, built up a following, and I'd say what he wants is to be a big overlord. Maybe he has a greater prize in mind.'

'Like the overthrow of Sealand?' Alfren said.

That could be it. Was this chief so ambitious?

'Look, I'm on the trail of missing children and I propose to carry on, subject to Handar's approval.'

If she received an order to break off from the pursuit, she would be dismayed. Although, she trusted Handar would not abandon the children. The niggle was, it had to be soon.

'Would you be able to meet the boss?' asked Tans.

'Yes, although I don't want to spook the raiders by being seen with rangers.'

'I see. Alfren, we'll find it difficult to make a case to Han that she should allow you to sail off with raiders, especially crazy ones. In any case, they may be reluctant to make a move while the ranger ketch is here, unless we put out to sea tomorrow in the storm, out of their way. Look, if you go with the raiders to their keep, how do we ensure your safety? How do we track you?'

'I scare them,' she said. 'They don't come near me.'

'If we find board here in Landing for Zal, we could leave to track the tramper,' suggested Faran. 'My uncle knows the coast well.'

'Can a sailing sloop match a tramper for speed?' asked Tans.

'Yes,' said Faran. 'We have gas turbine propulsion.'

'What?' asked Jin in amazement.

'We crack and distil kerosene fuel from peat oil.'

Jin whistled softly.

'Alright,' Tans put down the distraction. 'Alfren, how do we ensure your safety when at the keep?'

'I don't know,' she replied. That was the problem with her plan: it led to her imprisonment in a fortress somewhere, surrounded by paid hirelings just as nasty as the ones on the tramper.

'We'll tell Han what you've told us, but probably she won't let you go until you've a better proposition.'

Alfren was disappointed and she tensed, ready to receive a slam. It didn't come. Anyway, slam or not, it had been a stupid idea all along. How could she take on a chief, a reiver, a madman? She saw Jin's kind eyes, Liffet's ready smile, Faran's open look. They weren't cowed, but she mustn't get them into trouble with raiders because of urges she felt.

But she had to reach the children. There was little time.

She took the cut-out from the navigation chart on the tramper. The wind blew fiercely, and rain had stopped for a moment.

'I kept this. I hope that the children aren't far away at a keep, somewhere on the coast shown by this chart. Look, we've come together and that's good fortune. The rest is up to us. What I propose is that I should play along and see what tomorrow brings, all the while trying to find out as much as possible. It may be there's something you can find in the burgh. Let's look again at what we've seen and heard. If there's a sign the tramper is about to leave, I'll jump off, or rangers and islesfolk together could storm it. What do you think?'

'Alfren,' asked Tans, 'are you sure you're free to leave any time you wish?'

'Yes, almost completely sure.'

'If we want you off the tramper, how do we signal?'

'Just tell Liffy or Faran.'

'Right. How do they signal?'

Alfren thought how she had changed over a few short days. She saw winds approaching and sent thoughts to Liffet. She could do the same with anyone, she supposed.

'Um, don't think about anything for a moment,' she told Tans.

'What?'

'Just try it.'

Tans nodded, then, 'Oh!' she said in surprise. 'Just like being on a sunny beach! Hey, that was good. Do it again!'

'Tans!' Jin scolded.

Faran

The problems the Landers faced were real and urgent, and Faran had never seen anything like that before. It was clear to her that the tension between two sides, Landers and raiders, engaged their resources and as a result her land, the Western Isles, had been left alone – not raided or colonised. Her folk had been lucky so far, but once raiders or the League overcame the other, they could spill over. Who would she rather have land on her shores?

Her folk had stayed away and stayed out of it, but it couldn't last. Folk on both sides were rising up. That's why she was there, wasn't it? She had heard their minds and it was disturbing.

On the other hand, these rangers were goodly, humorous and dedicated, as well as enormously practical, fit and hardy. Liffet, who she liked a lot, was light-hearted but profound too. Alfren, the wave girl, intrigued her.

Where would Alfren lead them?

Faran could learn a lot from these few folk and not only by reading their minds. In fact, their words and actions told her just as much or more.

Faran's family would want to be away soon, even into a storm. She would tell them to wait, live with uncertainty in their minds, and put it to good use; it would show them how to prepare themselves however they could for a future facing more unknowns.

'Yes, alright,' Tans said. 'You may return to the tramper, Alfren, on condition you jump off when we say.'

Tans was fair and decisive; *a safe hand* as Faran's brother would say.

'Yes, Tans,' said Alfren. It was an order.

Alfren looked pleased. The hunt for the children had not been called off. Faran read a strong compulsion in her and thought it possible a few more hours on the trail of the children could draw the next event to Alfren and this group of Landers. With such determination in their minds, they were the sort that brought adventure on themselves.

Faran read comfort in Alfren's mind from the support given by Liffet and the rangers. It was a source of strength to her.

Jin

Alfren was brave and determined, Jin thought. The problem was that the chief would want her for his scheme just as much as the children he had invested in by kidnapping and holding them captive for so long. Her plan appeared simply to offer herself in exchange for the children but this chief, this visionary fellow, would surely not release any of them because he couldn't risk revealing the location of the keep. Still, it was clear. This was a new patrol; they were in the jaws of the trap set by this chief, and they had to take one careful step at a time.

Just then, a heavy rain squall sluiced over the group. It was the right moment to break up.

Jin saw Tans and Faran hasten over to the quayside and descend to their boats, the ranger ketch and Western Isles sloop.

He lost sight of Liffet and Alfren – those two knew how to stay in the shadows. That rather confirmed they had been wall-runners, well-used to staying concealed.

Takes one to know one, he grinned. How many times as a child had he been scolded for straying too far and out of sight for too long?

Jin settled into his watch.

DAY 5

Keep

Jin

Together with the master sailor, the rangers gathered at the base at five o'clock in the morning. Jin had managed a few hours' sleep.

Handar spoke. 'I took a last look at the harbour minutes ago. The boat decks were approaching quay height due to high tide and a storm surge.'

Any storm was as big as the last, and all deserved attention. Jin had witnessed their impacts. All had earned his respect.

Never get caught out in one.

'We're unable to summon reinforcements to search for a keep,' said Handar. 'Communication is lost. There is no keep shown on our maps and it may be farther off than we've been led to believe. I have a mind to call off this patrol and regroup. Any thoughts?'

Falt shuffled on his chair and leant forward, chin on his knuckles.

'I know the burgh, Han, and the land around here. There's no keep out there – no fortress that could house and hide kidnapped children. There's nowhere big enough, nowhere with a good harbour or sheltered water.'

'That's true,' said the master of the ketch. 'I know every inch of this coast. There are many small fortifications, but no grand keep.'

'What does this mean for the report we have?' asked Handar. 'Surely there is a keep somewhere?'

He saw Falt and the master nod at one another.

'Could you follow me to the square?' Falt directed. 'I'd like to show you something.'

They followed Falt from the base, through the ginnel to the lane and into the burgh square, to the stone cross set on a large plinth. It was dark morning and even in the centre of the burgh the winds whipped fiercely.

'What is it, Falt?' asked Handar.

'We're looking for a fortification, with a large keep, on the west coast of Sealand, not far from Wallburgh, that raiders control, where they can hide and sally out on their raids, where they could hide our children.'

They nodded in agreement.

'Well, this is it. Right here.

'We're trapped in it.'

Star

Alfren

In her cabin Alfren sprang from her cot fully clothed. A moment later, there was a knock at the door, and she heard the Picker's raised voice.

'The seer Alfren. I must wake you.'

'What is it?'

'Come through to the galley.'

She gathered her bow and quiver and strapped on her knives, then released the cord from the door and stepped into the passage. In the galley, the Picker waited alone.

'The seer, I can assure you there will be no tricks. There is a deal between us and, despite what you think of our ways, I will honour it. We will enter into negotiation.'

'Alright. Good.'

'First, we want a reassurance from you.'

'Which is?'

'There is a ranger ketch in the harbour and a ranger squad in the burgh. You claim to be a ranger and it may be that you summoned them here. We will take them hostage if you attempt to contact them. We will not allow them to leave. They don't know it, but they are captive, and their lives depend on your honour.'

'Alright,' she replied.

'If you collude with them using your mind waves, we will sell them as slaves – and you too. Is that clear?'

'Yes.'

Was there a way they would know if she did?

'Do we have your word?'

'Yes.'

That was all she could say.

'While you are here, you will be monitored carefully. From now on, someone will be with you at all times.'

The Picker winced. It was because of his wounds.

What did the Picker mean by *while you are here*? How was it that he could threaten the rangers in Landing, a free burgh of Sealand? Was this a boast of power and influence by this chief? He must be close, only hours away. Why the delay? Surely it was because of the high wind. Why hadn't she received a slam in her mind since the cove? She was heading in the right direction, but this was wasting time and when she did that a slam hit her soon enough.

'Remember, we have a deal. Follow me.'

Slowly the Picker climbed from the galley onto the deck. The skipper was in the wheelhouse. He nodded to her. There were four hirelings with lamps on the quayside, two of whom leant over to assist the Picker off the tramper. The rain had stopped but the wind blew fiercely. She jumped off the gunwale onto the quay. There was a wheelchair, and the hirelings lifted the Picker into it.

'These guards are here in case your rangers attack us,' the Picker said. 'We have pistols.'

Pistols and the ammunition for them – if there was any – were expensive. Was she supposed to be impressed by the wealth of this chief?

'Follow,' called the Picker.

The hirelings were an escort for the Picker, not her. She

walked behind as they wheeled the chair across the paved quay to the funicular station. It was high tide, about quarter-past six.

The hirelings took the Picker into the car. She thought it would be fun to ascend in it – just like being on the tram on Wallburgh esplanade – but not then, not with the hirelings there. She bounded up the steps alongside the funicular.

Perhaps they were taking her to accommodation in the burgh awaiting fair weather for sailing?

At the top station, she found the lad from the tramper was waiting, holding a lamp. He stared at her, and she at him.

'I'm to escort you,' he said curtly.

'Where to?' she asked.

'Just here,' he said vaguely. 'I was right – you're a witch.'

'No, I'm not,' she replied.

'You are. How did you climb those steps without a lamp to see by?'

'There's a handrail, isn't there? You could do it if you tried. What's your name?' she asked.

'Why do you want to know?'

'So I can cast a spell on you.'

'Bjan.'

'I mean this nicely, Bjan. Is your dad alright? Will his leg mend?'

'Yes, he's alright.'

'Good. I hope you'll both get your silver.'

'Maybe. Your name's Alfren, isn't it?'

'Yes. Also, the Witch of Dingle Lane.'

'Thought so.'

The lad was wary of her, not frightened, that was all.

The car arrived at the top station and the hireling escort wheeled the Picker onto the main street. The street was cobbled, the surface bumpy. The hirelings fitted shafts to the wheelchair, lifted it and the four of them carried the

Picker up the street, about 70 yards along a narrow lane to a big square, probably the burgh's main square. They turned off along a wide lane that opened out to a courtyard and approached a large door set in a high wall. A wicket, a small door set in the larger one, was opened from inside and they stepped through. She and Bjan followed the Picker and his hirelings into a short passage that led to a well-lit and enormous hall. Alfren had seen only one such large indoor space, in the Burgh Hall at Wallburgh, but this was higher and with galleries all around. She saw several figures on all levels looking over. The hirelings lowered the chair and the Picker wheeled himself around on the wooden floor to face her.

'The seer Alfren,' he said. 'You are our guest here ... at the keep.'

'This is it? Clever rogues!' she realised.

They had deceived her, hadn't they?

She looked at the Picker for triumph on his face, but there was only satisfaction. Bjan looked sullen. The hirelings turned away with the Picker, then Bjan too.

They must have kept her on the boat overnight simply to check no one had followed them and to be sure of the whereabouts of the rangers.

From the shadows under the galleries, a fellow in a dark uniform dress stepped forward, perhaps a gaoler, although she had a kindly expression.

'Follow me, Miss Alfren.'

The fellow led the way to a corner of the hall, under the galleries, to a spiral stone stairwell. They climbed to the first level and walked along a gallery with a view over the hall on one side and several closed doors on the other. The fellow stopped and turned to her.

'This is your room. The key's on the inside, in the lock. Sorry there's no window, but that way it's not so cold. There's a bite to eat, and a wash jug and bowl there. Latrines are along the gallery. I'm Nurse Tulla, the children's steward. They rise at six. I'll be along in half an hour to take you to them.'

'The children?' she asked in surprise.

'Yes, of course. You're the new nanny, aren't you?' The nurse appraised her. 'You won't need all those arms about you. Look at you – knives and everything. It must be rough where you come from. Don't dither.'

The nurse left her.

Alfren opened the door and stepped in the room. She could have screamed! They were here and she had found them. She wanted to tell Liffet and Faran, but she daren't. How could she warn the rangers? And yet, flooding her with relief, Nurse Tulla had said she would see the children just as they rose for the day.

The slam hit her. She fell onto the bed and gripped the mattress. She tumbled through the waves and they tossed her wickedly. She was upside down and falling head over heels, spinning without end. 'Alright, what is it?' she cried. 'Yes, the children ... only a short time.' The spinning and falling stopped.

After a moment, she stood up slowly.

She was probably going mad.

There were woollen tunic and trousers hanging on a hook on the wall, and soft boots by the door. She changed out of her wind suit and hung it to air, then slid her weapons under the bed. A guard would search for them and remove them surely.

She sat to wait. How were the children? Would they be healthy? How many? How old?

Was she free to leave the keep? Not likely, or only under escort. Could she send to Liffy when she stepped outside the keep? Would the Picker know she had sent? Could she send to Liffy in a focused way, so that her send was not detected? The point was, if she did, could she control the actions of the rangers so as not to endanger not only themselves but also her quest to rescue the children?

There was a knock on the door and she sprang up to open it.

'Miss!'

There was a young girl about eight-years old dressed in a plain fawn gown.

'Nurse sent me. You are to follow me please, miss.'

'Thank you,' Alfren said. 'Who are you?'

'Please miss, I'm Star. Me and the other orphans have special names. I like my name.'

'Yes, it's lovely.'

Alfren followed Star to the stairwell. They descended two floors and walked along a passageway.

'These are the dormitories miss, and there's the refectory. Please wait here, miss.'

Alfren entered a stone-vaulted refectory lit by gas lamps. At one end was a kitchen stove where a woman in a grey dress stirred an iron pot.

'You're new, darling. Tea for you?'

'Thank you. I've just arrived.'

'Stay the right side of the chief, lass, and you'll do alright.'

'I will, thanks.'

She collected a hot cup of tea and sat down to wait.

The first few children dressed in long fawn gowns entered and stared at her.

Here they were at last.

They looked pale and glum, but healthy. They collected bowls of porage and plates of oat cakes and cheese. She smiled and said, 'Good morning,' and the boldest of the young ones came to sit with her. The older ones – around the same age as her – sat apart. Although she had many questions to ask them, the youngest children were the ones to begin, so she answered.

'I come from Wallburgh, it's a big burgh on this island.

'I've always had long hair.

'I'm not too thin really. Porage is my favourite.

'Yes, I'm here to tell you stories.

'Yes, I hope we can play in the cloister later, but I think the high wind will last all day.

'My best friend is called Liffet.

'No, I'm prettier.

'I have another friend called Faran. Yes, she's quite pretty.

'No, I don't have a boyfriend.

'No, I'm not married.

'Yes, I can sing. Yes, let's.

'I like to play *Catch You*, with a scarf over my eyes so I can't see.'

Except she cheated at that game.

Nurse Tulla entered. 'That's the last of them, plus two in the infirmary; twenty-three in all. Two will be leaving us soon.'

'Oh, where will they go?' Alfren asked.

'To live and work in the burgh. They're old enough.'

'Oh, I see. Was Bjan here once?'

'You've met him? Yes, he was, before he went to live with his stepdad.'

Alfren would have liked to ask about Zal too.

She got to know the children as they played and took their lessons.

She enjoyed that morning. She felt drawn to the tenderness and innocence of their minds – she wouldn't let go of them.

Rooftop

Jin

Jin was cooped up at the base and wished he was at the ketch with Tans. Acting as though she was a seaman ranger, Tans walked between harbour and base freely but didn't veer from the main street and square so as not to alarm whoever was watching and thus bring out the guard. They had only to put one foot wrong and they could be locked up. Falt had sketched a map of Landing on the galley table. Handar and Falt had discussed escape or sending one of them to raise the alarm. Jin hoped it wouldn't be him. Here was where the action would play out. It would be days before relief arrived. Besides, Landing was impregnable and escape seemed just as impossible. If they tried to run the harbour mouth in the ketch, the guard would raise the chains across the entrance. Could they bribe the guard? Could the master of the ketch pass under sail through the narrow harbour mouth in this wind?

Something had put Handar on edge. She had told Jin she supposed it was a matter of hours, no more than a day, before the guard came for them.

Tans came in and Handar called the squad together.

'Ma'am, I've been talking with Scout Liffet and Faran Steersman from the Western Isles. Faran says that Alfren is in the keep and has seen the kidnapped children. When I asked how she knew, she said she's a mystic and knows Alfren's thoughts.'

Falt nodded.

'Can that be right?' asked Tans.

Falt shrugged to say maybe so.

'Ma'am, they say we should wait. She says Alfren is close to finding out something and not to worry – the situation will change and soon. Faran said if we do nothing then Alfren will make sure we are safe from arrest.'

'That's reassuring to hear,' said Handar. 'I wish I could believe it.'

Jin sat down to salvage what parts he could from the radio set. After dismantling it, he straightened the frame and checked circuits and windings for continuity. Where there were breaks, he soldered repairs. He thought about the aerial; he should check it. He climbed into the attic and opened a hatch that let out onto the roof. The wind pulled heavily at the hatch.

The roof was made from planks of solid wood overlaid with tin sheet which made it a strong construction. Just as in Wallburgh, surely that meant that roofs could withstand folk walking on and crossing them. Jin climbed out and peered over the ridge of the roof into the square. He could see what must be the keep too. The small burgh was really an entire castle, with buildings packed together within the curtain wall. It should be possible to move over and between rooftops. He had an idea.

Back down at ground level, he crossed the yard towards the store and stopped, thought a little, and looked around. It was slightly odd. There was a circular stone slab in the centre of the yard much like the grindstone from a grain mill and set into it there was an ornate bronze disc two feet in diameter. He looked closely – it was a sundial. The passage of feet and hooves had worn at the design cast onto the surface, and there was an offset hole for a peg which would cast a shadow to show the time from the scale. That was interesting: Jin realised the sun would light the yard only at its highest in summer, if at all. The sundial must have another purpose.

But that wasn't all that was odd – it was the yard, which was square and precise. The same went for the main square, he thought, and that was a generous size. Packed-tight houses that seemed to compete for space, yet why hadn't they built on the squares?

'You alright there, Jinny? Lost something?' asked Tans, who was about to return to the harbour.

'Yes. Tans, listen a moment, will you?'

'Go on.'

'We're in Landing, right? They say Landing was the first burgh to be built after the Extinction.'

'Yes, it's the oldest continually occupied burgh. Shame it's so grim.'

'It has seen some destruction then, from storms.'

'Certainly.'

'And it's been rebuilt in a random way, judging by the buildings, except for our base, the old treasury.'

'Yes, I guess there were one or two storms up to a rip storm at force 14 that tore the place down.'

'And they kept this yard, maybe others too, and the main square, and didn't build over them.'

'It seems so.'

'The folk survived.'

'Yes.'

'It's a yard with a very big sundial plate.'

'Oh, let's have a look shall we. Do you want to get a crowbar? I'll fetch Han and Falt.'

Jin levered up the sundial. As he had guessed, it was hinged and folded back. He sat on the lip of the hole, found footholds and lowered himself down a twenty-foot-deep tube into a stone-lined narrow passage. He was concerned about foul air, but there was a draught. Brilliant, he thought. Why should the rangers escape from Landing when they could hide down here? He turned to a door, which he pushed at. It swung easily to reveal a large stone underground vault with an arched roof. It was dry. During the Extinction folk had constructed this shelter under the yard, he realised with appreciation for their forethought and industry. They could have taken sanctuary here the instant a storm struck. It might destroy their houses, but folk would survive. Had Landing folk forgotten this was here? Were there other refuges, he wondered?

That afternoon, he put in a request to Handar. She agreed after specifying certain precautions. He and Tans collected a few items from the store and made ready. Tans dressed in her storm suit.

Handar said she would go to see the guard that day to press their captain into a frank discussion about his loyalty.

Jin opened the hatch, climbed out onto the roof and Tans followed. The houses were so close together that no one below could see them should they look up. At a distance he saw no guards on the castle curtain wall or on the roof of the keep. Why would there be? Just as at Wallburgh, guards were few and were required only at the gatehouse and the harbour.

At roof level, they made their way up the main street and crossed where a building spanned the street. They waited for Falt who stood below to give them a nod when clear. From there it should be easy-going to the keep although wind gusts and rain showers were heavy, and they had to pay heed to their balance. They climbed up and over roofs, holding onto the ridge like a rail, hopping from one roof to the next over narrow passageways below.

At a step between two buildings they had a view of the courtyard before the door to the keep, but out of sight of the arrow slits. They watched the comings and goings through the wicket. Jin made mental notes. Folk entering showed a token to the guard, gave their name and the guard called out the number. He supposed that just inside the wicket someone checked and made an entry in a log.

He sensed someone close by. He started with surprise and looked to his side.

'Would you like some soup, Jin?'

It was Liffet.

'How the ...?'

He looked behind to see Tans sitting in a fold of the roof sipping from a flask.

'Yes, thanks, I would.'

'What are you watching for?' asked Liffet.

'To see who passes into the keep.'

'Are those pitons in your bag?' she asked.

'Yes.'

He had found steel pitons in the stores; pegs that he could hammer between stones to allow him to scale the curtain wall to the battlement.

'What are you doing here, Liffet?'

'Same as you. I came to see the keep. I thought it would be best to see Ally today. I'm sure she's alright – if she wasn't, she would let me know. Anyway, I wanted to check.'

'Right. How will you get into the keep?'

'Through the wicket, like everyone else,' she said plainly.

'Do you have a token?'

'Yes.'

'Who from?'

'The skipper's daughter.'

'Which skipper?'

'The one on the tramper we sank. Is there another skipper?' she asked.

'Wasn't he upset because you sank his boat?'

'Yes, and because I threatened to kill him,' she said.

He looked behind at Tans, who waved.

'Do you know where Alfren is? I mean, I know she's in the keep, but whereabouts?'

'First-floor gallery, north side.'

'Faran knows somehow?'

'Yes. Keep it simple. That's what they told me in training.'

'You know, Liffet,' he turned to resume his observation of the keep, 'we should let Handar know. We don't want you held hostage too ... Liffet?'

She had gone.

He turned to Tans, who shrugged.

Visionary

Alfren

Bjan came to the schoolroom and asked Alfren to follow him. She smiled at Blossom, a child she was helping with spelling, although she felt some trepidation; after all, this would likely be an introduction to the chief. Bjan led her to the ground floor, across the Great Hall and through a large door to a cloister; an open space with a rectangular lawn, a canopy and a walkway all around – a shelter from wind and rain. Even on the windiest days it would be pleasant here outside the confines of the keep. No wonder the children asked to play there. In the far wall was a locked door that Bjan opened from a bunch of keys. There was an unlit passage. Bjan held a gas lamp and sparked it. Alfren guessed this passed within the curtain wall of the castle.

They descended steep steps to a small door which Bjan held open to allow her through then closed it behind them both. She could hear the boom and roar of wind and sea. Bjan opened a second door and she was blown back. He stepped out, she pulled herself through and found a handhold on the rock face. She saw she was on a ledge above a cliff, the sea breaking on rocks far below. Clad in only her tunic, she felt chilled. There was no handrail and the ledge was narrow, wet rock. Bjan locked the door and strode off along the ledge. She followed but was pushed about. She looked up to see the sheer curtain wall and down to a deep grey-green sea. Ahead was a corner in the wall and a tower above. Bjan waited at an open door. The wind gusted; she had to face the rock and grip with both hands. Just inside, there was shelter at last. Before her was a staircase. Loud booms echoed round the stonework. As she climbed, she glimpsed the curtain wall and pounding sea through an arrow slit. She guessed they were almost at the top when Bjan stepped onto a landing where he unlocked and opened another door. He gestured she should enter a large cell and locked the door behind her.

She was alone.

Patterned tapestries lined the cell walls. There was a grand desk and chair and before it a small chair, intended for her she supposed, all set on a large rug. A blackened fireplace contained a smouldering peat fire. She stood near the hearth to warm up.

She needed a strategy for the negotiation and list of her bargaining points. She needed to know what the chief wanted. She was unprepared.

She jumped when she heard his voice.

'The seer Alfren.'

A large fellow in robes appeared from behind a tapestry.

'Marine Alfren of the Sealand Rangers, if you please, sir,' she replied.

This could be only the chief. He held a tapestry open for his assistant who emerged carrying a leather case, then he crossed the room to take his place behind the desk. A felt cap was tied under his chin so that she saw only a big face of heavy bone, with bold, open grey eyes.

'You may call me Chief. I am the visionary. Let us be polite and open with one another. Do sit. May I address you as Alfren?'

She nodded.

The assistant laid the case on the desk and removed the lid, then took a curved steel rod, inserted it upright and attached a pendulum so that a pointer hung over the centre. It was probably a device to test her. She bristled at the assumption and prepared to be indignant.

'Tell me, what happened to Zal,' the chief instructed.

'I don't want to tell you anything that could lead to harm for my friends, the rangers and me,' she replied. 'I believe Zal is safe and well. I hope she'll get better soon.'

'Good news, indeed. If my hirelings hurt her, they will be punished. And your friend, Scout Liffet?'

'Also safe.'

What was the point in telling him? He wanted to know their whereabouts so he could hold them hostage to her good behaviour and compliance, just as the Picker had threatened the rangers with harm.

She looked into her lap and wondered where to start.

'I am pleased your friends are safe,' said the chief. 'I will begin by explaining matters to avoid misunderstanding. I know about you: you have left a trail of clues as to your nature and abilities. You know little or nothing about me, so let me make redress. I look forward to a long, profitable collaboration with you. You have agreed to a negotiation and that is a good, first step.'

She nodded. His voice was calm but there was an underlying urgency. He was convinced of something and had little time to explain it. She didn't wait for him to start.

'I'm not a seer, not the sort you want.'

'There have always been seers, throughout time, but some of them never knew that's what they were,' he responded irritably. 'Some had an inkling; some could do a few tricks with their friends. They kept themselves hidden. Did you know that?'

'No.'

Although that described her exactly, didn't it?

'There were seers before the Extinction and after,' the chief stated.

'Oh?'

'What do you know of the Extinction?'

'A lot of people died suddenly and with them went their settlements,' she said.

What did this have to do with a negotiation? Talk of the Extinction was boring; too many folk rambled on about it.

'That is mistaken. The Last People died slowly and horribly from starvation, conflicts, and poisoning from their own pollution. That's the legacy of their civilisation – and I've seen lands we could not live in. Their *civilisation* caused the Extinction.'

'I know about pollution,' Alfren replied. 'Knowledge of chemistry and technologies for filtering water will help us.'

'Technologies? The Last People were proud of their technology,' the chief said dismissively. 'Technology was all they knew. There were wars, starvation, disease, poverty, exploitation ... a needless loss of life every day, in numbers we cannot imagine – all preventable. Theirs was a stupid, wasteful civilisation. They put more energy into controlling each other than anything else - whilst they ignored the world about them. That was the cause of their fate.'

He was full of contempt.

'When they realised they were dying, it was too late. They thought their technology could save them, but it was a deceit – they kept on poisoning themselves. Then they all died.'

'It's passed,' Alfren said. 'We can't change what happened. We must find a way on, without raiding or kidnapping.'

This wasn't a negotiation; it was pointless and just an argument.

'Yes, that would be ideal; an end to all this nonsense.'

She was surprised. Did the chief agree with her?

But then he asked scathingly, 'Really though, do you think folk care enough to change? Do you know what happened long ago? I've read the texts from those times. A few folk, those that had insight and intelligence, warned of the Extinction long before it occurred. The Last People ignored them. Don't you see? They received warning in good time, yet they carried on regardless. They didn't change their ways, even to save themselves.'

The chief softened his voice.

'Don't you want folk-kind to live? Don't you want your family and friends to live?'

'Yes, all folk.'

She knew she was sulking. The chief was boring.

He paused, then spoke up firmly. 'We need a seer, and now. Only a seer can tell us what will happen and when. A seer sees the latency, the build-up of forces that could sweep us away.'

'Do you mean storms? Or something else? Storms are just storms; there's nothing special about storms,' she said.

She was frustrated.

She added, 'You and others like the fortune-tellers on the market street have to put the Extinction and fear of what may come behind you. There is pollution in the world and that's what we should worry about. Maybe the storms released the pollution at the Extinction. No one knows. But the Extinction is behind us – mystery over.'

Her voice rose.

'Let me tell you, the world is not a better place when you kidnap children! How dare you! I will tear down your keep which is a prison for frightened children. They are not yours to take. I will ...'

The wave slammed into her and tossed her through the air. She reached out, but there was nothing to hold onto.

She spun and fell and felt the slam again, throwing her like a plaything. There was no escape. She tried to breathe and she flailed. Hands lifted her as she collapsed. She heard a voice calling, 'Let it run, Alfren!'

She couldn't escape so allowed it and went to the only place that was safe – her mind. Immediately she saw vast waves, new to her in their expanse. She settled, in awe of them and floated among great, colourful waves as they towered and crashed. Behind them came more waves. She marvelled at the whirling, great mass of them. Slowly, she withdrew. She was sitting on the chair; there were hands on the sides of her shoulders in support – the assistant's hands. The chief stared at her, then nodded at the fellow.

'Here's a towel, dear, to wipe your eyes,' said the assistant.

She realised she had been crying, not from sadness but simply from the turmoil of the waves.

'A drink of water too?'

'Yes, please,' she said, and took a draught from a mug offered.

'We'll take tea,' said the chief.

The assistant went to one wall of the cell where Alfren heard the creak of a gas tap and the snap of a spark to a light a gas stove.

'Alfren,' said the chief, 'after the seizure, you were in a trance for an hour.'

'Oh?'

That was a long time. She knew she had lost time when with the waves before, sometimes for hours, but she felt she had been away for a short time only, although she realised these new waves were vast and probably had taken her much longer to explore.

'I suppose that to you it seemed only a moment. Bring your chair to the desk. I will explain this device to you.'

She felt a little wobbly, otherwise her mind was clear, and her strength was fine.

The chief waited for her. She shuffled up to look closely. In the case there was a patterned disc, like an ornate clock face.

'I should tell you; I claimed this keep in a contest with a client when I was young. I was able to draw good hirelings to me, keen for silver. I was successful and now I have great wealth. One day, I came across a mystic. He told me heard the waves but could not navigate their way. I came across learned folk with an interest in the Extinction who hoarded old texts. I took them – a *raider*, as you would call me, takes what he wants. In time, wealth and adventure were not all I sought. I taught myself the skills of a scryer. Thus, I read the clouds and the winds, migrations and seasons, currents, tides and swells. One hour, one day, one year ... there are always signs.

'Long ago I traded for this device before you on the desk. It took many hours to deduce how it works.'

The assistant brought tea and oatcakes.

'Thank you,' Alfren said and picked a handful of biscuits to munch on. She wasn't listening to the chief. The disc was ornate, containing bands of concentric circles. There was a ring on the outside marked with the points of the compass, and inside that another ring with the phases of the moon. Within that was a ring engraved with the rain, folds of clouds and the sun. There was a wide ring next with four quadrants to it: one contained an engraving of a whale; the next, a lighthouse; then, a castle; and a planet. On the next ring there were several symbols like a writing, swirls and shapes, and on the next too. In the centre was an engraving of a sundial. Alfren heard ticking and leaned closer. The pendulum started to swing; not simply side to side but round, in an oval and off-centre. It swung round

the castle quadrant, back to the centre of the plate, and round again.

'Oh!' Alfren leaned back, and the pendulum came to rest.

'Those are your mind waves, Alfren. The castle quadrant represents folk in a settlement, which reveals your motivation.'

She was intrigued but annoyed that the chief could use the device to read her mind. She crunched on her biscuits.

'What's it called?'

'I call it a wave assayer.'

'What do you know about waves?' she asked.

'There are energies in all matter and living things - which radiate waves. Or, put another way, waves condense into energies we interpret as *life*.'

'Did the device do anything when I fell over?'

'Yes. It showed a great deal of energy in the planet quadrant, which means our Earth is trying to communicate with you.'

'I didn't hear Earth. Earth doesn't say anything.' She had never heard 'Earth' waves.

'Have the waves overcome you like that before?'

The answer was 'yes', recently and for the first time when she was on the shingle beach.

'Not like that.'

She thought they had spent too long in the chief's cell and not getting anywhere. The chief wasn't so overbearing; she was emboldened.

'Sir, I'm here to negotiate in cordial terms the immediate release of the children into the care of the rangers. Also, before we start, you must withdraw all threat to the rangers. Also, I should be free to meet with the rangers to take advice.'

The chief regarded her.

'I will agree to your demands on condition that first you submit to a test with this device. No harm will come to you.

Until then, my original conditions remain. You must not contact your rangers. I propose to carry out the test this evening. You have the afternoon to prepare. I shall see you before sunset, at seven o'clock.'

He stood. 'Alfren, it matters not to me that you deny you are a seer. What matters is you could save us all.'

He and his assistant slipped behind the tapestry and were gone.

She pocketed more biscuits and waited. The door opened and Bjan summoned her. The return along the narrow ledge in the high wind was just as treacherous as earlier.

Liffet

In the Great Hall, Bjan left Alfren on her own. There were three galleries high above her. She sat on a bench and watched folk come and go: hirelings, sailors, tradesmen, clerks and scribes. It dawned on her that this was the place where deals were made for raids around the League. No doubt the raids were underwritten by the chief. Surely they plotted how to dodge the customs, how to extort silver from vulnerable settlements. They conspired and arranged everything in this keep at Landing, in the badland on Sealand.

Until then, her world had been the Watch. Raiders had been their foe, their character unknown to her. There, in the keep, raiders were close, all around, and they blended in like Landers. How much influence had they in Wallburgh?

Who could she trust and how far?

The chief must have given her free run of the keep to see if she was tempted by the raider life. The intent was that she would be drawn to help with the care of the children and want to stay. The chief intended she should use the wave assayer in some way to examine energies – the waves she saw. He meant she would be a trusted aid to a wealthy chief and intended to impress on her that she could ask for anything she wanted.

They meant to lure her to accept a life at the keep.

Alfren climbed the stairs to her room. Everything there was as she had left it that morning; the chief didn't trust her, she was sure, but he wouldn't show that by searching her room. She meant to go and see the children but there was something on her mind. She sat on her bed and allowed the waves to wash over her and went to the vast waves she had seen in the chief's cell. She had never seen the like of them before. She didn't know what they were trying to tell her, if anything. Waves spoke of seasons and migrations, heaving seas and storms. There were folk waves, too many to know well, except for Liffet and Faran. These were the new Earth waves. She rolled around them, but they were so big she hopped from one to the other, going up then down. There seemed no limit. Their strength had grown in the hours since the tower. They were building up. For what? She let them go. There had been no slam this time. These Earth waves hadn't overpowered her then because she had accepted them and listened.

Just at that moment she sensed Liffet was near. She ran to the door and opened it to look along the gallery. A figure approached on all fours, hidden from the hall by the parapet.

'Liffy!' she called softly.

'Is anyone watching?' whispered her friend.

'Probably, but I don't think it'll matter if they see you.'

'Why not?'

'I'll explain.'

Liffet crawled into the room and Alfren shut the door. They sat together on the bed.

'I'm a scullery maid, do you see?' said Liffet.

'You, in a kitchen? Not in a thousand storms. How's Zal?'

'Better. Awake and taking food.'

'Rangers?'

'On the rooftops last time I saw them. Jin was making ready to climb the battlement.'

'That could be good. Liffy, listen, there are new waves, and this chief wants me to tell him more about them. I think it would be good to know. They're strong and I felt them first at the beach. I have to go to his cell at seven o'clock. Will you come?'

'Yes, alright.'

'I have to do what he wants first. He says we'll negotiate afterwards. I wasn't any good at dealing with him. Anyway, that's one of the reasons you should be there too. Also, he has this device he calls the wave assayer, which sort of shows which waves I'm with when I see them. It's beautifully made. You'll see it. The path to the tower is a slippery ledge, exposed to the wind. You've got your suit on underneath all that, haven't you?'

'Yes. I'm too warm.'

'Take off your suit. We'll go to see the children.'

Alfren explained to Nurse Tulla that Liffet was a trustworthy friend, and that afternoon they took the children to the cloister. She told the older children about herself and Liffet growing up in Wallburgh. She told them about her work monitoring the water supply, and how she had trained as a watchman. One lad pointed out the keep didn't need watchtowers. He said they ate fish landed in the harbour and lamb brought by farmers. They had all they needed and the keep had always protected the west.

Really, had it – or had the keep exploited the land?

She realised those were provisions traded at a price set by the chief for his profit, and his hirelings made certain no one opposed him. The lad said he would work for the chief one day and would be a great dealmaker.

She and the older girls played with the youngest

ones. Her heart trembled for them; they seemed dull. Liffet entertained the middle-years children performing handstands and cartwheels. They played ball and chase and whenever Liffet pretended to fall over they jumped on her for fun.

They left for dinner in the refectory. Afterwards, she and Liffet bade goodnight to the children who were excited the nurse said and needed to calm before bedtime.

'Still thinking about those new waves?' asked Liffet as they climbed the stairs to the gallery.

'Yes. They're not so bad: they're like the others, just from a new place. You know, Liffy, I should listen and find their message ... if there is one, I mean.'

'I'd say beware, as they might harm you.'

'Yes, they're strong.'

'Though, if you don't listen to them, they slam you and you become all at sea.'

'That's right.'

They changed into their suits. Liffet wore the knives that Alfren had taken from the scavengers at the cove, then they waited in the Great Hall. The hirelings and other folk noticed them immediately and kept away.

'The chief doesn't live in the keep,' Alfren explained. 'He has his own stronghold: a new tower. He doesn't trust me with the main entrance, which I suppose is secret. We have to use the *windy way*.'

Wave Assayer

Bjan appeared at the door to the cloister. He had a look of surprise when he saw Liffet. They followed him. Just as earlier that day, he locked and unlocked doors using a bunch of keys.

Alfren was steady on the windy way this time because her boots gripped the slippery ledge.

'Hold on a moment!' she called.

Bjan and Liffet stopped to wait. In the dim light, she looked down at the deep green sea over 200 feet below. The tide would ebb that evening and although waves spilled over rock, this was a lee shore and conditions were not so rough.

'No way to escape,' called Bjan.

They followed him to the tower where they climbed the stairwell to the chief's cell. Bjan closed and locked the door behind them.

The wave assayer was open on the desk. She and Liffet puzzled over it. She sent a little message to say, 'Cold room, isn't it?' to Liffet, and the pendulum swung over the castle.

'What does that mean?' asked her friend.

'I think the whale must represent life and nature; the lighthouse is the sun raising the wind over the sea; the castle is all individuals living together in settlements. But the planet, that's supposed to be the Earth waves which are the ones I didn't know about. When I used waves to send just now, that's why the pendulum moved over the castle.'

'Oh, that's clever. We should nick it.'

'Yes.'

The chief entered followed this time by the Picker and then the assistant as before.

'Ah, this is a surprise,' exclaimed the chief. 'This must be ...'

'Yes, it is, sir,' said the Picker.

'Scout Liffet. You are welcome. Alfren, your guest is important to us. I hope we can make Scout Liffet comfortable.'

Liffet spoke, 'Hello, mister.' She ignored the Picker.

'Shall we begin?'

The chief sat with the Picker standing at his side and the assistant seated behind. Alfren took her place.

'Alfren,' said the chief, 'as I said earlier, I am a scryer. I have read the signs. In my calculations, I input the sway given to me by the children. I trust you found them well looked after. By sway, I mean their sense of the waves. As a result, I have deduced we are about to reach a critical point in the Extinction. But I lack clarity and a seer must guide us. Your ability to see the waves is extraordinary.'

'I want nothing to do with the Extinction,' Alfren said. 'I told you; it's over.'

It was maddening. Even Jin had mentioned the Extinction. Folk had to forget about it. The Extinction wasn't the problem, pollution was. Water was tainted.

'Before the test,' replied the chief, 'you should know what Earth may be telling us. Pollution caused the Extinction and Earth resents that.'

Oh? She nodded. She was willing to listen where it concerned pollution.

'The sun has shone on our Earth, and the living world has had an abundance of life over vast numbers of our lifetimes and for aeons before. There was so much sunlight and warmth that the world created stores of energy, trapped in oil and coal. The sun provided more than enough energy for life, even when the population of the Last People overran the world. There were millions upon millions of people, Alfren, not the few thousands of folk in the League. Foolishly, the Last People relied on energy stored by the world, not that which was given freely by the sun. They burned vast amounts of fuel in just a few lifetimes and released noxious fumes. The world was resilient. Earth, which is, I believe, the intelligence that guides the world, shifted energies. The seas moved, the clouds cleared, the land grew warmer. Earth helped to maintain the equilibrium in the world, albeit poisoned with fumes. Then, one day, the world's resilience collapsed. Earth could no longer guide or constrain the world, and the world's climate buckled, and the weather ran wild.'

The chief had removed his gaze from her and was looking within his own mind.

'Earth must help the world release energy to a level much lower than at the Extinction. Then, one day, when the energy is spent and the pollution absorbed, there will be a new steady climate, not chaos, in the world.'

Alfren was silent. It seemed to explain a lot. The chief had said Earth had made a clean world for the Last People to live in, but the Last People had polluted it and Earth had been unable to do anything about it.

Earth waves weren't known to her until they had slammed her. It could be true that some of the Last People could have known about them at the Extinction.

Seers, the chief had said.

Waves flooded her then – all waves, and without a slam. She floated among them. She found Liffet's waves and knew

286

she could trust Liffet to keep her safe. She heard Liffet speak, telling the chief not to interfere.

She had to admit the chief was right: Earth waves were vast and beautiful; they wrapped around all other waves. To the Earth, life itself was a wave, not simply each animal or plant – those things that came and went – but the energy of life. This was a new idea to her; Earth seemed concerned for life, but not necessarily for folk. That was the message.

'I see the message.'

Earth wanted to preserve life in the world, any life. Yet, Earth saw the world was hurt and that might bring about a new Extinction that could finish life altogether. There it was, the Earth's intent – save life.

Why then? Why the urgency? She had seen it in Earth waves. Even the chief knew it. She shifted to the waves she knew: wind waves. It was a waxing quarter moon that day. The winds flew over her land. All was well: high wind-force 7. She dived into the waves and moved forward, feeling the draw of wind, the blows, rising heat and cyclones. She counted the tides and watched the winds shift, rise and fall. She had never explored so far ahead: so many tides, so many days of a growing, gibbous moon. The autumn equinox passed. A day later there was a spring tide at a new moon.

She leaned forward in her chair and groaned.

The coming storm was enormous. It was too big; she couldn't see all of it. Storm waves swamped her mind. It was overwhelming and she was about to give up, then had an idea. She sought Earth waves and brought along her sense of the storm waves she had seen, until she encountered Earth's vibrations – memories of life lost – which told her Earth had felt this storm a few times.

Had she just questioned Earth and received a reply from the waves? Did this mean the Earth knew her? She let the waves ripple and ebb away.

She knew. She sat straight and opened her eyes. The cell was dim and quiet. The gas lamps hissed and spat. The pendulum on the wave assayer swung gently. The chief stared at her, frowning. She turned to check on Liffet whose face was straight and calm.

'What we must do is tell folk,' she said, quietly. 'In eight days, at the new moon, there will be a spring tide and a high storm – a rip storm-force 14. As you know, any living thing in the path of a rip will perish. We must sound the alarm.'

'Well done,' said the chief. 'Don't you see? You have saved us. We will make preparations, just as you say.'

'Release the children to me.'

The chief looked at her. 'You will be safest with the children here in the keep. You can trust me to manage this, for the good of folk-kind.'

He dissembled!

'I want to leave with the children right away!'

She was alarmed. The chief had agreed to negotiation. She saw he had planned to deceive her. She had to release the children from imprisonment and warn Sealand of the rip storm, but the chief wanted to keep secret the news. Many folk could die.

She wanted to fly at the fellow in a rage.

The chief nodded to the Picker who rose to slip behind the tapestry.

'Calm, Alfren. I will look after you and your friends. You will survive the storm with the children, I promise. I have planned carefully. We are survivors, you and me.

'At times like this, when you feel your friends are threatened, my folk fear you will shriek with your mind. My hirelings told me it is unendurable. You cannot shriek because I have promised to guarantee the safety of those you care for.'

She saw the Picker appear and behind him came two

hirelings gripping a woman in a ranger storm suit, a hood over her head.

Handar.

The hirelings removed the hood. Handar took in the scene in the cell.

'Alfren? Scout Liffet!'

'Lieutenant,' said the chief, 'I am sorry to inconvenience you. I am the Chief, and my role is that of visionary. Your ranger, the seer Alfren, has foreseen a rip storm-force 14 at the full moon in eight days. We will have her to thank for warning us. You will remain here safe under my protection.'

'Sir,' replied Handar, 'rangers do not require your protection. I can add that, in due course, rangers will purge the guard who today have informed me of your influence. You do not have authority here.'

The chief turned to the Picker and the hirelings. He spoke abruptly.

'Hold them in gaol. Make certain it is secure. Make ready to sail. We have business abroad.'

The chief stood and made to leave.

'Marine Alfren,' called Handar calmly. 'Get us out of here. That's an order.'

'Yes, ma'am,' she replied.

Children

The chief turned to look at Alfren. She knew why. Could she send out a shriek that would disarm them all? No, she didn't know how. She remained seated because she had sent to Liffet to say 'Now!'

Liffet reached behind a tapestry, found the gas tap that supplied the lamps and closed it. The light faded in the wall lamps almost immediately. The cell was in darkness. Within a few seconds, the two hirelings had sparked their tinderboxes.

Handar, still bound, shoved one of them over.

The chief shouted, 'Bring aid!'

Alfren bolted from her chair to run behind the tapestry. She found the door, pulled it closed, and barred it. Hands thumped on the other side. In the darkness, she saw Liffet count out the steps over to the chair where she had sat. Alfren made for the desk and on the way tripped and kicked the second hireling; he was almost too big and heavy to unbalance, but when he did fall, he made a big thump. She kicked away his tinderbox, took hold of Handar and guided her to the chair. Liffet took the small knife from her chest harness and cut the bindings from Handar.

Alfren pulled the wave assayer device towards her,

dismantled it and folded it shut.

'Alfren,' called the chief, 'you can't save everyone. There are too many. If you try, no one will survive. Think on that!'

'Don't come after us. If you send your hirelings, I will turn them on you!'

She hoped that sounded convincing.

'Everyone in this cell, stand still!' called Handar. 'You sir, the Chief, under the regulations of the land I should arrest you. However, events are at large, and you have many hirelings. You may withdraw. If you cross my path and prevent me from carrying out my duty, I will have the right to incapacitate you. The regulations permit me because I have given you fair warning.'

'I cannot control all my followers,' the chief replied.

Alfren heard calculation in his voice. She saw a hireling raise his arm. She jumped, caught his arm and a pistol fired. He had aimed at Handar's voice.

Suddenly, the chief yelped. 'I've been stabbed!' he cried.

'That was me,' called Liffet from beside Handar. In the dark, Liffet had guessed where he stood, jumped silently onto the desk, pricked the fellow in the upper arm and hopped off.

'I'm militia. We don't do chat and fair warning. Mister, when this is over, watch out for me.'

Alfren groped around on the floor and collected pistols from both hirelings, then handed them to Handar who tucked them away in her webbing.

She took Liffet's hand and her friend held Handar.

'Lead on, Ally.'

She pulled the two Landers away, found Bjan's waves, and sent a feeling of release so that he should unlock and open the door. They slipped out into the stairwell.

'Thank you, Bjan,' she said.

By his lamplight, he looked downcast.

'Yes, well ...'

'Please, lock the door and come with us. Thanks for staying outside when you heard the chief.'

He locked the door. 'That's alright. What next?'

'We'd like you with us,' she said.

By lamplight, the company made their way down the stairs and out onto the windy way. Alfren was in front and ran ahead, well-balanced on the rock ledge, she noticed. At the door to the keep, she felt the presence of someone familiar. She looked up.

'Jin!' she called.

Jin

Jin looked over the parapet into the darkness below. No one. He heard only the roar of wind and waves. His eyes wept in the force of the updraught. He cursed and put on his goggles. Sixty feet below and 50 yards along he saw figures on a ledge carrying lamplight. He heard his name called, turned up his gas lamp, adjusted the beam and shone it downwards. Alfren beckoned. He took a rope from his pack and handed it to Tans, who set up a belay. He put on a harness, attached a descender to the rope, pivoted over the edge and rappelled down to Alfren and three others at the ledge.

'Hello, Jin! Brilliant! Look, what I propose is that the older children should go with Faran from here, out of harm's way.'

He could hear in her voice that her plan, whatever it was, was urgent. He looked down into the darkness below. If it was possible ...

'Ma'am,' Alfren addressed Handar, 'Tans should bring Zal to the keep at dawn. We'll meet them at the door.'

She turned to a hireling lad.

'Bjan, you should come with us when we leave.'

'No, miss, this is my home, for me and my dad.'

Jin had seen that often enough: so many without a

home were glad to find one wherever there was just enough provision for life.

'Bjan,' said Handar, 'I'd like you to report with your dad to Jin at the ranger base tomorrow. You will receive orders.'

Alfren spoke to Handar but he didn't listen in. He shook hands with Bjan, who was maybe a year younger, taller and stronger. Jin saw Bjan notice his fine but worn storm suit, his latest high-pressure gas lamp, a harness and gear, and slung over his shoulder, his rifle.

'I'll be glad to have you aboard, Bjan,' he said.

'Thanks, mister,' Bjan replied.

'Rangers,' said Handar, 'I have to put the guard straight with help from Falt and these pistols. I'll see you at the door to the keep just before sunrise, six o'clock.'

'Yes, ma'am,' Jin chorused with Alfren.

Handar put on the climbing gear lowered by Tans and ascended.

One moment Jin had been on watch on the curtain wall, wondering if he was in the likeliest place; the next, when Alfren had appeared, he had found it was exactly right. From the spot he had chosen, he had had a view of the keep and the courtyard, but a crook in the wall hid him from a search lamp of any kind. He nodded to himself. An old ranger had once impressed on him, *on patrol always go forward*.

Jin followed the others into a narrow passage in the curtain wall which led to a cloister. Alfren explained what had happened that afternoon and the plan she had formed. He settled in a corner to wait. In a short couple of hours, he would strike his lamp to signal out to sea.

Alfren

Alfren, Liffet and Bjan continued through the keep to the dormitories. They surprised Nurse Tulla who was sitting in an armchair with a cup of tea.

'Nurse Tulla, ma'am,' announced Alfren, 'I have news and it has to come from me. I've been to see the chief who I expect will flee the burgh by boat, and without telling you or anyone but his closest aides. The news I have is that there'll be a big storm which could raze the burgh. I would like to put the children in a place of safety and frankly, ma'am, I can't see that it's safe anywhere here, not to my satisfaction. I've misled you. I'm a Sealand ranger and Liffet here is a militiaman and there are rangers in the burgh ready to help. The chief's time here is over. We've discovered his raider base and we'll restore the burgh to order before long.'

'Well, good riddance to him,' the nurse replied. 'Is this true, Bjan?'

'I see it was never right,' Bjan replied. 'We all of us had no choice, we were kidnapped, we know that. It has to end. We can be free of the chief.'

'The evacuation should begin this evening, with the older children first,' Alfren said.

'We have to let them go,' confirmed Bjan. 'We should wrap them well. The witch Alfren – the *ranger* – says it's a force 7.'

The nurse left to rouse the older children of twelve years and over.

Nine of them filed into the refectory and Alfren explained why they had to leave.

'There's a big storm coming in only a week's time. It'll be the biggest ever for many years. We'll take you somewhere safe. From there, we'll find where you belong and your families. The little ones will go tomorrow morning. You're first, this evening. The first of two boats will take you to visit the Western Isles, because it's really safe there, and then after the storm, sail to Wallburgh.'

It was a surprise to the children, of course. They had questions.

'What if we want to stay?'

'We'll look after you well until you're ready to come back here to the keep, if that's what you want. We mean to put you somewhere safe.'

'The little ones will miss us.'

'They will. Someone you know will be here soon to look after them.'

'Who?'

'Zal.'

She paused while they took in all that she'd said.

'Zal's been ill but she's better.' *Better not tell them I shot her.* 'You'll see her again when this is over.'

The children cheered.

'We thought she had got on the bad side of the chief,' said a girl.

'The chief has gone,' Alfren said. 'That's why we're going to take care of you.'

She addressed the girl. 'Please, would you take this case? It contains a special device called a wave assayer. Give it to a girl called Faran on the sloop.'

'Can we trust you?' asked a boy.

'Yes, you can,' Bjan replied for her.

Faran

Tans climbed down from the quay into the cockpit of the Western Isles sloop followed by a second figure whom she introduced to Faran's family. This was an officer called Handar who was in a hurry, but it took only a moment for Faran to read her mind which she saw was was fair and resolute. Handar explained what was asked of her family.

Faran's family wouldn't need her persuasion. Faran didn't need to read their minds to know that.

Alfren

They hurried to prepare the children. Alfren noticed Bjan was tender with the children, yet this was the same lad that had been a rough, violent raider, such had been the demands on him. He must have barely any recollection of his childhood before he had been kidnapped. His stepfather must have been an anchor for him as he grew up.

She went to collect her bow from her room. It was still there undisturbed under the bed. Then she joined the troupe of older children led by Liffet as they passed through the Great Hall. The hirelings and dealers were milling around, too busy shouting to one another to bother with the children and the girls. A guard came running over from the main door to challenge them. Bjan stopped the guard with a hand on her chest. Whatever he said, it worked. The guard turned about.

The children each had their own night lamps and filed through the cloister and into the passage in the curtain wall to the ledge over the sea. The wind pummelled the children on the ledge and those waiting in the passage. The waves and wind boomed powerfully. She saw that the children were frightened. This must be the first time in their recollection that they had stepped foot outside the keep.

Jin

Suddenly, dark night turned to daylight as the most mighty lamplight shone onto the rock cliff below. The brightness was intense but not aimed at Jin. He could make out a figure on a rock platform who directed the lamp, probably Faran. The platform was exposed by the tide although waves sloshed over it.

The oldest boy went first. Jin fitted a harness and from above on the wall Tans lowered the boy over 200 feet. He saw figures assist the boy: islesfolk who also wielded pikes on the rocks to steady the sloop. He saw that the mast on the sloop was down and the foaming wash was from a propeller – the turbine drive which Faran had mentioned. The steersman kept station skilfully among the waves.

What other innovations could these islesfolk have?

The other children found courage and followed one by one. At the last, the bright lamp was extinguished.

'Can I go?' asked Liffet cheerily.

'No,' said Alfren.

'Soup again?' asked Jin.

Liffet smiled.

'I hope I'll get to visit the Western Isles one day soon,' he admitted. By the deck lamps on the sloop, he saw that the islesfolk had boarded. Over the noise of the wind, he heard the whine of the turbine. Those on the rock ledge waved at a figure on deck. Faran. The sloop glided away from the rock bluff of Landing. The children would have a rough trip in these seas, Jin thought. Yet, Alfren was right. He was sure they would be safe.

Alfren

It was near midnight.

'Jin, let's get some rest. Come with us.'

Alfren waited while Tans, who was above on the battlement, with Jin's help below sorted out the ropes. Tans would join Zal who was then aboard the ranger ketch. Jin followed Alfren and Bjan closed and locked the doors.

In the Great Hall, hirelings recognised Jin's ranger garb straightaway and jeered. He smiled and waved, which was bold and funny. Alfren realised hirelings regarded rangers as trouble, but fair too. Besides, it was clear that word of the high storm was out – most likely from the hirelings from the chief's tower – and no doubt word of the chief's withdrawal. With each passing moment there would be less risk of confrontation. Here were hirelings and dealers making ready to leave the burgh for their strongholds and hideaways.

Where next might they find a new meeting place for their plotting?

Below, in the dormitories, Liffet sat on a stool on guard. Bjan went to find his father. Alfren and Jin fell onto empty beds for just a few hours before their turn on watch.

DAY 6

Great Hall

Alfren entered a dormitory, went to Liffet's bed, and poked her friend.

'Get up,' she said.

Liffet rose groggily and followed her up the stairs to the Great Hall.

'I was having a nice dream about sailing to the other side of the world.'

'Was I there?'

'No.'

Alfren grinned.

Folk milled around the hall, no doubt making last-minute deals before they embarked on their boats. The girls crossed to the main door where the wicket was closed and guarded. Bjan was waiting there.

Alfren gave him a smile – he was good really – and Liffet said a cheery, 'Good morning, Bjan.'

He nodded.

Alfren saw he needed confidence, that his upbringing in the keep had marred him.

The guards formed up at a loud rap on the door. One opened the wicket but blocked Alfren's view. Bjan pushed the guard aside and stepped through. She caught a glimpse of a wheelchair like the one the Picker had used, carried by two seaman rangers. The guards stepped aside for Bjan as he pushed and lifted the wheelchair through the small wicket.

Zal was pale, wrapped in blankets. Alfren leaned over to embrace her.

'Two days ago, when I left, you were poorly.'

'Yes, I was, and I'm weak still. Faran has helped a lot. Let's be quick, I don't have strength.'

Bjan carried the front of the wheelchair and Liffet held the back on the descent of the stairwell to the children's quarters. Nurse Tulla roused and dressed the children and Alfren made hot milk and porridge. In the refectory, the children danced around Zal with delight. Liffet, Bjan and Nurse Tulla brought two sickly children from the infirmary.

They were all dressed and ready. Cajoling the children to follow, Liffet and Bjan carried Zal up to the Great Hall. Tans and Jin followed; he had unslung and loaded his rifle. Why, Alfren didn't know. There had been no sign of trouble. Who would make trouble with children present? The chief had to leave the burgh soon if he hadn't already. His stronghold had been uncovered. He had said the evening before that he had business abroad. Where and what for she couldn't guess. She had to admit this might not be the last of him unless he found a seer somewhere else and soon, which was unlikely.

The point was that neither she nor the chief could say where their paths would lead after a rip storm. They could count on finding nothing except destruction. Everyone would have to make the best of what was left on the other side of the storm and many would have to start all over again.

She and Nurse Tulla carried the two unwell children who hung onto them closely with arms around their necks. They should be in a bunk on the ketch as soon as possible. At the top of the steps she heard Liffet call her forward.

She gave the child to Tans, set down her bow and stepped into the hall.

Alfren faced a great rank of hirelings and other folk. In the centre stood the chief, their visionary, and his master, the Picker.

Several hirelings held crossbows, although none raised them or aimed at her. There were folk in the galleries, above and behind her. She walked forward and, as she did, she skimmed over the waves. Foremost, vast and folding, were Earth waves, wrapped around all other waves. There was no message, except that it was clear a rip storm approached.

The chief stepped forward too. His voice boomed in the hall.

'Alfren, as you know, I brought you here so that you might save folk. You have succeeded in this task and folk have fair warning of the greatest storm to strike for decades, an Extinction-level storm. I *facilitated* your journey. Your foresight, the gift of a seer, was given a frame of reference by my research. Remember this: we will survive because I brought you here and guided you.

'It has been a confusing journey for you – with peril of your own making. You are resourceful when faced with new challenge but there was never need for alarm or injury.'

He nodded to Zal.

'I had made provision for you. I must avoid wasteful conflict at this critical moment for our survival. We will survive!'

'Aye,' the folk replied.

'You find your strength in your friendships and your folk. You mistake me, as I will not harm them.'

Neither will you save them, Alfren thought.

'Without a threat, you cannot shriek in our minds and disarm us. Alfren, I am determined to save folk-kind.'

He meant his own folk foremost.

'I know it will be hard to understand, but I do this for you and your friends. Return to the dormitories. I will summon you to explain how I will save the folk you love. It will be the best for all. You will thank me when the storm has passed. The Extinction comes again. We will survive!'

The folk in the hall growled their 'ayes'.

The chief had appealed to his hirelings, but it meant nothing to her. Survival could not be built on a foundation of kidnap and bullying.

'No, sir, stand aside. We intend to leave.'

'Alfren, we have little time. You and your friends will come to no harm. I have no choice.'

The chief beckoned and hirelings walked forward to surround her. She was trapped. One hireling carried a bottle and pad to administer anaesthesia.

'Do not harm her or her friends, any of them, in any way,' called the chief. The hirelings grabbed her.

She meant to resist but instead felt Earth waves building and flooding her mind.

'Save life,' she heard from the waves. She felt wobbly but didn't fall because she was gripped by the hirelings. Earth waves wrapped everywhere and around everyone; they rippled and prickled throughout her body. Earth sent tendrils worming their way into her. She writhed to resist but the hirelings gripped her firmly. The tendrils rooted in her. She wanted to fight, but knew the fight wasn't in her body – it was with Earth. She endured threads pulling her body to pieces. She had to think. That was it – Earth waves knew what they were doing. They looked for the message folk carried.

She had looked for messages in waves, but the Earth looked for the message in folk. Why? She knew. Earth cared about life, any life that would not harm the world. The tendrils wormed into her and she writhed with the irritation.

Jin

'Stop, ranger at large!' Jin called above the shouts and screams. 'Weapon at hand!

'Unhand the ranger marine! Sir! Give the order! Arrest of a ranger with malicious intent is unlawful. Weapon at hand! Sir!'

It was worth a try. Although, looking around at the assembly, it was clear Jin faced a good number of hirelings, any of whom could shoot him.

He glanced to his side. Tans, Liffet and Bjan had shielded the children as best they could. He heard a commotion at the door. Uniformed folk entered through the wicket.

He heard Handar's voice before he saw her.

'You, sir! I gave you fair warning. Marine Jin, take aim on this fellow and fire on my order.'

'Yes, ma'am. In my sight, ma'am.'

He couldn't say for certain his old rifle and the well-worn cartridge in it were dependable.

'Sir, release the ranger,' Handar ordered.

Handar intended to take control by force of character because that was her only option as the chief's hirelings outnumbered her squad of guards. However, like the chief, Handar knew the hirelings' motivation – they were there to make silver, not take up a fight.

There was a moment of silence as both sides weighed the outcomes of a skirmish.

'Stop!' came a weak voice beside Jin.

He saw Bjan wheel Zal before the chief.

'All of you!' she rasped; her frailty clear. 'I am Zal, a native of this keep. I am weak with illness and know not whether I will live or die this day. Listen to me!'

There was complete silence in the hall.

'I see the Extinction wraps around every one of us right here. The Extinction could take us all – and leave no one alive. We might die unless we do what we know is true. At this, the Extinction, each of us must face our destiny. We must not quarrel. There is no time. Go, every one of you. Find your place at the Extinction. It comes again to take us. May every one of you fare well. Go, I say!'

The chief glared. Then Jin saw the fellow's face soften at the sight of Zal. Finally, the chief nodded to the hirelings.

'Let the seer go.'

Jin couldn't have known that Zal had a profound influence over the chief.

Liffet appeared and held up Alfren as the hirelings released her. She tottered, leaning on Liffet.

The chief and hirelings filed from the Great Hall. All other folk backed away and turned to each other. A mumble grew. It was over.

Jin looked to Handar and nodded. It had been close – an action won by force of will.

One more scrape he could notch up as a win.

Tans came over to congratulate him. Falt waved, then climbed the stairs to the galleries to look for anyone left behind with a grudge. Jin released the cartridge from the rifle chamber and checked before pocketing it.

It looked alright; it could have fired.

Alfren

Alfren saw Earth waves dissolve, their tendrils slipping from her body. As the last of them left, she opened her eyes. She was in the Great Hall in the keep on a bench, in Liffet's embrace, Zal before her.

She had a sense that Zal knew the waves in some way, but not the same as she did. Zal might understand her.

'Crikey, Zal. We came close then, you know, the waves, they might not have waited for the storm before taking us. What happened?'

Zal was too weak. It was Handar who knelt before her.

'Zal appealed to the chief. She defused the stand-off and saved us from harm.'

Handar rose, with other matters to look to, not least the fact that they were vulnerable still whilst in the keep.

'Marine Alfren, make ready to leave.'

'Yes, ma'am.'

All Alfren knew was that Earth had tested them, riddled her with tendrils, and somehow Zal had averted a terrible end.

'Bjan!' she called. 'Let's get Zal into her cot on the ketch, right now. What you've done for us was brilliant!'

She rose and stumbled, to half fall on him.

Ketch

In the courtyard before the keep, Bjan lifted Zal from the wheelchair to carry her.

Liffet helped Alfren into Zal's place, then Alfren wheeled herself down the cobbled main street. At the funicular she smiled at the thrill of her ride in the rail car down to the quay.

Her strength had returned after the Earth tendrils and she was able to help Bjan and the master of the ketch lift Zal into a cot. Faran had left instructions for Zal's care. Bjan was nervous when he administered antibiotic to Zal, but his confidence was growing. He had found purpose, Alfren reckoned.

She had recovered by the time the children arrived with Liffet and Nurse Tulla a half hour later. The youngsters scrambled aboard eagerly. She laughed in relief but had to explain that Zal should be left alone in quiet.

She climbed onto the quayside. There would be no delay. The wind had dropped. The sooner they were on the open sea and far off the coast the safer they would be.

Bjan was there, standing back and watching. His help had turned events, she was sure. He had been gentle with the children; the little ones especially had jumped happily to his kindly commands. It was a part of his nature she couldn't have guessed at when on the tramper. She approached him.

'Look out for whoever needs help here, won't you?'

'I will, witch Alfren.'

'You were a massive help, thank you. I've got to go. Find the best shelter you can before the storm. Be seeing you,' she said.

Bjan nodded, eyes downcast, and then met hers with a smile.

She smiled too.

There was no time.

She saw Handar and rangers run over from the funicular.

'Alfren,' Handar called out, clearly in a hurry, 'your orders are to take these children and Zal to the storm shelter at the ranger barracks. You are to alert Wallburgh. I know you'll do all that is necessary.'

'Yes ma'am. Ma'am?'

The question was why her squad would not come too.

'Jin will be interim governor of Landing. The seamen rangers will commandeer boats to sail to the outlying islands to alert all folk. Falt, Tans and I will split up to alert settlements along the west. I hope to reach the north islands before the storm strikes.'

That was it? Why couldn't she go with them, all the way north?

'Ma'am?'

'The master will take you and together you must sail the ketch. Follow your orders, Marine.'

'Yes, ma'am.'

It came to her, why was she the only one to assist with sailing the ketch?

'Liffy!'

Handar turned to her. 'Scout Liffet will cross the badland back to Wallburgh, alerting anyone on the track, and a certain ferryman.'

There was no point in arguing with Handar and certainly not with Liffet.

'Yes, ma'am.'

She would be without Liffet at a testing time with the waves.

'Ma'am, please could you instruct Scout Liffet to arrive in Wallburgh no later than three days before the full moon.'

'Scout Liffet, you heard. Please comply.'

'Yes, ma'am,' said Liffet.

Alfren hugged Tans, Falt and then Jin the longest. She had an idea that without Jin she would right then have been stuck in a cell in a tower.

She drank in the sight of her squad. It was possible she might never see them again if they failed to find good shelter before the rip storm struck. Even then, in the aftermath, they would have much to contend with on their journey home to Wallburgh.

She had only a minute before the ketch sailed. She pulled at Liffet and they dashed along the quay to a tramper and hailed the fellow in the wheelhouse.

'Skipper, well done!' she called.

'Aye, well,' he called in reply and forced a grin.

'Skipper, please see Marine Jin at the ranger base, and tell him Marine Alfren sent you with your daughter. I hope he'll arrange some recompense for the loss of your tramper.'

'Marine, is it? Oh aye,' he nodded. 'Aye, will do.'

Alfren and Liffet faced one another.

'You'll get lost, you know,' Alfren said.

'Yes, and you'll fall overboard,' said Liffet.

Alfren smiled. 'Remember what Handar said about being in Wallburgh before the storm.'

'What was that?'

She aimed to kick her friend on the shin, who sprang away.

'Right-oh,' said Liffet.

'Don't muck about.'

'Still bossy.'

'Bye, Liffy.'

'Bye, Ally.'

She turned and ran to board the ketch. When she looked back, the rangers and Liffet had gone from the quay.

The wind had dropped to breeze-force 5. Alfren was pleased because she would learn the ropes in this her first sailing. 'There's nothing like jumping in at the deep end,' Liffet would have said.

She went to see the children, some of whom were seasick, as the ketch bobbed on its way. It was crowded in the cramped cabin, but they were safe.

It was a moment to relish. She had found them.

She couldn't be sure which, but some must be returning to their home burgh of Wallburgh.

The master of the ketch was a kind fellow who sailed the boat as evenly as was possible. Alfren found a sea suit then went forward to adjust the sails on the main mast so that the master could stay in the cockpit to navigate and steer. She took a few minutes — it was longer probably — to sit on deck alone. There, she wouldn't be distracted by the children.

She went to the waves. There were Faran's faint waves, not too difficult to find this time: there was a message of wellness and certainty, to say their sloop with the older children was not far off the Western Isles. She found Liffet and saw contentment and solitude, which told her to mind her own business. She laughed. Then she went to Earth waves because she had to see what they were doing ... to see if they had changed. Still they scrolled around, looking for weakness. She shuddered.

She settled to find the waves of two folk she knew well, which wasn't easy at all. Unlike Liffet, and Faran for that matter, their minds were not open and sensitive to wave messages. Nevertheless, she spent time sending as clearly as she could. She made the send fearful and rousing and sent an itch, so they felt they had to do something about it. She sent again and again.

Vaults

Jin

Jin made the open market square his base so that all should know where to find him. He began with an instruction to the guard to list the folk who intended to stay in the burgh at full moon. Also, he instructed them to open the gate to the barbican. Anyone who wanted could take refuge in Landing.

Earlier he had seen that few boats remained in the harbour. Clearly, hirelings and dealers had sailed. Landing was safer without them.

Bjan came to him with his father, who limped with the aid of a crutch. Jin gave a ranger token to Bjan who would be required to assist in any duty. Bjan's father had decided to stay with his son and make a new life in Landing rather than follow the raiders. Jin asked Bjan's father to open the ranger base off the square and repair the door.

Jin and Bjan found vaults in other yards around the burgh and instructed folk to fit them out for occupation. He reckoned bunks for up to five hundred folk should be enough. After the storm, folk would stay in the refuges while the burgh was inspected, made safe and reconstructed. They could be there for weeks.

He called boat owners to him and urged them to pool

resources to lift boats onto the quay and strap them down or, better, beach them nearby and haul them high onto land.

He and Bjan sat on the plinth under the cross in the market square. He was puzzled as to where to shelter livestock that would be brought down off the fells. He asked if there were mines or quarries outside the burgh: the answer was no. He thought about the keep, its cloister, dungeons, barbican or anywhere that might do. But he knew that wind and falling masonry would batter open spaces in the burgh. The storm could topple even stout buildings.

A thought occurred to him. He gathered a team of burghers. They rigged an A-frame to lift and remove the cross in the square, then the thick stone slabs underneath. Revealed was a steep ramp that curved down to a vast, low underground chamber fitted with stalls and stables. All along there had been a large shelter for livestock. Jin was impressed that the survivors of the Extinction had gone to such great effort to build these catacombs. Clearly, they had expected Extinction-level high storms to pass again.

He asked Bjan to show him around the keep and the chief's tower. The chief had removed everything. He had received reports from the guard that boats had lined up under the tower on the chief's last day. It must be that the tower was not the chief's true stronghold – there could be another, most likely somewhere remote.

Jin detailed the guard to make an inventory of any treasury and carry silver and valuables underground. Then he visited the gaol where Handar had imprisoned the disloyal guard officers who had betrayed her to the chief. He gave them a letter to deliver to the militia in Wallburgh and sent them on their way.

Each morning and evening, he joined the guards on the roof of the keep, to watch for sign of the storm.

Alarm

The Vicar

It was midday. The vicar was arranging a class for children on the repair of fishing nets in the chancel of the church. The children were running around in the nave where Alfren and Liffet had often looked after them. Strange that the two girls came to mind.

That day he was irritable which was most odd; there was nothing to worry about and goodness knows he had little to do. Maybe he was getting old or sickening? Maybe he should take a walk to the West Gate and take the air? Or maybe find a good fish for supper? There must be something on his mind – that's what he told his parishioners when they were out of sorts, when he gently teased out their worries.

He looked at the porch at the other end of the nave just as Yarla, Alfren's mother, entered. She seemed agitated. Really, today was not a good day for helping parishioners, distracted as he was.

He strode down the nave and forced a smile. 'How are you, Yarla,' he asked politely. 'Can I help?'

He wanted her to get to the point.

'Vicar, I've been worried. Alfren has been missing for five

days. Just today, a ranger called to say they were tracking her but when I asked where he said out west and not to worry. She's never been farther than the voe and she's out west! That's the badland and you know what they're like out there. You can't tell them and raiders apart, can you?'

The vicar felt extraordinarily tense. He was almost beside himself and for the first time in his life he felt he might snap.

'Well, I keep thinking of all the horrible things, you know,' said Yarla.

'Yes, yes. She's a tough girl though. She'll manage as best she can.'

If Yarla didn't leave right then, he would push her out.

'Yes, she is, I hope so. It's strange though, Vicar, but I think she's been speaking to me.'

'What?' He didn't want to listen to the imaginings of an overwrought mother. But hold on, *speaking* to her?

'What does she say?'

'Well, it's probably silly, and I'm just exaggerating things ...'

'Go on,' he almost pleaded.

'Well, it's like a message, about something that could happen at the full moon.'

'What is it?' He could have screamed at her.

'All I have in my mind – there's nothing else – is ... is rip storm. There, I'm glad that's out. Rip storm. It's a bit like the flood, do you remember? What do you ...?'

He must have frozen with wide-open eyes and mouth agape. The same message flooded him. There was only one explanation.

Alfren.

He spun round, bounded to the church tower and slipped the bell ropes looped to a hook on the wall.

'There's no time to waste, Yarla. I heard it too.'

He arranged the ropes.

'Children,' he called, 'don't be alarmed. It's bell-ringing practice.'

He jumped up, hung on the rope and the bells clanged.

'Is it true?' Yarla asked over the din.

'Yarla,' he cried, 'go directly to the Watch barracks. Tell them to sound the sirens and light the beacons. Tell them they must. Folk will come and I'll explain. Go to the rangers and tell them everything, about the flood too. I'm sure the militia will be here soon. Go, Yarla, let's not lose a moment!'

Late that evening, when the last of the parishioners had gone from the rectory, the vicar slipped a bottle of whisky from its hiding place and poured himself a dram. He took his precious diary and began to write. Would his diary survive him and the storm ... the Extinction? Would someone read his words in a few generations? Would a few folk survive at all?

Folk had heard the church bells that day and, soon after, sirens from the watchtowers above the burgh. They had flocked to the church where he told them the forecast was trustworthy, the high storm was real, and they should prepare in earnest.

Some had said it must be a false alarm and there was no evidence for a high storm, certainly not a rip storm, and it was just a scare. Some said that the whole Extinction was a myth anyway and had feigned to carry on as usual. He saw them as the day wore on when they had shown signs of a growing feeling of dread and had scuttled home to prepare.

Some said they would leave the burgh the following day to be first to the interior of the island. Others said those that left were too hasty and they should all act together.

Warnings were sent by telegraph and radio to any outposts with the receiving equipment. Folk told him the few rangers at the barracks had left immediately by boat and pony, no doubt according to a pre-arranged plan to cover the settlements and islands in the outland.

A couple of fishing boats raced eastwards to the League towns, their masters native to those lands, to warn of storm surges and high winds.

Throughout the day, on the hour, he had heard the watchtower sirens and that evening he had climbed the church tower and seen the beacons ablaze.

Over the next days, the burghers lifted all the fishing boats ashore and transported them to a large quarry to the north of the burgh.

The militia were on hand to prevent looting and theft. They inspected houses and issued certificates of storm-worthiness. They searched for hoards of food and goods and returned them to the burgh stores.

Just as it had been written in the old texts when warned of a storm, folk took fishing nets and threw them over their house roofs, then weighted them with large stones. They boarded up windows, roped together furniture in lower rooms, propped their cellars to resist collapse, tore down the children's dens, and carried any loose debris to a large bonfire. The burghers flushed and inspected the main sewer in case it became necessary to use it as a refuge.

Outside the burghs, farmers checked their underground stores and heaped more earth and stones over them. They herded their livestock and filed them into their double-walled and covered boundaries, or into large barrows, low and dark but overtopped with deep earth, and safe.

The vicar heard the farmers noted how the wildlife sensed the storm. Some birds flocked and flew away. Others found deep burrows between stones or at the roots of wind-bent trees.

Faran

Faran's home island was small, a couple of miles across, a rock outcrop really. Sometimes storm spray had swept over the whole island, but she had never been allowed outside the *clochán*, her family's stone 'beehive' hut, to see it.

There was much to do. They sank their boats in the deep harbour, ready to raise when the storm had passed, and carried their stores and herded their livestock into the underground halls, high in the hillside.

They didn't wait – they took to their shelters, except for a few who were in their minds drawn to the high storm.

They climbed high to the stone lookouts to watch for its approach.

Home

Alfren

The ketch glided into the harbour late that day. Alfren heard a peel of bells from the church and the wail of sirens from the watchtowers for a minute on the hour.

There was no one to greet them at the harbour. She raced to the barracks where she found two rangers making ready to depart. They helped her bring the children, Zal and Nurse Tulla to the barracks. Then the rangers jumped onto the ketch, which sailed for the remote western isle of Turnaround.

Elderly, retired rangers came to help with the children and opened the barrack's infirmary, where they cared for the two poorly children and for Zal, who was exhausted. Alfren trusted Zal would rest and gain strength for a few days before she had to move again to shelter.

When all was settled, Alfren left for home. On seeing her, her mum collapsed with relief on her rocking chair. Alfren recounted her adventures and told how she had chased raiders to find the kidnapped children, but not much had happened really. She admitted that yes, she had had a premonition of a big storm but really folk could feel it anyway, couldn't they?

Alfren asked her mum to find her good friend, Gleth — the one who, with her children, had come to stay with them in their home after the flood six years before.

Then she went to see the vicar to find a throng of folk in the nave of the church. In the chancel, the older children were busy making wooden boxes in which to transfer items to the storm shelter; the younger ones played with their wooden toys. She noticed the folk here were elderly or young mothers in the main — vulnerable folk who might be overlooked in the rush for the shelters. The vicar told her how relieved he was that she was safe and asked after Marine Jin. She told him he was safe too, but he would remain out west for the storm. Then she climbed into the pulpit to address the folk.

The Vicar

The vicar was relieved to see Alfren. It was clear to him that she had a strong purpose in mind. The folk fell silent when they saw her in the pulpit. She spoke firmly.

'I have something to say. My name is Alfren, and although some of you knew me as a watchman, I am a marine with the rangers. I am the only ranger who will be here in Wallburgh when the storm comes. My orders were to raise the alarm and to provide help to you. A high storm will come. A soothsayer who we came across in the west, in the badland, alerted us. We can rely on this soothsayer.'

The vicar saw her hesitate, no doubt because this was the most awful and fearful news.

'We have until the full moon. I am sure you're wondering what would be best. You're free to join other burghers who'll shelter in the mines. If you wish to stay in Wallburgh, please let the vicar know and we'll provide shelter here. You should bring what you can: food, carbide for lamps, blankets and mattresses — whatever you have we will make go around.

Those of you who're fit should meet me here tomorrow and we'll fetch barrels to fill with water. Are there any questions?'

'How long will the storm last?' asked an elderly lady, standing near the vicar.

'Three days or thereabouts. It's not clear really,' Alfren replied.

There was a gasp from the crowd of folk. A high storm of such strength and duration would be terrible. He overheard the lady say to her friend, 'She's sure about that,' and her friend replied, 'She must be the one – the one with the sight.'

The vicar was worried for her. Wasn't that a burden? Whom did Alfren have to support her?

'Alright?' asked Alfren and having delivered her message, she smiled encouragingly. 'Until tomorrow.'

Alfren

Alfren went to sit outside the church on a bench. There were two days until Liffet returned. Earth waves, quiet and rippling, crept up and niggled at her. She didn't understand: were they looking for a weakness in her?

She didn't want to face them alone and without a friend around to catch her.

She thought about the chief. How much more of Earth did he know that he hadn't told her? She hadn't given him a chance to tell her much.

What more was there in the connections between Earth, the world and pollution?

She returned home. From there, she led her mum and Gleth to the ranger barracks. In an office, she invited Gleth to sit down.

'I have a pleasant surprise for you, but there is some bad news too. It'll come as a shock and I'd like you to prepare as best you can. My mum is here by your side to comfort you. Don't worry, it's not very bad.'

Both looked puzzled.

'I was on patrol in the badland for a few days and ... I've found your missing daughter – your youngest.'

Gleth frowned then trembled.

'Her name is Zal. In a moment, I'll take you to see her. She's in the infirmary; she's poorly. We've given her the best antibiotics from the Western Isles, and she's responded well.'

Now the bad part. 'But she hasn't rested well, she's weak.'

That's the truth, she thought.

'She needs love and care. Please, expect nothing from her and in your hands, she may live.'

I am brutal, she thought. That's what they say: that a seer must tell the truth, hard as it may be.

An elderly ranger nurse took the two mothers through to the ward where Zal lay, and Alfren withdrew.

I have the wrong energy within me; I give out the wrong waves. I shouldn't be close to Zal at this time, she thought. *Zal needs giving energies. I carry and offer only fear – a high storm in fact.*

It was sunset, half past seven in the evening. Alfren strolled from the barracks to the esplanade where she found a copper thruppence deep in a pocket in her wind suit and bought a whole seared fish from Tally's fish shop. She sat at a tram stop to eat. She thought about what change might follow the storm. That's what folk were not prepared for. Who could think that far ahead?

She sent a message to say all was well to Liffet who was in her bivouac sack somewhere in the badland. She heard curiosity from Faran to say their rune master was examining the wave assayer, accompanied by urgency to reflect their preparation for the storm.

She went to the Bald Lady pub where the watchmen

gathered. She smiled at her memories of the telling of the tale of how the pub got its name. It had been told many times, sometimes over the course of a whole evening, always made funnier than the time before. Gal, the owner, had in her early days as a watchman waved every day from her watchtower at a fellow in long dress and shawl passing by carrying peats on her back in a kishie and knitting while she walked. Gal waved and waved and enjoyed the sight of the peat gatherer passing on fair days late that summer. But one day the wind was up and blew away the shawl; the fellow was bald, and a raider too. The fellow dropped the kishie and ran for the hills. Gal gave chase but had to stop; she wasn't permitted more than a mile from the tower. Needless to say, the kishie contained work tools stolen from the shipwrights' quarter.

Alfren drank a beer, listened to more of their funny stories and sang a song for them.

Then she went home to wash and sleep.

DAYS BEFORE THE STORM

Wallop

Alfren awoke. She was fifteen years old. She would be 16 years soon. Her age didn't matter so much. She was a watchman turned ranger. She was a seer, sort of; not the grand seer the chief wanted, one like they had in times past. She had rescued the kidnapped children which had been a great adventure, but Faran and the islesfolk and the rangers had done all the work.

She dressed and then walked through the burgh on her way to the ranger barracks, passing the fortune-tellers on the market street. They called to her that the end was coming, just as they had always said it would, and she should wear one of their charmed crystals to ease her soul. She was tempted. Would it help?

'No thanks,' she said.

She collected her water test equipment from the laboratory to take for safe keeping at the church.

She watched the water from the esplanade. The tide was high at ten minutes before ten in the morning that day, then half past ten the next, then eleven o'clock the day after. She loved the rhythm of the moon waves. She belonged between the land and sea. This was her anchor; this place – Sealand. If she had any doubts, she thought, remember, an anchor.

Each day she had made herself busy attending to folk at church and the children at the ranger barracks. They were as settled as could be. Already, Wallburgh families had claimed five of the fourteen children: the remainder were from the League and would have to wait until after the storm – and after winter – to return home, if the rangers could find out where their homes were. She knew Jin would search for records in the chief's tower in Landing.

When she had a moment's rest, she thought of Zal, Liffet, Faran, Jin and Bjan. Though she preferred not to rest as when she did Earth waves intruded. She felt them, brushing her skin. It was unsettling.

She was glad when late one evening Liffet arrived and reported to the militia barracks. They met at the esplanade the following morning.

'Liffy, you took your time!' she said. 'What was it like?'

'It's good out there. I could've wandered forever. I saw folk, scavengers from afar, and raider gangs too. Lieutenant Handar told me to leave messages for them on their tracks, saying "Go inland to the caves or to Landing", with coins as a reward. So that's what I did. The ferryman wouldn't budge. He said he was waiting for the word and I told him he would get it up his arse if he didn't shift. What about you, missus ranger?'

'I've been busy but ... We're preparing and waiting. I'd rather have been with you or my squad, except they're all split up.'

She had had too short an experience of the rangers and right then all she had to do was wait.

'I mean, it's Earth waves, Liffy. They're a nuisance.'

Alfren spent the morning at the church and then went to wait at the bowling green. Liffet arrived and sat next to her. It was usual that they didn't always speak at first, but instead exchanged some funny messages. Liffet's were wobbles on entering the ranger barracks for the first time, and angelic manners while there. Alfren sent stacking boxes at the church until she was surrounded and no way out.

'Zal's well,' Liffy reported. 'She's not out of it, but over the worst. She got such a boost when reunited with her mum. We did our best for her, you know, on the tramper and everything. But look what happened. She led us to the children and she saved us, you know, at the keep, when she said what she did about the Extinction and stuff.'

'I wasn't aware of that, Liffy, I was out of it. Extinction? Oh well, it doesn't matter, not anymore. Anyway, I was thinking of her. It was all unfair on her. She deserves to live.'

'She will.'

'Do you know that, Liffy?'

'Yes.'

The news made everything better.

'Did she tell you anything, you know, about Earth?'

'She said she must think about it and tell you herself.'

'Right.'

The problem was how could they meet when she might trip Zal back into illness, all because she held the storm, whereas Zal needed life-giving energies?

'Liffy, there's something else, about Earth waves, I mean. I'm worried that when the storm comes, I'll shriek, and send everyone mad. I think I can manage not to, but I don't know. I want to be sure you can block me as you used to, but we haven't tried for a while so we're going to have a test, alright?'

'Yes.'

'I'm going to focus on your waves and send an almighty wallop and you have to block me, alright?'

'Yes.'

'Are you sure? Because I must send a big ...'

'Get on with it.'

'Ready?'

Alfren saw it then. Liffet had walked through the badland and the time alone had helped her friend in ways she couldn't know and didn't need to know because it was private. It was the first time Liffet had been away for any length of time too. They had to stay friends yet grow apart, each in her own way she realised, and Liffet had found a way onwards.

'Right. Now!'

Alfren went to her mind, found all the waves and moved to Liffet's. She tried to feel as angry and as loud as she could, then sent out a wave with all the force she could muster. She let it drop and opened her eyes.

Liffet lay on the grass next to her.

Alfren sighed.

'Get up, you daft winkle.'

She kicked her friend gently.

Liffet sprang up, grinning. 'Not an oat flake.'

'Good. Idiot.'

They walked to the militia barracks. The wind was dropping she noticed and was a blow-force 4. The air was light and chill with no rain. It was fresh, quite pleasant, with no portent of a storm.

Liffet reported to the commander, who told her she should find something useful to do – there was no need for a scout at that time, and training was suspended.

Alfren followed Liffet who asked a few questions and found a clerk in a small office up a long corridor. Liffet introduced herself, explained quietly what her request was for, and the clerk leafed through a few files. It took an age, but eventually the clerk told them an address.

They stood before a row of houses along a narrow path off

High Step Lane.

'You do it,' Alfren said.

'Alright,' said Liffet and knocked on a door. Alfren heard children's excited screams. A mother opened the door and five children, aged from three up to eight, crowded round her legs to see who called.

Liffet introduced them both and Alfren smiled at the children – two in particular she recognised.

'Ma'am,' Liffet explained, 'the raider who brought the two children ashore two weeks ago is detained in the ranger barracks. It's not what it seemed – the girl was their nanny and had made a bid to escape a chief from the badland who was responsible for kidnappings.'

'I see,' said the mother uncertainly. 'You're militia?' She looked at Liffet's uniform and then at Alfren. 'Why do the rangers have her? And good riddance to raiders, I say.'

'She was innocent,' said Liffet patiently. 'I have an interest in this matter, ma'am. Please forgive me if I don't explain everything in detail. I believe it would help if the nanny and her wards were able to see each other before the storm comes.'

'Will you be there?'

'I'll escort you and the children and I'll be on hand at all times.'

The mother wavered. 'They have been a bit of trouble, the two of them. I can't understand what they say. They speak a language unknown to me. Let's say this afternoon.'

'Thank you, ma'am. Until later.' Alfren and Liffet smiled at the mother and the children, then turned about and left.

They went to help in a chain of folk who passed boxes of provisions from the stores up the lanes to the West Gate, and from there up the hillside to the mines. Then they went to the ranger barracks, Alfren to help clean the storm shelter and Liffet to collect the two children to take them to see Zal in the infirmary. Later, Liffet joined Alfren who was practising with a longbow at the archery butts, there simply to free her mind for half an hour. Alfren was keen to hear news.

'The mother was pleased,' said Liffet. 'She said she'd prefer to shelter from the storm here at the barracks, if that's alright with you. The children were happy to see Zal, of course. It seems she's the only one here who knows their language. Their visit made a big difference to her. I think even she didn't know how much she had worried about them. Her wound is healing well. She's awake for longer.

'Zal said to tell you don't give in to the Earth, and you would know what she means. She suggested something and if it works, that's fine by me.'

Following this, they walked to the Watch barracks at the West Gate. Alfren put in her request and it was authorised there and then.

'Right-oh, Liffy,' she said, 'we're on. That'll be us on watchtower Barb when it comes. Thanks,' she said.

'Oh, believe me, given a choice I would rather not be stuck down a mine with a load of snoring militiamen, there just to clean out the latrines.'

'Just two more days to go, Liffy. They need help at the church. Could you go? I'll be at the barracks for a bit.'

'Right-oh,' her friend replied. 'One more push to collect supplies.'

Liffet walked off and then turned, came back and stood before her.

'I thought things through these last few days in the badland. I don't think you meant to kill Zal when you shot at her. You did the only thing you could because of who we are. Sealanders, that is. You, me, Handar, everyone ... we have to shoot, as folk did before us ever since the Extinction, otherwise we wouldn't be here. But I think you knew something was amiss and you loosed that arrow precisely. From then on, Zal was going to live, without question, until the point when the raiders kidnapped us.'

'Thanks, Liffy.'

Her friend half turned to go, then looked at her again.

'You could do with a new suit, scruff.'

Alfren walked down the lanes. She looked down at herself, at her scuffed and torn watchman's wind suit. She should purchase a ranger's storm suit. Not then, though. She didn't want to change anything. It was as though what she had and was used to was a protection from something.

Zal

Two days before the storm, folk marvelled at settled weather. The wind stilled to barely a flurry-force 1. The sun shone and sheep-fleece clouds sailed slowly overhead in a blue sky. Folk strolled along the esplanade enjoying the clear air and flat-calm water. Alfren and Liffet brought the church children and those rescued from Landing to the bowling green, where they had a run around and played madcap games. Liffet wheeled Zal from the infirmary to watch for a few minutes. Alfren and Zal waved at one another, then she saw Zal beckon her over.

'Alfren, I'd like you to know two things. First is that you saved the children – and me too,' Zal smiled. 'That's what I'll always think. The second is beware Earth. Only you can see it, maybe I see a little bit too, and Earth knows that. It seeks the intelligence that brought harm to the world. You and I don't know what Earth might do. Keep Earth out at the time of the storm, Alfren. Just keep it away.'

'I will.'

Zal was older and clever. 'I could learn from her if we live,' Alfren mused. 'I thought I was odd and alone, but I have Liffet, Faran and Zal, and all the others, Handar, Tans, Jin and Falt, even Bjan, who understand me in some ways better than I do myself. Which is alright, really.'

On the morning of the last day, the sirens sounded and church bells tolled. Folk filed through the burgh, climbing to the West Gate, and under militia escort they trooped over the fell to the mines. Some folk stayed in the burgh in their deep cellars. The elderly and infirm went to the barracks or the crypt under the church. The vicar had told Alfren that the crypt had withstood all storms and he expected it would do the same again. She and Liffet helped folk all day. She saw the militia search the burgh to make sure no one had been forgotten. By the early evening, the burgh was quiet. She and Liffet walked down the lanes to the esplanade. It was slack water – half past five. The sun was low above the hills behind them.

'There'll be a forty-foot storm surge above our heads tomorrow,' said Alfren, when they were sat in the tram stop.

'Blimey. That'll flood Tally's and Finnie's, and the Bald Lady too. Ally, do you think we'll live through this, or will this be the last bit of the Extinction?'

'I don't know. If we do, it'll take a lot of work to put us back on our feet. Raiders will come and the storms – and more storms and more raiders, most likely.'

'Will it ever get better?'

'For you and me, who knows? I think if we learn to stop pollution then maybe, but a long time hence.'

'The children of the Extinction will live,' said Liffet.

'I hope so. Come on, we should go. We must be there at six. Race you.'

They hastened up the empty lanes and, instead of taking the West Gate, out of habit they climbed onto roofs, jumped onto the wall and climbed down the outside. They ran up the fell to the west watchtower Barb.

The watchmen were light humoured as usual but serious too.

'Tell the raiders there's nothing left in the burgh. You know, when you see the storm, you could make a dash for it.'

They meant to the shelter deep underneath the Watch barracks.

'There should always be someone at the tower,' Alfren said.

'Farewell, girls. Hold fast, watchman!'

'Hold fast, watchman!' she answered.

She took up her routine. It was late in the day. The air was still. There were no boats in the sound. No birdsong. Over the sound on Whaleback there were no sheep, no farmsteaders. The water was blue-green and glinting in the low sun. She climbed up to light the beacon. In the failing light, she saw the watchtower beacons to the south, glowing like stars at night. At eight o'clock she and Liffet put on their ear covers and Liffet cranked the siren for a full minute.

'I won't get any sleep if we have to do that every hour, will I?' Liffet said.

Horizon

Jin

Jin was on the roof of the keep, sharing the watch with Bjan and the guard as he had done every night. It was clear moonlight; they would see the storm should it arrive earlier than expected.

All burghers, livestock and stores were underground. The gate to the barbican was open and there was a guard detachment on the main gate to the burgh with orders to admit any stragglers. More folk than he had expected had arrived by boat, sent there by rangers, but there were sufficient places available in the vaults. A good number of scavengers had also been emboldened to seek shelter in the burgh. Bjan had reported the arrival of a motley band, two of whom were wounded. They gabbled something about a girl with a bow and taking the road to the west, Bjan relayed. Jin had laughed.

Bjan had found a register of children in the dungeons of the keep. The nurses had kept it unbeknown to the chief, and it would certainly help them find where the children had come from.

Jin marvelled at the light under the full moon. The sea shimmered under a light wind. It was rare he had a chance to gaze at the constellations and pick out the planets and brightest stars, with Venus brightest away to the west. He named them to Bjan who took a keen interest.

Bjan asked why the storm was coming.

It was the Extinction, Jin said. It had started long ago and it was a mystery why.

Now, they faced it again. Yet, a seer had given them warning.

A storm seer.

Alfren.

When the next day dawned, Jin sent the guard to the vaults. He and Bjan remained on the roof of the keep. In the early morning he felt a flurry of wind and looked out to the west to see a sliver of black on the horizon. The blue skies misted over.

He wanted to stay and watch, drawn to it. How fascinating it would be to see an Extinction-level storm.

He felt Bjan tug at his arm.

They had to go.

North

Falt

Falt met Handar and Tans on Land's Edge, the farthermost island of the Sealand chain, at the northernmost settlement of Last Hope. It had been a race to cover the distance, but they had succeeded: the word had gone out. Whoever they had met, they had alerted them to the rip storm and folk had spread the word.

For the duration they would shelter with their ponies in a cramped barrow. Folk had said the people who had built the barrow had lived long before the Last People. It was old indeed. There were solid stone pillars and slabs, overtopped with deep earth.

In the last hours of the morning, they raised a slab to block the entrance and packed earth and stones behind it.

There was no more to be done.

RIP STORM

Rip Storm

Alfren

Alfren and Liffet watched the sun rise over Whaleback at seven o'clock and made a big serving of porage. Alfren made Liffet clear up, as she didn't want her friend larking about out on deck.

It was Liffet who saw it first and by then it was almost upon them.

The blackness of night loomed over the hill tops to the west.

'Sound the alarm, Liffy!' Alfren called.

Liffet cranked the siren and the wail echoed over the burgh and the hills.

At the entrances to the mines, the guards hastened inside and barricaded the doors.

The Vicar

The vicar heard the siren.

He looked up into a misty blue sky and wondered if he would see the world again. He hurried into the church and under the church tower, he closed, bolted and barricaded a thick, heavy door and descended the steep stairs to the crypt where folk were settled. Gently, he found the frightened ones and told them to pass their fear to him, for he would carry it for them.

Alfren

From the deckhouse, Alfren grabbed the logbook and a backpack. Outside, she gazed at the heaving storm front, entranced as black clouds billowed to fill the sky. The first licks of wind and rain swiped at her. She felt fingers of Earth all over her body and suddenly the waves she sensed became hot and she felt her mind start to boil.

Shakily, she descended the ladder followed by Liffet. At the shaft to the bunker, Alfren felt the first punches of wind. She had to go underground but the storm was there to take her folk away and she yearned to defend them – out there on the fell. She turned to face the storm. She would stay and watch, experience the magnificent waves and be taken up by them. The storm was wonderful: it was all waves summed together but more colourful, more thrilling. She was ready to leap into the storm.

Liffet tugged her arm.

They had to go.

They descended into the bunker and Liffet closed and secured the hatch. The bunker was spacious enough, containing stores, desk, galley and bunks.

'Liffy,' Alfren trembled. 'Earth is here and strong.' They sat close together, as they had on the tramper when they were six years old.

But this time, it was different.

Alfren recalled clearly what Zal had told her the day before at the bowling green. Earth was intelligent but undecided to the nature of folk-kind. It was because Alfren could see all

waves that Earth had called upon her to rescue the children and had slammed her when she had veered from the path. Earth saw that the children were innocent and could survive to build a new world. However, Earth didn't understand her because she was interested in pollution – the same pollution that had brought havoc to the world. Earth might throw all its fury at her if Earth mistook her for the cause.

Liffet must show her how to shelter from Earth, as that same Earth would rise with the storm to seek out and take life that might bring pollution to the world.

Alfren went to her friend's waves. She saw all of them and Liffet's self-wave too; it was the wave at the heart of her friend. She tried but couldn't shut out the ripples of all other waves, but she did her best to concentrate on the self-wave. She stayed with her friend as Liffet showed her how to stay in one place, with the one wave gently coiling and flowing, as Liffet let go of her other waves. It was too tempting to go to all other waves, even Earth's, but she must try not to otherwise what would become of her?

She looked inside her own mind. She had never seen her own waves and how many there were! Among this jumble, she had to find her self-wave. Alfren floated around, dismissing many, until she found a wave that kept appearing and was steady, unchangeable. She focused on her own wave and then opened her eyes.

There was Liffet, just a girl, simply there.

'Oh, that worked, Liffy.'

'Keep it up, Ally.'

It would help her focus, help her to block out all waves, especially Earth's. She saw and heard everything but without waves. She supposed that was what it was like to be ordinary.

The bunker shook. There was a howl as if all burghers

together had screamed. Alfren heard a screech, a crash and knew the watchtower had fallen. The air pressure in the bunker fell and she swallowed. There was a high wailing sound, silence for a moment, then a thunderclap that made the bunker tremor. She heard a rattle as though a giant tried to tear the hatch away, and water trickled into the bunker. Liffet peered up the shaft, then climbed to check the latches. She reappeared, took chains and shackles from the store, and once more climbed the ladder.

No one could survive out there.

The screaming wind and maelstrom of the tempest were deafening. Liffet jumped off the ladder, put ear covers on, and on Alfren too. In the dim gaslight, they waited. Alfren focused on her self-wave, a meditation it seemed, while the clamour and shocks raged above.

From the clanks and bangs, like a thousand smiths at their anvils, it seemed the storm would open up the bunker and drag them out.

Earth sought to find where life cowered.

A rip storm.

The claws of wind tore at the ground to find them.

It was endless. Was it possible that the storm would never end?

This was the Extinction.

There was no way of knowing how long three days would be, as there was no way to mark the passing of time in their bunker.

The gas ran out.

The booms, explosions and strikes continued, sometimes far away, sometimes overhead. Water seeped and lightning flashed down the shaft although the hatch was shut tight. Alfren supposed there would be an inferno through the burgh.

She thought of the children. The ranger shelter and

the church crypt were deeper, more sheltered than the watchtower bunker.

At times, it was like being in the hold of a steel-built boat with many folk striking the hull with giant hammers. Sometimes the roar was deeper than the steam valve lifting at the power station; sometimes more shrill than the screech of tram wheels on rail; always with a moan of sadness or a howl of pain.

Alfren blocked all waves.

She clung on when it seemed the bunker was sliding down the hill into the sea; or hurtled over and over a sea cliff; or buried, airless, under heaped stones and earth. Heat rose and the air was unbreathable. Next, there was an ice chill. The bunker rocked like a tramper on high sea waves. It tremored as a crescendo of wind built and then tumbled.

The bunker began to fill with water.

If she or Liffet opened the hatch to pump it out, the wind would tear the hatch away. If they put their heads above the hatch they would be struck by shards of ice and wind that might snap their necks. There was nothing to do but move to the top bunk. As the water rose higher, Liffet moved a bunk so that it was set under the entrance shaft. They would stand there, then climb the shaft as the water rose, release the hatch at the last possible moment, and then the Extinction would take them.

Earth had won.

Alfren let go of her self-wave. She wanted to experience all waves before the end of her life.

Shoots rooted into her body, every part of her, even her joints and bones. She wanted to scream at the needling irritation but forced herself to be patient. It was as though Earth sought every fibre, every memory, every thought. She endured it. After an age, the tendrils began to withdraw. She shivered with relief.

Earth had won.

All other waves were overpowered. Instead, she recalled her memories of all the waves she had seen: tide waves, sun, moon, magnetism, life, folk, her friends, stillness, wind, and storm. She wondered at Earth waves. Surely Earth – the real Earth – must be capable of not only threats but nurture too? Not during a great storm though.

She gathered up her strength and sent out wave after wave of calm and reassurance to the children. Maybe they heard her. She did it again and again. No child should be frightened.

She opened her eyes.

'Blimey, Liffy, look at all this water!'

'Yes. I can't see. There's no light, but I know we haven't long. I wrapped up your logbook.'

'It should survive even if we don't, Liffy. Folk after us, some of them, if there are any, will collect books and stuff. How long have we been here, do you think?'

'No idea,' replied Liffet. 'Come on, stand up!'

Liffet climbed the shaft. Water cascaded down. Alfren shouldered her backpack containing the watchtower logbook, collected some items from the bunk and followed. Liffet released the chains from the hatch and passed them to her. She dropped them into the rising water. They waited a little, then Alfren climbed alongside her friend.

'Brought you these.'

Alfren handed Liffet a pair of goggles and helped with a climbing harness.

The hatch rattled furiously and the howling wind screamed above.

They buttoned their collars and drew their hoods close. Alfren attached a rope to Liffet, belayed to the ladder and clipped on.

'Ready!' Alfren called.

'Slack!' called Liffet and Alfren payed out a short length of rope. Liffet climbed to release the latches. Instantly, the wind whipped the hatch open and tore it away. Liffet put her head a little above the opening and drew back in again.

'It's dark. You'll have to go!'

They exchanged places. Alfren poked her head out.

'I see the stump of a watchtower leg,' she shouted. 'About 20 feet! Our anchor! Liffy, you can rappel from here!'

'Alright!'

They exchanged ropes. Alfren heaved herself out of the opening. The wind bowled her over, but she was held. Liffet payed out and Alfren slithered over to the stump of a watchtower leg, where she fought to wrap a rope around the stump as a belay and attached her harness to it.

It was black night with a violent, tearing wind.

She pulled sharply on the rope once.

Soon after, Liffet tumbled and bumped into her. They embraced, the wind snatching at them, lifting, pulling them up into the maelstrom.

No one could survive a rip storm.

Thunder crackled and they felt blows of sound in their bellies. Large ice balls struck them. They wrapped legs around one another to prevent any part of them flailing and kicking in the wind. A deluge drenched them, and they held their breath until they could hold it no longer. Just as suddenly, the water cleared in a blast of warm air.

Alfren looked up. It was black. A gust of wind pulled at them. The belay rope would surely snap.

The gust passed and there was nothing.

No, there was a storm ... but just a storm; a strong gale-force 9.

The girls shuffled and sat against the stump.

Alfren looked up. Over the hill appeared a patch of grey.

More grey cloud swept in with a new dawn.

They waited. The storm dropped to a high wind-force 7.

There came a heavy mist with dark-grey daylight. They released themselves from their belay.

They arose and dropped their harnesses. Alfren searched the wreck of the watchtower deck until she found what she wanted.

'Here it is, Liffy!'

Together they lifted a piece of wreckage and Liffet lashed it upright with the rope. Alfren checked around, far through the mist. There was no threat. In the waves, there was no storm to come.

She was a watchman.

All clear.

She cranked the siren and the wailing cried around the hills.

Was there anyone left alive to hear it?

All clear.

She and Liffet tumbled down the hillside through the mist to the burgh. She saw that much of the wall still stood; other parts had collapsed. They climbed the great boulders of a breach and looked down.

Were there survivors?

Or were she and Liffet the only ones?

As they made to pick their way through the rubble of the burgh, she heard it.

A single church bell pealed.

Comment

Author Note

Could the Extinction really happen?

Yes.

Weather patterns will tip into instability when the world succumbs to rising heat. The winds will heave and tumble. Farmers won't be able to rely on fine weather to cultivate food over a growing season. In each part of the world, the weather will be unstable one year to the next.

There will be extremes of weather, there will be crop failures, and the ineffectiveness of governments will stoke anxiety and eventually chaos.

Unlike the premise of catastrophe movies, the future won't lie with some fortunate folk who have endured the worst but have the means to start again and thrive. Instead, throughout the long years of climate change, a hardy new folk will migrate again and again, running before the storms, spending a generation at most in each new land.

They won't quite forget everything of this our age, thus there will be no return to the Stone Age, not that it would be bad. Neolithic peoples were enterprising and widely travelled. Orkney had a major centre at Scara Brae, active 5,000 years ago. Later, the 2,000-year-old stone brochs of

Shetland kept people sheltered in the North Atlantic – I can see a well-preserved broch from my window; the clefts in the stone are a breeding ground for storm petrels that spend their lives in wild seas. I hope they will survive the climate change we have brought upon the world.

Just as our stone age forbears, the new folk must be adaptable and resourceful. It is regrettable that ours is the first generation of people who have lost their self-sufficiency, which could be the undoing of many. But those folk that follow may quickly become just as enterprising and resourceful as those at the stone age.

They will need to be.

Alfren's folk will live in these coming times, maybe in a lull in the Extinction that allows settlement and trade to flourish.

Eventually, an age beyond Alfren's time, heat energies in the world will be spent and gradually a new steady climate will take hold and extreme weather will subside.

No one knows if this new world climate will be habitable.

It is evident now that due to rising population and exploitation of the world's environment and energy stores, heat in our world will continue to rise for many years.

Only a complete fool says nothing will come of it.

Appendix: Tide Table

Day	Low	High	Low	High	Low	High	Sunrise	Sunset	Moon
			05:09	11:33	17:25	23:43	06:19	19:43	●
			05:53	12:19	18:07		06:21	19:40	
		00:29	06:35	13:02	18:47		06:24	19:37	
		01:11	07:17	13:42	19:28		06:26	19:34	
1		01:53	07:57	14:20	20:09		06:28	19:31	
2		02:35	08:38	14:58	20:51		06:31	19:28	
3		03:18	09:20	15:38	21:37		06:33	19:25	◑
4		04:04	10:06	16:22	22:36		06:35	19:22	◐
		04:58	11:07	17:15			06:38	19:19	
5	00:14	06:13	12:40	18:33			06:40	19:16	
6	01:49	07:53	14:03	20:06			06:42	19:13	
	02:54	09:00	15:04	21:06			06:45	19:10	
	03:41	09:48	15:48	21:52			06:47	19:07	
	04:17	10:27	16:23	22:31			06:50	19:04	
	04:49	11:03	16:55	23:07			06:52	19:01	○
	05:18	11:37	17:26	23:40			06:54	18:57	○
Great Storm	05:49	12:09							

Printed in Great Britain
by Amazon

55901717R00214